Deemed 'the father   , **Richard Austin Freeman** had a long and distinguished career, not least as a writer of detective fiction. He was born in London, the son of a tailor who went on to train as a pharmacist. After graduating as a surgeon at the Middlesex Hospital Medical College, Freeman taught for a while and joined the colonial service, offering his skills as an assistant surgeon along the Gold Coast of Africa. He became embroiled in a diplomatic mission when a British expeditionary party was sent to investigate the activities of the French. Through his tact and formidable intelligence, a massacre was narrowly avoided. His future was assured in the colonial service. However, after becoming ill with black-water fever, Freeman was sent back to England to recover and finding his finances precarious, embarked on a career as acting physician in Holloway Prison. In desperation, he turned to writing and went on to dominate the world of British detective fiction, taking pride in testing different criminal techniques. So keen were his powers as a writer that part of one of his best novels was written in a bomb shelter.

THE GREAT PORTRAIT MYSTERY

R Austin Freeman

HOUSE OF
STRATUS

This edition published in 2001 by House of Stratus, an imprint of Stratus Holdings plc, 24c Old Burlington Street, London, W1X 1RL, UK.

www.houseofstratus.com

Typeset, printed and bound by House of Stratus.

A catalogue record for this book is available from the British Library.

ISBN 0-7551-0362-9

This is another of the excellent mystery stories by that master, R. Austin Freeman. Trained as a surgeon he was forced by ill-health to abandon his profession and turned to writing as a whole time occupation.

CONTENTS

The Great Portrait Mystery

PART I

As a collection of human oddments, the National Gallery on copying day surpasses even the Reading Room of the British Museum, and almost equals the House of Commons. The spectacle that it afforded was a source of perennial interest to Mr Joseph Fittleworth, as were also the productions of the professional copyists, humorously described in official parlance as students. For Joseph Fittleworth was himself a painter, with a leaning to the methods of the past rather than to those of the future, a circumstance which accounted for his professional failure. Which illustrates the remarkable fact that in these days, when even indifferent Old Masters sell at famine prices, while the unsold work of contemporary genius grows mouldy in the studios, an artist's only chance of popularity is to diverge as far as possible from the methods of those great men of the past whose productions are in such demand.

Hence it had happened that Fittleworth had accepted with avidity a not very lucrative supernumerary post at the National Gallery where he could, at least, have his being amidst the objects of his worship, which we may remark included an exceedingly comely young lady, who came regularly to the gallery to copy pictures, principally of the Flemish school.

On this particular Thursday morning Mr Fittleworth walked slowly through the rooms, stopping now and again to look at the work of the copyists, and dropping an occasional word of judicious and valued criticism. He had made a tour of the greater part of the building and was about to turn back, when he bethought him of a rather interesting copy that he had seen in progress in a small, isolated room at the end of the British Galleries, and turned his steps thither. The room was approached by a short corridor in which a man was seated copying in water-colour a small Constable, and copying it so execrably that Fittleworth instinctively looked the other way and passed hurriedly to the room beyond. The work in progress here interested him exceedingly. The original was a portrait of James the Second by Sir Godfrey Kneller, and the copy was so perfect a reproduction that Fittleworth halted by the easel lost in admiration of the technical skill displayed. The artist, whose name appeared from an inscription on his colour box to be Guildford Dudley, was seated, looking at his picture and the original, as he deliberately mixed a number of tints on his palette.

"I see you haven't begun work yet," Fittleworth remarked.

The painter looked up at him, owlishly through a pair of very large, double focus spectacles, and shook his head, which was adorned by a tangled mass of very long, reddish hair.

"No," he replied, "I am just having a preliminary look before starting."

"Do you think your copy wants anything done to it at all?" asked Fittleworth. "It's excellent as it stands, though just a trifle low in tone."

"Not lower than the original, is it?" demanded the artist.

"No," replied Fittleworth, "but it will be in a year or so, when the medium has darkened, and it's a good deal lower than the original was when first painted."

The painter reflected. "I'm inclined to think you're right," said he. "I ought to have kept it one or two degrees higher. But it isn't too late," he added, briskly. "A day's work or so ought to bring it up to the proper key."

Fittleworth was doubtful and rather sorry he had spoken. Raising the tone meant practically going over the entire picture afresh, which seemed a risky proceeding in the case of a finished, and highly successful, painting. He attempted gentle dissuasion, but, finding the painter resolved on the alteration, refrained from urging him further.

"I see," said he, "that the glass is on the original. Wouldn't you like to have it taken off?"

"Oh, no, thanks," was the reply. "There's no reflection in it from here."

"The glass lets the tone down a little," Fittleworth began; but there he paused, with his mouth slightly open, and the painter started and fell into a rigid posture, with his palette-knife poised motionless in mid-air. Astonishment was writ large on the faces of both men as they listened. And not without cause; for, clear and distinct, came the notes of a hautboy, playing a lively melody, and most evidently from somewhere within the sacred precincts of the building. Fittleworth remained for some seconds rigid as a statue, with his mouth open and his eyes fixed on those of the painter; but suddenly he recovered himself, and, without a word, darted from the room. Passing the water-colourist, who was looking over his shoulder and grinning, he entered the larger gallery, to find the easels deserted and the students trooping out of the door; and, following them, soon found himself in a momentarily-augmenting crowd of copyists, all surging towards the source of the music and all on the broad grin.

It was in the Venetian room that Fittleworth finally ran the musician to earth. There he found a dense crowd, collected round Titian's Bacchus and Ariadne, and at its centre, a tall, thin man of grotesque and whimsical aspect, who wore a steeple-crowned felt hat and a long cloak, apparently quite oblivious of his audience. At the moment of Fittleworth's arrival, he was giving a spirited and skilful rendering of the "Carnival de Venise" with somewhat florid variations, and meanwhile keeping a pensive eye fixed on the picture. Fittleworth, controlling his features as well as he could, pushed through the crowd and touched the stranger lightly on the shoulder.

"I am sorry," said he, "to interrupt your really admirable performance, but I'm afraid we can't allow it to continue here."

The stranger rolled a solemn, and somewhat reproachful, eye towards the official, and pausing for a moment on a low note, sprang up an octave and opened a fresh suite of variations, of really surprising agility. Fittleworth smothered a grin and waited patiently until the bravura passage came to an end with a most astonishing flourish, when he once more entered his polite demurrer. The stranger removed the instrument from his mouth and, having waited for the applause to subside, turned gravely to Fittleworth.

"Do I understand," said he, "that you object to music in this establishment?"

Fittleworth replied in the affirmative.

The stranger shook his head solemnly. "That," said he, "seems to be an extraordinarily mistaken view. Surely you do not dispute the essential kinship of the fine arts?"

Fittleworth smiled evasively, and the stranger continued, amidst a murmur of encouraging giggles from the students:

"You will not deny, sir, that the different fine arts are but various modes of a general sense of beauty."

Fittleworth was not denying anything; he only objected to the hautboy.

"Then," the stranger persisted, unmoved, "you will admit that each of the modes of beauty is reinforced by exposition and illustration through the other modes. For my part," he added finally, "I regard appropriate and sympathetic music as indispensable to the due appreciation of pictorial beauty," and with this, he turned away and moved off through the gallery followed, like the Pied Piper of Hamelin, by an attendant multitude.

Fittleworth was in somewhat of a dilemma. There was no explicit rule against the playing of musical instruments in the galleries and the act was not in itself unlawful; moreover, the stranger's plea, though fantastic and absurd, was advanced so suavely and plausibly that it was difficult to deal with. He was still smilingly considering what it were best to do, when the stranger halted before Claude's "Embarkation of St Ursula" and forthwith began a plaintive rendering of "Partant pour la Syrie." For a while the humour of the situation was too much for Fittleworth, and the performance was nearly at an end before he had recovered himself sufficiently to renew his protests; but as the stranger moved away, he once more addressed him with polite, but urgent, remonstrance. The musician regarded him with reproachful surprise and again urged him to consider the intimate relation between the different modes of beauty, instancing the performances of Miss Maud Allen as a familiar and popular example; and even while Fittleworth was racking his brain for a suitable rejoinder, the stranger drew up abruptly before David's portrait of Elisa Bonaparte, and fixing a fiery eye upon the picture, burst into the "Marseillaise."

Fittleworth felt himself becoming hysterical as the students cheered and the stirring phrases of the warlike melody rang through the building. It was useless to protest. The stranger only frowned, and rolled a compelling eye that demanded silence. Bewildered attendants watched the performance from afar with horrified stares and the crowd grew from moment to moment. After a brief appreciation of Fragonard's "Happy Mother" (to the air of "La Vierge à la Creche"), he moved on into the Dutch Gallery, and pausing before a picture of Van Ostade's, struck up with surprising spirit and verve "The Dutchman's Little Wee Dog"; which brought down the house and, incidentally, put a term to the performance. For at this point, to Fittleworth's great relief, an irritable old lady, who was copying a Rembrandt, came forward and demanded how she could "be expected to work in this disgusting hubbub." Fittleworth took the opportunity to point out to the musician that the galleries were at present filled with workers to whom his admirable performance, though delightful on a more seasonable occasion, was, just now, a distraction and a hindrance.

The stranger turned, and raised his steeple-crowned hat.

"That," said he, with a low bow to the old lady, "is an entirely different matter. If my presence is a source of disturbance, there is nothing for it but for me to wish you a very good morning.

With this and another low bow, and an elaborate flourish of his hat, he turned, and adjusting the mouthpiece of his instrument, walked away briskly towards the entrance hall, playing "The Girl I left behind me."

It was some considerable time before the galleries settled down again. The students, gathered into groups, eagerly discussed the fantastic stranger, and Fittleworth, passing from one group to another, was assailed by innumerable questions. It was getting on for lunchtime when he found himself once more in the neighbourhood of the isolated room where the portrait was in progress, and he noticed, as he passed through the corridor, that the water-colourist had already left. He found Mr Dudley staring discontentedly through his great spectacles at the picture on his easel, and a single glance showed him that there was abundant cause for discontent.

"What do you think of it?" the painter asked, looking up doubtfully.

Fittleworth pursed up his lips. "I'm afraid," said he, "you haven't improved it. The tone is certainly higher but the likeness has suffered, and the whole thing looks coarse and patchy."

Dudley gazed gloomily at the canvas and nodded. "I'm afraid you're right," said he. "I've mucked it up. That's the plain truth."

"You certainly haven't improved it," agreed Fittleworth, "and, if I might venture to advise, I would recommend you to clean off this morning's work and consider the picture finished."

The painter stood up and surveyed his work savagely. "You're perfectly right," said he, "and I'll follow your advice." He closed his folding-palette and began rapidly to pack up his materials, while Fittleworth stood, gazing regretfully at the spoiled painting. When he had packed his box and brush-case, Dudley proceeded to secure the canvas, which was very neatly arranged for safe transport, being fixed by catches to the bottom of a shallow box, the sliding lid of which served to protect the wet surface.

"Are you going to take it away with you?" Fittleworth asked, as the painter slid the lid into its groove and fixed on the carrying straps.

"Yes," replied Dudley, "I will take it home and then I shan't be tempted to tinker at it again when I've cleaned this mess off."

Having closed and packed his easel, he picked up his heavy colourbox, his brush-case and a leather bag, and Fittleworth, seeing him thus encumbered, politely offered to carry the box which contained the painting; and so they walked together to the entrance-hall, where Fittleworth delivered up the shallow box to its owner, wishing him luck in his efforts to obliterate the traces of the unfortunate morning's work.

About eleven o'clock on the following forenoon, Fittleworth halted by the easel appertaining to Miss Katharine Hyde for a few minutes' confidential chat. He did not often allow himself this luxury, for the two young people had agreed that their relations inside the building had better be kept on a business footing. But every rule has its exceptions, and besides, as Katharine had not been present on he previous morning, she had to be told about the musical stranger. Fittleworth was in the midst of a spirited narration of the incident, when one of the attendants approached with a mysterious air.

"Beg pardon, sir," said he, "but there's a Mr Dudley has come to work at his picture and we can't find it."

Fittleworth frowned. "Dudley, Dudley," he muttered, "isn't that the – yes, of course." And, as a red-haired person with large spectacles advanced in the wake of the attendant, he said, "have you been asking for your picture, Mr Dudley?"

The artist replied that he had.

"But, my dear sir," laughed Fittleworth, "you took it away with you yesterday morning."

The painter gazed at him with owlish surprise.

"I wasn't here yesterday morning," said he.

Fittleworth stared at him, in silent astonishment, for a few moments. Then he exclaimed impatiently:

"Oh, nonsense, Mr Dudley. You can't have forgotten. You were working at the picture all the morning, and I helped you myself to carry it to the entrance-hall."

The painter shook his head. "I was working the whole of yesterday in the National Portrait Gallery. You must have helped someone else out with my picture."

Fittleworth started, and was sensible of a chill of vague alarm. The painter's appearance was so remarkable that a mistake seemed impossible. And yet he began to have an uneasy feeling that this was not the same man. There was the same long, red hair and the same enormous spectacles, but the face was not quite that of the man whom he had talked to yesterday, and the voice and manner seemed appreciably different. And again, a vague and chilly terror clutched at his heart.

"Shall we go and look at the attendance book?" said he; and as the painter agreed with alacrity, they hurried away.

"Your name is Guildford Dudley, I think," said Fittleworth, with his finger on the page that recorded yesterday's attendances.

"Yes," replied Dudley, "but that's not my handwriting."

Fittleworth reflected for a moment in a state bordering on panic.

"I'm afraid," said he, "there's something wrong; but we'd better run round to the Portrait Gallery and verify your statement."

They hurried out together, and turning round into St Martin's Place, entered the Portrait Gallery, where a very brief investigation proved that Mr Dudley had been engaged the whole of the previous day.

Fittleworth broke out into a cold sweat. It was evident that a fraud had been committed; and a most elaborate fraud for, among other matters, an attendance card must have been counterfeited. But what could be the object of that fraud? A copy, no matter how good, seemed hardly worth such deliberate and carefully-considered plans. Fittleworth and the painter looked at one another, and with the same horrible suspicion in both their minds they hurried away together to put it to the test.

As Fittleworth entered the small, isolated room where the counterfeit Dudley had been at work on the previous day, he drew a breath of relief; for there, at least, was the original, secure in its frame. But his relief was short-lived; for Dudley, who had followed him closely, strode up to the picture and, after a quick, critical glance, turned to him with raised eyebrows.

"That is my copy," said he.

Fittleworth felt all his terror reviving, and yet this awful thing seemed impossible.

"How can it be?" he exclaimed. "You see that the canvas is quite uninjured and the frame is screwed to the wall."

"I know nothing about that," replied Dudley. "I only know that that's my copy."

Fittleworth directed an agonised stare through the glass, and as he looked more closely, he felt a growing suspicion that the painter was right. The brush work and even the surface of the original had been closely and cleverly imitated, but still – here Fittleworth turned sharply to an attendant, who had followed them into the room.

"Go and fetch a screwdriver," said he, "and bring another man with you."

The attendant hurried away and returned almost immediately accompanied by a workman, carrying a screwdriver. The frame of the picture, unlike some others in the gallery, was fitted with brass plates which were screwed to hard wood plugs let into the wall. By Fittleworth's direction, the workman proceeded to unscrew one of the plates while his assistant grasped the picture frame. Fittleworth impatiently watched the screwdriver as it made about a dozen turns, when the man stopped and looked up at him.

"There's something rummy about this screw, sir," he remarked.

"It seems to turn all right," said Fittleworth.

"Oh, it turns all right," said the man, "but it don't git no forrader. Let's try another."

He did so, but the second screw developed the same peculiar properties. And then a most remarkable thing happened. As the workman stepped back to direct a puzzled look at the screw-plates, his assistant must have pulled slightly at the frame for it began to separate visibly from the wall. The workman dropped his screwdriver and seized the frame which, with another pull, came away bodily, with the four screws loose in the plates.

Fittleworth uttered a cry of despair. A single glance at the back of the brand new canvas put the fraud beyond all doubt, and another glance at the screws left little to be explained as to the methods adopted by the robber. To Dudley, however, who was unaware of the events of the previous day, the whole affair was a profound mystery.

"I don't see how they managed it at all," said he, "unless they got in in the night."

"I'll tell you about it presently," said Fittleworth. "Meanwhile, if you will lend us your copy for a few days, we will put the frame back; and mind," he added, addressing the attendants, "nothing is to be said about this at present."

When the picture had been replaced and the men had gone away, Fittleworth gave the artist a brief account of the happenings of the previous day, to which Dudley listened thoughtfully.

"I see the general scheme," said he, "but what I don't understand is how that man managed to do it all in such a short time, and with people moving about the galleries, too."

"I think that's all clear enough," said Fittleworth. "You see, the actual exchange of the pictures need have taken less than a minute. Everything had been carefully prepared beforehand. The thieves must have come here on previous days with the dummy screws in their pockets, and it would be the easiest thing in the world to take out the screws one at a time and push the dummies in in their place. And as to loosening the canvas in the frame, two men could easily do that in a minute or two, when once the screws were removed, if they had a sentinel posted in the corridor. Comparatively few people come to this room, you know."

"But that would need three men at least," objected Dudley.

"Exactly," replied Fittleworth, "and I think there were three men; the hautboy player was one; his business being to draw everyone away from the scene of action, and I feel no doubt that the water-colourist was another; a sentinel posted in the corridor to keep watch while the third man made the exchange."

"I see," said Dudley; "and when he'd made the exchange he oiled out the original, rubbed on some colour and put in a few touches on the highlights."

Fittleworth nodded. "Yes," said he, "that is what he must have done; and it would have been fairly easy since the picture was in such good condition and there were no cracks to cover up."

"Yes," agreed Dudley. "It would, it would. But, all the same, he must have been a pretty fair colourist and uncommonly skilful with his brush."

"Yes, he must," agreed Fittleworth, "and that suggests a very important question: this man obviously knew you well, as is proved by the exactness with which he personated you. He also knew exactly what you were doing and has known for some time past, for this was evidently a premeditated scheme, most carefully thought out. Moreover, the personator was clearly a painter of some skill, and even allowing for his make-up must have resembled you somewhat in appearance. Now, Mr Dudley, can you think of anyone to whom that description could apply?"

The painter reflected awhile, and Fittleworth added, somewhat abruptly: "Who commissioned this picture?"

"This copy," replied Dudley, "and the one I was doing next door were commissioned by an American gentleman, named Strauss, who is staying at the Savoy."

"What is Mr Strauss like?" Fittleworth asked.

"He is a tall, lean man, somewhat like the portraits of Abraham Lincoln."

"Ah," murmured Fittleworth, recalling the hautboy player. "How did you come to make Mr Strauss' acquaintance?"

"He introduced himself to me a month or so ago, when I was copying at the Luxembourg; in fact," added Dudley, with a sudden flash of reminiscence, "it was he who suggested that excellent box to protect one's work. He had one made for a copy that I did in Paris, and he provided me with two more for these two copies."

Fittleworth reflected profoundly. The *modus operandi* of this clever fraud was becoming more and more obvious. Clearly, it would be necessary to make inquiries about Mr Strauss, and meanwhile, the Director of the Gallery would have to be told about the catastrophe; a horrible duty, to the execution of which Fittleworth braced himself with a sinking heart and with a suspicion that his official days were numbered.

An unwonted air of depression brooded that evening over the modest apartments of Miss Katharine Hyde, for Fittleworth had just recounted, in minute detail, and a hushed, funereal voice, the appalling history of the robbery.

"It's a hideous affair," he groaned, in conclusion. "The Director took it very well, considering all things, but, of course, I shall have to go."

"Did he say so?" asked Katharine.

"No, but you know the sort of howl that will be raised when the thing becomes known. It'll be frightfully uncomfortable for him, and the least I can do is to take the full blame, seeing that I actually carried the picture out. I shall have to offer to resign and he'll have to accept my resignation. What I shall do for a livelihood after that, the Lord only knows."

"It's dreadfully hard on you," said Katharine, "with all your talents and accomplishments, too."

"It is hard," agreed Fittleworth; "just as there seemed a chance of our being able to marry after all these years. I suppose I ought to release you, Katie, now that our prospects seem hopeless."

"Why?" she asked simply. "I shouldn't want anyone else, you know; and as to my freedom, well, I'm free to be a spinster now if you don't marry me. But we won't give up hope. Perhaps the picture will be found, after all, and then you won't have to resign. Is it a very valuable picture?"

"It's worse than that," said Fittleworth. "It was a loan, and I should say of priceless value to the owners for sentimental reasons."

Katharine looked interested, and being anxious to divert her lover from the subject of their personal misfortunes, asked for more particulars.

"The picture has quite an interesting history," said Fittleworth. "It was painted by Kneller in 1688, and the story goes that the king was actually sitting to the painter when a messenger arrived with the news that the Prince of Orange had landed in Torbay. The portrait was intended as a gift to Samuel Pepys to whom the king was greatly attached, and in spite of the agitation that the bad tidings naturally produced, he commanded Kneller to proceed and get the portrait finished so that his old friend and loyal servant should not be disappointed."

"And did Pepys get the picture?" Katharine asked.

"Yes; and what's more, it remains in the possession of the family to this day, or, at least, it did until it was stolen. So you see, apart from its intrinsic value as a painting, it has this especial value to the family. I had sooner those brutes had stolen almost any other picture in the gallery, even the Raphael Madonna."

"Is there no clue whatever to the identity of the thief?" Katharine asked.

"There was one clue," Fittleworth replied, "but it has broken off short; an American gentleman, named Strauss, who commissioned the portrait. We looked him up at the Savoy, but he has disappeared, and nothing whatever is known as to whence he came or whither he has gone. He was undoubtedly one of the robbers, but he seems to have vanished into thin air."

"Oh, well," said Katharine, "I daresay the police will soon catch him and he'll be sure to have taken care of the picture;" and with this hopeful prognosis the subject was dismissed, at least from speech, though in the minds of both the young people the missing picture remained as a sombre background to all other thought.

As he walked to the gallery on the following morning, Fittleworth considered, for the hundredth time, the most prudent form of procedure. Should he write an official letter tendering his resignation, or should he adopt the less final and deadly plan of offering verbally to resign. He was still undecided when he turned in at the gate and began to ascend the steps; but he reached a decision as he reached the third step from the top, at the very moment when he collided with a commissionaire who was also ascending in company with a brown paper parcel. He would resign, in the first place, at any rate, by word of mouth and see how they took it.

And having formed this decision, he proceeded without further delay to put it in execution.

The Director and the Keeper had apparently talked the matter over, anticipating this course of action.

"Well, Fittleworth," said the former, "the matter doesn't rest with me. If it did, I should say – Who's this from, Jenkins?" The question was addressed to an attendant who had just brought in a brown paper parcel, addressed by name to the Director.

"Don't know, Sir John," was the reply. "A commissionaire brought it. He said there was no answer and he's gone."

The Director nodded, and as the man went out he scrutinised the parcel critically and examined the typewritten address label. "If the matter rested entirely with me," he resumed, "I should say – er – now, what the deuce can this be?" He turned the flattish, oblong parcel over and over, and finally, picking up the office penknife, applied its edge abstractedly to the string. "I should say," he repeated – "if the matter rested with me, that is, which, of course, it doesn't, that – it's a box. I haven't ordered any box. I wonder what the deuce – " Here he pulled the paper fairly open and Fittleworth uttered a cry of astonishment.

"What is it, Fittleworth?" Sir John asked; to which the former made no reply, but leaning across the table, quickly pulled out the sliding lid of the box. And then there fell on the room the silence of utter amazement, for, from the shallow box, there looked out composedly the familiar features of James the Second.

"Well," Sir John exclaimed, at length, "this is the most astonishing affair of all. I suppose it's all right," he added suspiciously, unclamping the picture and lifting it out of the box. "They're such uncommonly artful dodgers; still, I think there's no doubt this is the genuine original. But why on earth have they returned it, after taking all that trouble to steal it?"

The three men pored over the canvas, searching suspiciously for any sign of change or substitution. But there was none. The surface of the painting was unaltered and apparently none the worse for its recent vicissitudes.

"They seem to have handled it carefully," Mr Barnard remarked. "No one would dream that it had been covered up with fresh paint."

"No," agreed Sir John; "it hasn't left a trace. They must have used a slow-drying oil and cleaned it off immediately. But," he added, turning the picture over, "they've had the canvas off the stretcher. Do you notice that?" He held the picture towards the other two, who examined it narrowly.

"It seems to me, Sir John," said Fittleworth, after running his eye round the edge of the canvas, "that it's only been off at one end. The tacks at the top and the upper part of the sides don't seem to have been disturbed."

The Director looked at the picture once more. "You're quite right, Fittleworth," said he. "The canvas has been off the stretcher at the lower end only; and what's more, the bottom bar of the stretcher has been removed and replaced by a fresh piece. Do you see that? The piece that has been inserted is old wood but it's different from the other three, and you can clearly make out the fresh surface that has been left in cutting the tenons. It is a very astonishing thing. What do you make of it, Barnard?" Mr Barnard could make nothing of it and said so. "The whole thing is a complete mystery to me," said he. "They may have damaged the old stretcher-bar and had to replace it; but I don't see why they wanted to unfasten the canvas at all."

"Neither do I," said Sir John, "but the main thing is that we've got the picture back uninjured, and, that being so, perhaps you would like to reconsider your resignation, Fittleworth."

"I don't think I will, Sir John," replied the latter. "The affair is known to several people and there's bound to be some sort of inquiry."

"Perhaps you're right," rejoined the Director. "At any rate, we will hear what the Trustees say. Of course, if the matter rested with me – but it doesn't; so, for the time being, I must accept your resignation."

PART II

It was perhaps fortunate that Saturday is a public day at most galleries, and so, an off-day for copyists; for in any case there would have been no work on this disastrous morning for Miss Katharine. Within a few minutes of Fittleworth's arrival at the Gallery, she had taken up a position at the foot of the Nelson Column to await the promised report on the course of events. Fittleworth, on leaving the Director's room, made straight for the trysting place, and was received with a bright smile and a small, outstretched hand, as they turned away together towards Whitehall.

"Well," asked Kate, "what has happened?"

"I've offered to resign," replied Fittleworth.

"And of course Sir John scouted the idea?" said Katharine.

"Oh, did he?" exclaimed Fittleworth. "Not at all. He did say that if the matter rested with him, he'd – "

"What?"

"I don't quite know, but the great news is that the picture has come back."

"Oh, good!" exclaimed Katharine. "But, if it has come back, why on earth should you resign?"

"You'll see if I tell you how it came back;" and here Fittleworth described the mysterious return of the picture and the still more mysterious change of the stretcher bar.

"But I still don't see why you're resigning," Katharine persisted.

"Then," said Fittleworth, "I'll explain. You see, Sir John and Barnard are concerned with the picture, *qua* picture, and from that point of view, a stretcher-bar is just a stretcher-bar and nothing else. But there's one point that they've overlooked – at least, I think they have. This was not only a picture: it was a family relic."

"But what has that to do with it?" asked Katharine.

"That question, my dear girl, is best answered by another. What did those men want with the old stretcher-bar?"

"Well, what did they?"

"I don't know," replied Fittleworth; "but as soon as I saw that the bar had been changed, I realised that there was something more in this robbery than met the eye. Consider the facts, Katie. First you will see that these men were not common thieves, for they have not only returned the property, but have obviously been most careful not to injure it; which is quite unlike a criminal, who is usually perfectly regardless of the amount of damage he does. In the second place, you will notice that these men wanted the bottom stretcher-bar of the canvas, and wanted it so badly that they were willing to go to great trouble and expense to get it. Next, you will see that these are men of very superior intelligence. One of them is quite a skilful painter, and another an expert musician, and one of them, at least, is a person of great ingenuity. And now, consider the picture itself. It was painted for the King when the Revolution had actually begun and was to be given into the custody of a man who was the King's trusty friend, who was a man of unswerving loyalty, of infallible judgment and discretion, and who was so perfect a man of the world that he was practically certain not to be involved in any of the troubles that were to follow. What does this suggest to you?"

"It doesn't suggest anything," she replied, with a vague little shake of the head. "What does it suggest to you?"

"Well," he replied, "you will agree that for a small and precious object, the stretcher-bar of a valuable picture would furnish an ideal hiding-place; and seeing that three men who are obviously not fools have gone to immense trouble to get possession of this bar, I am inclined to assume that it had been used for that purpose."

"Really, Joe!" exclaimed Katharine, "what a delightfully romantic idea! And how Machiavellian of you to have thought of it! Shall we turn into the Park for a little while?"

Fittleworth assented, and as they had now reached the gates of the Horse Guards, they passed through, furtively watched by the gaudy sentinel, who stood, like some gorgeous tropical bird, keeping guard over the tunnel-like entry. The two lovers walked soberly across the great gravel expanse, and it was not until they had passed through the small gate into the Park, that they took up the thread of their talk. It was Katharine who spoke first.

"Have you made any sort of guess as to what it was that was hidden in that bar?"

"No, I haven't," replied Fittleworth; "and it's no use guessing. But this much I think is plain: those men must have had some pretty definite information, and as they couldn't have got it from the picture, they must have got it from somewhere else; and the question is, where else could they have got it?"

"Could someone have told them?" Katharine suggested.

"No, certainly not, for if anyone had known of the hiding-place, the hidden object would have been removed long ago. The only possible conclusion seems to be that a written record of the hiding-place exists and has been overlooked."

"I see," said Katharine. "You mean among some of the old family papers."

"Possibly," replied Fittleworth, "but I think not. You see that, wherever the record is, these men have obtained access to it. Now, they can hardly be members of the family, for if they had been, they could have abstracted the stretcher-bar when the picture was in the private collection instead of waiting until it was in a public gallery. So that it seems to follow that the record that they have seen, is in some place which is accessible to the public. And if it is accessible to the public, why, you see, Katie dear, that it must be accessible to us."

"Yes," agreed Katharine. "I suppose it must; if we only knew where to look for it. But perhaps my Machiavellian Joseph has thought of that, too."

"I haven't had much time to think about it at all," replied Fittleworth; "but there is one likely place that occurs to me, and probably much the most likely: my old college."

"At Cambridge?"

"Yes, Magdalene. That was Pepys' college, you know, and he bequeathed to it, not only the famous Diary, but a large number of manuscript memoirs on naval and other affairs, as well as prints and collections of ancient poetry. It is highly probable that the document of which we are assuming the existence, is among the papers in the Pepysian library; but if it is, there is one little difficulty which will have to be got over."

"What is that?"

"Why, you remember that the prudent and secretive Samuel had a way of writing his private memoranda in shorthand, which he evidently used for security rather than brevity; and that being so, we may be pretty certain that our hypothetical document would be in shorthand, too. That is rather a serious difficulty, though I fancy that the system that he used was not a very complicated one. I must find out what Rich's system is like."

Katharine clapped her hands. "Rich's!" she exclaimed. "How delightful! Have you forgotten that I am an expert in Rich's shorthand?"

"I never knew," said Fittleworth.

"Oh, but I'm sure that I told you. It was when I used to copy drawings and manuscripts at the British Museum that I got a commission to make a facsimile of a volume written in Rich's shorthand. Of course it was necessary to know something about the system or I should have got the characters wrong, so I learnt it up from an old handbook, and by the time I had done my task I had become rather skilful. It's really quite simple, you know, as compared with modern systems like Pitman's."

Fittleworth regarded Katharine with admiring surprise. "What a clever little lady it is!" he remarked, "and how opportunely clever, too! Do you think it would take you long to teach me?"

"But what is it that you propose to do?" she asked.

"I propose to go down to Magdalene, and go through all the Pepys papers of the Revolution period, keeping a specially sharp look-out for any written in shorthand. There are not likely to be many of these, for poor old Pepys' eyesight became so bad that he had to give up keeping a shorthand diary after 1670."

Katharine reflected earnestly, and as they took possession of an empty seat in a secluded path, she slipped her hand coaxingly around his arm.

"I'm going to make a rather bold proposition, Joe. Of course you can learn Rich's shorthand without any difficulty. But it would take some time and a good deal of trouble, whereas, I already know it and have had quite a lot of experience in copying and deciphering the characters. Now, why shouldn't you take me with you to Cambridge and let me decipher the shorthand papers?"

Fittleworth took a critical survey of the toe of his boot, and reflected on the personal peculiarities of a certain mythical female of the name of Grundy; and Katharine, stealing a cautious glance at him, deciphered a cryptogram that was easier than Rich's.

"Maggie Flinders would put me up, I know," she said à propos of the decipherment. "She's a something at Newnham, and we're quite old friends."

Fittleworth's face cleared. "That gets rid of one difficulty," said he, "and the other difficulty I must get over as best I can."

"You mean the expense that the inquiry will involve?" said Katharine.

"Yes. You see, I have no doubt that something of considerable value has been stolen, and stolen through my thick-headedness; and if that something can be recovered, it's my duty to get it back if I spend my last halfpenny in doing it."

"Yes," said Katharine. "I quite agree with you, excepting as to the thick-headedness, which is all nonsense; for of course the Director himself would have been taken in if he'd been in your place. So I'm going to make another proposition. I am just as keen on your getting this thing back as you are; in fact, your credit is my credit. Now, I have a little capital put by for a contingency that doesn't seem likely to arise just at present, and I should like to invest some of it in our joint undertaking."

It is needless to say that Fittleworth objected violently. It is equally needless to say that Katharine trampled on his objections with scorn, and that when they rose from the seat, the inevitable thing had happened. As the poet expresses it: "Man has his will but Woman has her way." The joint expedition to Cambridge was an accepted fact.

PART III

The services of Miss Flinders were not required after all. An old friend of Fittleworth's, a tutor and fellow of the college, who had married and settled down in Cambridge, had accommodation in his house for a pair of industriously studious turtledoves, and was even willing to provide them with a small study in which to carry out their researches.

So, Mrs Grundy being thus appeased on extremely advantageous terms, the doves aforesaid took up their abode in the residence of Mr Arthur Winton, M.A., LL.B., and the permission of the Master of the College and that of the Curator of the Pepysian Library having been applied for and obtained, the great investigation began.

It was a Tuesday morning, bright and sunny, when Fittleworth set forth on his quest. He carried with him, in addition to a quarto notebook, a half-plate camera of the most approved construction, the property of Mr Winton, who was an expert photographer and who had made the excellent suggestion that any likely documents should be photographed in order that they might be studied quietly at home and facsimile copies retained permanently for subsequent reference. So Fittleworth went forth with the camera in his hand and bright hope in his heart, picturing himself already restoring to its unconscious owner that (presumably precious) object of unknown nature, the very existence of which was unsuspected by anyone but himself. It would be a great achievement. His credit would be thereby completely restored and he must infallibly be reinstated in his not very lucrative office.

The first cool draught which blew upon his enthusiasm came from the material placed at his disposal. It was a colossal mass. Apart from the prints, drawings, maps and collections of poetry, none of which could be entirely disregarded – for even the poems might contain a concealed hint – there was an enormous bulk of miscellaneous papers, all of which must be gone through before any could be rejected. And, as he gazed at the collection with growing dismay, he realised for the first time the extraordinary vagueness of his quest. What was it, after all, that he was looking for? The question admitted only of the most ambiguous answer. He had but two fixed points; the Revolution and the portrait by Kneller. Of the connection between them he was totally ignorant, and so might easily miss the clue even if it were under his very eyes.

The famous Diary he dismissed after a brief glance of fond curiosity, for its last sad entry of May the 31st, 1669, was long before the stormy days when the catlike obstinacy of James brought its inevitable catastrophe. Other dated papers, too, could be set aside; but when all that was possible in this way had been done, the residue that remained to be studied was positively appalling in its bulk. The first day was entirely taken up by a preliminary inspection, of which the chief result was profound discouragement. Then followed a fortnight of close and strenuous labour, involving the minute study of countless documents on every possible subject, with fruitless efforts to extract from them some information bearing even indirectly on the picture. Day after day did he return to Katharine with the same dismal report of utter failure; and though his spirits revived under the influence of her bright hopefulness, yet as the time ran on and the joint capital dwindled, so did his confidence grow less. It was a bigger undertaking than he had bargained for. The mass of material and the formalities accompanying the examination of such precious relics involved an expenditure of time and labour that was quite beyond his calculations. And there was another discouraging element, of which for the present he said nothing to Katharine. As the days passed without a hint of any clue, a horrible suspicion began to creep into his mind. Suppose the whole thing was a delusion! That the substitution of the stretcher-bar was due merely to some chance accident, and that he was searching for something that had no existence save in his own imagination. Then all this labour and time and ill-spared money were utterly thrown away. It was a dreadful thought; and as it came to him again and again at increasingly frequent intervals, his heart sank and the future grew dark and hopeless.

It was on the fifteenth day that the first faint ray of hope pierced the gloom of his growing despair. On that day, amidst a collection of unclassified papers, he lit on something that at least invited inquiry. The find consisted of three small sheets of paper, evidently torn from a pocket memorandum book, each about four inches by two and a half, and all covered with microscopic writing in a strange, crabbed character which Fittleworth immediately recognised as some kind of shorthand. There was nothing to indicate the date, and, on applying to the librarian, Fittleworth was informed that nothing was known about the little papers excepting that they had belonged to Pepys, and were almost certainly in his handwriting. The script on them had never been deciphered, although several persons – one quite recently – had examined them; and the librarian was of opinion that they were never likely to be, as the writing was so small and so excessively shaky and badly written that it appeared to be practically undecipherable.

The librarian's report was, on the face of it, discouraging. But to Fittleworth the very illegibility of the writing gave it an added interest, hinting, as it did, at a late period when the use of the shorthand had become difficult. At his request the Diary was produced for comparison of the style of handwriting; and, on comparing the first of the six volumes with the last, it was evident that there was a change in the character of the script, though even the last entry, where Pepys records the failure of his eyesight, was far clearer and better written than the microscopic scrawl on these three loose leaves. Which was highly satisfactory, provided only that the illegibility was not so complete as to render decipherment utterly impossible.

Having applied for and obtained permission to photograph the three leaves – each of which had writing on one side only – Fittleworth exposed three plates, and then, suspending his labours for the day, set forth homeward full of excitement and revived hope.

He was just approaching the house when Katharine overtook him and, judging by his early return that something had happened, asked eagerly: "Have you got it, Joe?"

Fittleworth smiled. "I've got some sort of document in shorthand," he replied.

"Do you think it says anything about the picture?" asked Katharine. "But there," she added, with a laugh, "my excitement is making me talk nonsense. Of course, I've got to find out what it says."

"Yes," said Fittleworth, "you have; and I wish you joy of the job. It's a fearful scrawl; so bad that nobody has been able to decipher it yet. The librarian tells me," he added, with a knowing glance at her, "that only three months ago, an American scholar, who had obtained permission to go through the collection, spent more than a week trying to decipher it with the aid of a watchmaker's lens and had to give it up after all. So you see, my dear, that you have a very pretty little task before you."

Katharine looked at him thoughtfully. "That doesn't sound very encouraging," she said; and then after a pause, during which she reflected profoundly, with her usually smooth forehead furrowed by cogitative wrinkles, she looked up suddenly.

"I suppose, Joe, he *didn't* make anything of it after all."

Fittleworth laughed genially. "I was waiting for that," said he. "You are thinking that the American scholar may be a gentleman of musical tastes. I expect you are right and I hope you are, as that would prove that we are really on the track of our friends; but we shall be able to judge better when you have given us a sample of your skill. We shall be rather up a tree if you're not able to decipher the thing."

The latter contingency Katharine declined to entertain, and the pair, resisting the attractions of tea, made straight for Mr Winton's dark-room. The three plates were developed without a hitch, and while two were drying in the rack, the third was taken to the window for inspection.

"Well," said Fittleworth, as Katharine stood at the window, holding out the wet negative towards the sky, "what do you think of it?"

For some seconds Katharine made no reply, but continued to gaze at the crabbed lines on the black surface with a frown that gradually deepened.

"It's very small writing," she replied, at length, "and frightfully indistinct."

"Yes, I was afraid it was," said Fittleworth; "but do you make out anything of the – er – purport, or – er – or, what it's about, in fact?"

There was a brief pause; then Katharine, looking him tragically in the eyes, exclaimed:

"My dear Joe, I can't make out a single word. It's absolute scribble."

There was another pause, at the end of which Fittleworth murmured the single and highly irrelevant word, "Moses!"

24

The impatience of the investigators would not allow them to wait for the natural drying of the negatives. One after another, the plates were plunged into methylated spirit, and when dry, printed off rapidly on glossy bromide paper; and with the prints before her on a table by the study window, the agonised Katharine fell to work with Fittleworth's pocket lens and a most portentous frown.

Five minutes passed. Fittleworth moved stealthily, but uneasily, about the room on tiptoe, now forcing himself to sit on the edge of a chair, and now forced by his excitement to rise and tiptoe across to another. At length, unable to contain himself any longer, he asked in a hushed voice: "Is it very awful stuff, Katie?"

Katharine laid down the lens and looked round at him despairingly.

"It's perfectly frightful, Joe," she exclaimed. "I simply can't make anything of it."

"Perhaps it isn't Rich's shorthand at all," suggested Fittleworth.

"Oh, yes it is. I can see that much and I've made out a 'with' and two 'the's,' but the rest of it looks like mere scribble."

Fittleworth sprang from the chair on which he had been seated nearly ten seconds. "Oh, come," said he; "if you can make out that much, you can make out the rest. Only we shall have to go to work systematically. The best way will be to mark each word as you decipher it and write it down on a piece of paper. That's the best of working from a photograph which it doesn't matter about spoiling."

"I don't quite see what you mean," said Katharine.

"The method I suggest is this," he replied. "First mark the three photographs A, B and C. Then, number the lines of each and prepare three sheets of paper lettered and numbered in the same way. Then, when you decipher a word, say on photograph A line 6, write it down on the sheet marked A, on the sixth line and the proper part of that line; and so on. Could I help you?"

Katharine thought that he could, and accordingly, he drew a chair to the table and proceeded to prepare three sheets of paper in the way he had suggested and to mark the photographs.

There is something about a really methodical procedure that inspires confidence. Of this Katharine was immediately sensible, and when the two "the's" and the "with" had been set down in their proper places, she felt that a beginning had really been made and returned to her task with renewed spirit.

"There's a 'his,' " she announced presently, "at the end of line I, page B, and the first word of the next line is a longish one ending in 'ty.' "

"It isn't 'Majesty,' I suppose," suggested Fittleworth.

"Yes, of course it is," exclaimed Katharine, "and the next word is 'at,' followed by two short words ending in 'll.' "

"White Hall?" queried Fittleworth; and White Hall it turned out to be on further examination. The next proceeding was to search for a recurrence of these words with the result that "His Majesty" occurred six times in all, and "White Hall" twice.

"Now try the words adjoining 'His Majesty,' " Fittleworth suggested. "Take the one on page B. We've got 'His Majesty at White Hall.' Now, what is before that?"

"There's a 'me' and then 'attack' or 'attach.' "

"Me attack His Majesty,' " murmured Fittleworth. "That doesn't sound right. Could it be 'attend'?"

"Yes, I believe it is, and then the word before it must be 'bidding.' We're getting on splendidly. Let us try the 'His Majestys' on page A. Line 5 seems to begin: 'As to its' something, 'His Majesty has' something, 'his' – now, what has His Majesty done? Oh, I see, 'written.' 'His Majesty has written his – ' "

"Instructions," suggested Fittleworth.

"No, nor wishes, nor – oh, I see 'commands,' and the next words are 'in full in a' something, 'which he' something 'to me in a small' something 'box.' Now, let us see if we can fill in that sentence. 'As to its' something, 'His Majesty has written his commands'; now, as to his what? It seems to begin with a 'd'."

"Destiny?" suggested Fittleworth, and as Katharine shook her head he proposed "destruction," "deposition," and finally, "disposition."

"No, it's not 'disposition.' It's 'disposal.' 'As to its disposal His Majesty has written his commands in full in a paper which he' – something 'to me in a small' something 'box which he – ' "

"Gave, sent, presented, showed, exhibited, delivered – "

" 'Delivered,' that's it. 'Delivered to me in a small' something 'box.' "

"Wooden, ivory, leather, silver – "

"Gold," announced Katharine triumphantly, " 'a small, gold box'; and the sentence runs on: 'the said box being' something 'with His Majesty's' something, something, 'and this box he bid me put by in some safe and' – it looks like 'secret place.' I'm getting to read it much more easily now. Let us go back to that 'box.' 'With His Majesty's' something 'seal,' I think."

"Private seal, perhaps."

"Yes, of course. Then it reads: 'The said box being sealed with His Majesty's private seal and this box he bid me put by in some safe and secret place.' This is splendid, Joe. We shall make it out yet and you can see already that we're on the right track."

"Yes; and we can see how those other gentlemen got on the track. But as you seem to be getting more used to the writing, wouldn't it be as well now to try to begin at the beginning and go straight on?"

"Perhaps it would. But the question is, which is the beginning?"

"The best way to solve that difficulty would be to work out the first line of each page. Don't you think so, Katie?"

"Yes, of course; and I'll begin with page A. Now the first line seems to read: 'bids me to carry' – no, it isn't 'carry'; I think it's 'convey' – 'convey it to Sir' – Andrew, I think – 'Sir Andrew Hyde – ' "

At this point Katharine laid down the lens and turned to gaze at Fittleworth with a very curious expression of surprise and bewilderment.

"A namesake of yours, Katie," he remarked; "an ancestor, perhaps."

"Yes, Joe, that's just it. Only, in that case it would be 'Sir Andreas.' " She scrutinised the paper again through the lens and at length exclaimed triumphantly, "and it is 'Andreas.' Let us see how it goes on: 'To Sir Andreas Hyde, a cousin of my Lord Clarendon' – yes, that is the man – 'who is to deposit it in some secure place in one of his houses in Kent'. I wonder if he means the picture!"

"We shall see presently," said Fittleworth; "but meanwhile it is evident that this is not the first page. Just have a look at page C."

Katharine transferred her attention, as well as her excitement would permit, to the latter page; but after a prolonged examination she shook her head.

"This isn't the first," she said, "for the top line begins with the words: 'had concluded the business'. Then page B must be the first. Let us try that." She brought the lens to bear on the opening words of page B, but after a brief inspection she sat up with an exclamation of disappointment.

"Oh, Joe, how tantalising! This isn't the first either! There's a page missing. You will have to go back to the library and see if you can find it."

"That's rather a facer," said Fittleworth; "but I think, Katie dear, we'd better work out what we've got as these pages will have to be deciphered in any case, and then we shall be able to judge how much is missing. Let us have the first line of page B."

With a dejected air Katharine picked up the lens and resumed her task, slowly reading out, with many a halt to puzzle over a difficult word, the contents of page B.

"...to me a messenger bidding me attend His Majesty at White Hall. Whereupon I set forth and found the King in the Matted Gallery, talking with divers officers and noblemen. When I had kissed his hand he spoke to me openly on the affairs of the navy, but presently, making an occasion to carry me to his closet, did there open the matter concerning which he had sent for me. It appeareth that he hath caught some rumours of certain noblemen and bishops – even the Archbishop as he do think – having invited the Prince of Orange; which he did condemn as most fowle, unhandsome and treasonable. Now, recalling the misfortunes of his brother the late King and their royal father, he would make some provision lest he should be driven into exile, which God forbid. Hereupon he spake very graciously of our long friendship and was pleased to mention most handsomely my faithful service and judgement in the *affairs of the navy, and then he did come to the matter in hand. First he spake of Sir William Phips who did bring his ship the 'James and Mary'…"*

This was the end of page B, and, as Katharine turned eagerly to scan the already deciphered first lines of the other two pages, her eyes filled.

"Oh! Joe dear!" she exclaimed in an agonised voice, "what an awful disappointment! Don't you see? It doesn't run on at all. These are only odd leaves!"

"M'yes," said Fittleworth. "It does look rather a take in. Still, we'd better go on. And as page C seems to refer to the conclusion of the business, whatever it was, we may as well take A next. Keep up your courage, little woman. I may be able to find the missing pages at the library. Now, what has page A got to say?"

Once more Katharine addressed herself to her task, wiping her eyes as a preliminary measure; and slowly and with many a halt to wrestle with an almost undecipherable word, the crabbed scrawl was translated into good, legible longhand.

"…bids me to convey it to Sir Andreas Hide, a cousin of my Lord Clarendon, who is to deposit it in some secure place in one of his houses in Kent. As to its disposal, His Majesty hath written his commands in full in a paper which he delivered to me in a small golde box, the said box being sealed with His Majesty's private seale, and this box he bid me put by in some safe and secret place, and to speake of the matter to none, not even Sir Andreas himselfe, until after His Majesty's death and that of the Prince of Wales (if God should spare me so long) unless, in my discretion it should seeme goode to do so. Also that I do make some provision for the delivery of the said paper in the event of my own death.

"When I had returned home I considered at length where I should bestowe the golde box, and presently I bethought me of the King's picture which Sir Godfrey is now about painting and which His Majesty do design to give to me, and it did appear to me that the wooden frame whereon the canvass is strained should furnish a moste secure hiding-place. I made no delay to seek out Sir Andreas at his house at Lee in Kent, to whom the King had already spoken about the matter, and did deliver into his hand the said…"

Here the page ended, and, when she had written the last word, Katharine, after a brief interval of numb silence, fairly burst into tears.

Fittleworth stroked her hand consolingly. "There now, Katie darling," he said in a soothing tone. "We won't cry about it, though it is most confoundedly disappointing. You have done splendidly; and we are really picking up quite a lot of information."

"But what was it that he gave Sir Andreas? It couldn't have been the picture, because he hadn't got it then."

"No, evidently not. Let us work out page C. This is quite a short piece and looks rather like the end of the record."

Once again, Katharine dried her eyes and took up the discarded lens; and slowly – but less slowly than before – the decipherment proceeded.

"*...had concluded the business, the tide serving, I did take boate to White Hall and there reported to His Majesty what I had done but said naught about the picture, reflecting that the secret shall be safer if 'tis known to none save myselfe.*

"*This is a weighty business and do trouble me somewhat; indeede I do mistruste the King's plan which hath too much of secrecie, and leaveth too much in the hands of one man, though that man be, God knows, honest in intention and wishful to serve His Majesty in all things, especially at this sorrowfull time. But I shall do as I am bid and if it please God that the affaire miscarry, at leaste it shall be through no lacke of zeale on my parte.*"

As Katharine wrote the last word, she closed the lens and handed it back to Fittleworth. "There!" she exclaimed, "that is certainly the end of the record and we are just as wise as to what it was that he gave to Sir Andreas as we were before. You will have to go back to the library tomorrow and search for the missing leaves."

Fittleworth held up an admonitory finger. "Now don't be an impatient and unreasonable little person, Katie. It is most likely that the missing pages have disappeared altogether, so, before we spend precious time in searching for them, let us consider what we have got out of these.

"First, we know that the lost stretcher-bar contained a small gold box in which was an important document. That is a great point scored; a very great point, Katie; because, you will please to remember, it was pure guess-work as to whether there was anything at all in the stretcher until you deciphered these papers. Then we know that Pepys handed to Sir Andreas a something that was evidently of considerable value. We don't know what that something was, but we know where it was deposited – at least we should if we could find out where Sir Andreas' houses in Kent were."

"I can tell you that," said Katharine.

"You can!" exclaimed Fittleworth, gazing at her in astonishment.

"Yes," she replied complacently, "I can tell you all about it. You seem to forget that I am a Hyde. This Sir Andreas was the head of our branch of the family and I know all about him. We were just plain country gentlefolk, unlike our great connections, the Clarendons, and the Rochesters, but we have pretty complete family records, and I have studied them in great detail. Sir Andreas had three houses; one at Lee, near London, one at Snodland, near Maidstone, and a third, a small place called Bartholomew Grange, in the Isle of Thanet. Sir Andreas, who was a Catholic, was killed at the Battle of the Boyne, and the family seems to have become considerably impoverished soon after, for his son, Matthew Hyde, sold the houses at Lee and Snodland and went out to New England."

"And what became of those two houses?"

"I believe they were both pulled down and rebuilt. At any rate, they went out of the family. Well, Matthew remained out in New England until the beginning of Queen Anne's reign – 1703, I think – and then he set sail for home in a merchant ship called the *Harvest Moon*. The *Harvest Moon* sailed out of Boston Harbour in December, 1703, and was never heard of again, nor, of course, was Matthew Hyde; and the estate – what little there was of it – went to his son, Robert, who had remained in England."

Fittleworth considered these facts in silence for some time, toying abstractedly with the papers. At length he spoke.

"I think we can guess what happened. Pepys kept his own counsel during the whole reign of Dutch William, but when Anne came to the throne (she was a daughter of Anne Hyde, by the way, and a kinswoman of yours), he looked on the succession as settled, and being then an old man, thought it time to inform Matthew of the existence of the document hidden in the picture and that other something that he had given into the custody of Sir Andreas. I imagine that he sent a messenger to Matthew with a sealed letter containing this information, that Matthew immediately sailed for England and was lost at sea; and that before the news of the shipwreck reached this country Pepys himself was dead (he died on the twenty-first of May, 1704). Thus the secret was lost, even as wise old Samuel Pepys had feared that it might be."

"But it isn't lost completely," Katharine reminded him, "for this ingenious 'American scholar' seems to have got on the track of it; and the question is how are we to get on *his* track?"

"Do you know who owns the third house – Bartholomew Grange?" Fittleworth asked.

"Yes," replied Katharine. "I own it."

"You do!" exclaimed Fittleworth, staring at her incredulously.

"Yes. I thought you knew. My father was the last male of this branch of the family and I am actually the last descendant. The little house in Thanet is all that remains of the family estates, and the rent of it is what I live on – that and my copying."

"Then you could get access to it?"

"Of course I could. The present lease runs out next year, I am sorry to say – for my rent will cease then and I shall have to pay the wages of the housekeeper, who is an old servant of our family. So I could easily ask to make a survey of the premises. But of what use would it be? We have no evidence that the mysterious 'it' is hidden there, and if we had, we don't know what it is or where it is concealed."

"No, my dear, that is perfectly true. But you are forgetting that we are in search of three men who probably believe (and perhaps with good reason) that they have the clue; and who almost certainly have the stolen gold box with them. If Bartholomew Grange is the only house remaining in the family, those gentlemen will undoubtedly look round there first; and if we are not too late, there we shall find them; and if we can't make them disgorge by fair means I shall have them arrested for the robbery of the picture. Remember, the gold box is our immediate object; the rest of the inquiry can wait."

"And what do you propose to do next?" Katharine asked, as a flush of pleasurable excitement mounted to her cheek.

"I propose that you send a letter to your tenant tonight and that we start for town the first thing tomorrow morning and from there go straight on to Thanet. We can talk over details as we go."

Katharine gazed at her lover admiringly. "What a clever old thing you are, Joe!" she exclaimed.

"I should think I am!" laughed Fittleworth. "If it hadn't been for my expert knowledge of Rich's shorthand and the neat way in which I deciphered that – "

"Oh, go along, you old humbug!" Katharine exclaimed, making not very alarming hostile demonstrations. And, in a symbolical and strictly Pickwickian sense, he went along.

PART IV

The Isle of Thanet has a certain peculiar charm which lingers even to this day, despite the too-successful efforts of the speculative builder to annihilate it. A few years ago – at the date of this history, for instance – before the unlovely suburban streets had arisen to disfigure it, the north-eastern quarter of the island wore a pleasant air of remoteness that disguised its proximity to busy Margate and prosperous Broadstairs. It was in this quarter that the business of our adventurers lay, and, having risen with the lark and been fortunate in the matter of trains, they reached it quite early in the day.

"Ah!" exclaimed Fittleworth, sniffing the salt air with the joy of an escaped Londoner, as they left the outskirts of Margate behind, and took their way along the broad path by the cliff's edge; "your worthy ancestor wasn't such a bad judge, Katie. I shouldn't mind living here myself. By the way, I suppose there is no chance of your tenant objecting to our looking over the house?"

"She can't; and if she could, she would not. She is quite a nice person, a widow lady with two daughters. I told her in my letter who you were, and that we wanted to see what would have to be done to the place if the tenancy was not renewed. I also mentioned that you were an artist, and greatly interested in old houses; which is perfectly true, isn't it?"

"Certainly, my dear. But I am a good deal more interested just now in three very ingenious gentlemen and a small gold box."

"It will be frightfully disappointing if they haven't been here after all," said Katharine.

"It will be much more frightful if they have been here and gone away. That's what I am afraid of. They have had a pretty long start."

"They have; but they couldn't have ransacked the place without the consent of Mrs Matthews, my tenant. But we shall soon know everything; that is the house, in among those trees."

The sight of their goal stimulated them to quicken their steps. Soon they came to a high flint wall enclosing thickly wooded grounds, and, skirting this reached a gate on the landward side. Entering, and advancing along a moss-grown path, they presently came in sight of the house, a smallish building of cut flint and brick, with the quaint, curved Flemish gables that are so characteristic of this part of the world.

"What a jolly old house!" exclaimed Fittleworth halting to run his eye admiringly over the picturesque building with its time-softened angles and its rich clothing of moss, lichen, and house-leek. "Sixteen-thirty-one, I see," he added, glancing at the date-tablet over the porch, "so it was a nearly new house when Sir Andreas had it."

He rang the bell, and the door was almost immediately opened by a staid-looking middle-aged maidservant, who was evidently expecting them, and who greeted Katharine affectionately and cast an interested glance at Fittleworth.

"I am sorry, Miss Kate," she said, "that Mrs Matthews is not at home. She had to take the young ladies up to town this morning, and she won't be back for a week or more; but she left all the keys for you, and this note, and she said that you were to make yourself quite at home and do whatever you please. There are three gentlemen looking over the place, but they won't be in your way."

At the last sentence, Fittleworth's eyes lighted with a warlike gleam, and he glanced at Katharine. "Do you know what these three gentlemen are, Rachel, and why they are looking over the place?"

"I heard Mrs Matthews say, sir, that they are archæologists, whatever that may be. But they are wonderfully interested in the house. They have been about the place for more than a week, making sketches of the rooms and staircases, drawing plans of the grounds, tapping at the walls, and looking up the chimneys. I never saw such goings-on. They spent two whole days in the cellars, making sketches, though what they can see in a plain brick cellar beats me, sir. They went all round them tapping the walls with a mallet, and they even wanted to take up some of the floor, but, of course, Mrs Matthews told them she couldn't allow that without the landlady's permission. Perhaps you'd like to see them, miss."

"Are they here now?" asked Katharine.

"One of them is – Mr Simpson. He is in the Chancellor's Parlour, making sketches of the woodwork."

Katharine glanced at Fittleworth. "I think we had better see Mr Simpson," said he; and on this, the maid ushered them through a long corridor to a remote wing of the building, where, at a massive door she halted and turned the handle.

"Why, he's bolted himself in!" she exclaimed; and added under her breath, as she applied somewhat peremptory knuckles to the door: "Like his impudence!"

The knocking evoked no response, nor was there any answering sound from within when it was repeated and reinforced by loud rapping with Fittleworth's walking-stick. Rachel listened at the keyhole, and, as still no sound was audible, she exclaimed indignantly: "Well, I'm sure! It's a pretty state of things when strangers come to bolt people out of their own rooms."

"But," said Fittleworth, "the odd thing is that there doesn't seem to be anybody in there. Can we see in through any of the windows?"

"Oh, yes, sir," answered Rachel. "The window looks out on the Chancellor's Garden, a little garden closed in by a yew hedge. If you'll follow me, I'll show it to you; though, of course, Miss Kate knows the way."

As they followed the maid out into the grounds, Fittleworth asked: "Why is this room called the Chancellor's Parlour?"

"It is named after the great Lord Clarendon, the head of the family, you know," Katharine replied. "The tradition is that he used sometimes to come down here for rest and quiet, and that he occupied this wing which is cut off from the rest of the house and has its own separate garden. This is the garden, and that is the window of the parlour, fortunately not fastened."

The old-fashioned leaded casement was slightly open, so that Rachel could reach in and unhook it from the strut. As she threw it wide open, she announced:

"There's no one in the room, but I can see that the bolt is shot. He must have got out of the window. I call that pretty cool, in another person's house. And why wasn't the door good enough for him, I should like to know?"

"Perhaps he didn't want his work disturbed," suggested Fittleworth. "I see he has a large drawing on an easel. However, I will step in through the window and unbolt the door, while you go round."

He climbed in easily through the window, and, having unbolted the door cast an inquisitive glance at the absent Simpson's arrangements. On a sketching-easel was a large drawing board covered with a sheet of Whatman, on which was the earliest beginning of a drawing of the carved mantelpiece. A table close by bore one or two pencils, a water-colour palette, a jar of water, a slab of rubber, and a number of brushes. The drawing — what there was of it — was expertly done, but represented, at the most, half an hour's work.

"How long had Mr Simpson been in this room?" he asked, as Rachel and Katharine entered.

"The three gentlemen came here yesterday and made some sketches, but Mr Simpson didn't bring his things till this morning. He came about nine, and at half-past eleven he came to me for a jar of water."

Fittleworth reflected, with a cogitative eye on the drawing.

"Well," he said at length, with a glance at Katharine; "I think we can manage without Mr Simpson: As we are here, we may as well begin our survey with this room. Don't you think so?"

Katharine agreed; and when she had explained to the hospitable Rachel that they had lunched in the train, the maid said:

"Then I will leave you now. If you want anything you have only to ring. It's an old room, but it has an electric bell. And if I might make a suggestion, it would be as well to close the window, so that Mr Simpson will have to come in by the door in a proper and decent way."

As soon as she was gone, Fittleworth and Katharine looked at one another significantly, and the latter exclaimed: "What an extraordinary thing, Joe. Do you really think he got out of the window?"

"I doubt it very much, Katie. But, at any rate, we will adopt Miss Rachael's suggestion, and see that he doesn't come back that way; and then we will have a good look round."

He closed and fastened the window, and stood awhile surveying the room. It was a smallish apartment, rather barely furnished with five carved walnut chairs, an oaken livery cupboard, and a ponderous Elizabethan draw-table with the thick foot-rests and massive melon-bulb legs of the period. A wide fireplace with a richly-carved mantel, and a door – apparently that of a built-in cupboard – were the only constructive features that presented themselves for consideration, excepting the panelling, which extended over the whole of the walls.

"There's evidently something queer about Mr Simpson's proceedings, as we might expect," said Fittleworth. "According to Rachel, he was in this room from nine o'clock until at least half-past eleven. Now, what was he doing? He wasn't drawing. If you look at the work on his board you can see that either you or I could have done it in ten minutes. But the handling shows that he is not a duffer. Then at eleven-thirty, he went to the kitchen for a jar of water. What did he want that water for? He wasn't going to colour. He had barely begun his outline, and there is a good day's drawing in that mantelpiece."

"Yes," said Katharine, "that is rather suspicious. It looks as if he had gone there to see what the servants were about."

"Yes. Or to make a demonstration of being at work before he bolted himself in. That would suggest that he had already made a discovery. I wonder, by the way, what he has in that bag. Would it be improper to look into it?"

Whether it was improper or not, he did so, and as he opened the flap of the large sketching bag, which hung by its strap from a chair back, Katharine approached and peered in.

"That's rather a queer outfit for a water-colour artist," she remarked, as he fished out a leather roll-up case of tools.

"Very quaint," replied Fittleworth. "So is this: what ironmongers describe as a case opener, and Mr Sikes would call a jemmy. And what might this coil of rope be for? It is thin stuff – what sailors call a 'lead-line,' I think – but it is too thick for an easel-guy, and there's too much of it. There seems to be about a dozen yards. But there! It's of no use looking at his appliances; we know what Mr Simpson was after. The question now is: Where is Mr Simpson?"

"I suppose," said Katharine, "he couldn't be in that cupboard?"

Fittleworth stepped across and gave a pull at the projecting key.

"Locked," he announced. "He couldn't very well have locked himself in and left the key outside. I wonder if there is anything to be seen in the chimney. These wide old chimneys were favourite places for hiding-holes."

He slid the old dog grate out of the way, and, stooping under the lintel, stood up inside the roomy chimney. It was evident that the flue was not straight, for no light came from above, and, as very little was reflected up from the floor, the cavity was in almost total darkness. Fittleworth struck a wax match, and, by the aid of its feeble light, explored that part of the interior that was within the range of vision. But closely as he examined it, nothing met his eye but the uninterrupted surface of blackened brickwork. Reflecting, however, that hiding-holes would not be made ostentatiously conspicuous, he stooped, and, reaching out to the andirons, picked up the poker.

"You are not going to hit him with that poker, I hope, Joe," laughed Katharine, who had unlocked the cupboard, and was now standing with the open door in her hand. Fittleworth reassured her as to his intentions, and, ducking under the lintel, stood up once more in the dark chimney. Having lit another match he began systematically to sound the brickwork, comparing critically the notes given out by the successive blows of the poker, and noting the resistance and feeling of solidity. But the result was no more encouraging than that of the ocular inspection; the "percussion note" exhibited a disappointing uniformity, and the sense of resistance conveyed through the poker was that of a very solid brick wall.

He had been working several minutes, his attention concentrated on the unresponsive mass of brickwork, when he was startled by the slamming of a door. He stopped to listen, and then, after a brief interval, he was aware of a muffled cry and the sound of thumping on hollow woodwork. Instantly he stooped to look out, blinking at the unaccustomed light, and as he looked he uttered a cry of amazement.

The room was empty.

He sprang out across the hearth, and as he reached the floor the muffled call was repeated in a familiar voice, framing the word "Joe!" and the thumping recommenced, both sounds clearly proceeding from the cupboard. Striding across to the latter, he seized the key and pulled at it vigorously, but the door refused to yield. Then he gave the key a turn, whereupon the lock clicked, the door flew open, and out stepped Katharine, laughing heartily, and yet not a little agitated.

"Oh, my dear Joe!" she exclaimed, "that wretched door gave me such a fright. I believe it is possessed with a devil. It seemed to entrap me with intelligent, calculating malice."

"Tell me exactly what happened," said Fittleworth. "How did you get in there?"

"I walked in, of course, you old absurdity. You see, while you were rummaging about in the chimney, I stood here with the door open, looking at all that clutter on the shelves. Then my eye caught that delightful old jar on the top shelf, and I stepped in to reach it down; but no sooner was I inside than that miserable door slammed to, and the wretched lock snapped, and there I was, like a mouse in a trap. It's a mercy you were at hand."

"It is, indeed. But now that we've got you out, I think we will have a good look at that trap. It's a queer arrangement for a cupboard. It has a spring lock, and you notice that the very solid brass hinges are of the skew pattern to make the door self-closing. I don't see any reason for either."

"No; that was what I was thinking when I was inside. You want to keep people out of a cupboard, not to fasten them in."

"Exactly. So we will just prop this door open with a chair and examine this singular cupboard, or closet, minutely."

He pulled the door wide open, and, having fixed it in that position by means of an elbow chair, began his investigations, taking the door itself as the first item. Having tried the lock and examined the exterior, he ran his eye critically over the inner surface, and then he made a discovery. Near the top of the door was a small, square patch of wood, which yielded to pressure, and on pressing which the bolt of the lock slid back.

"Ha!" he exclaimed, "I smell a fox, Katie. Do you see? This is an internal release. Now what could that be for?"

"Why, obviously, to enable a person who was shut in to let himself out. It is a hiding-place, Joe. Don't you see? A fugitive who was closely pursued could step in and the door would shut behind him. Then the pursuers would come and give a pull at the key, and say, as you did, that a man couldn't lock himself in a cupboard and leave the key outside. And then they'd go away."

Fittleworth smiled, and shook his head. "That is all very well, my dear girl, but suppose there happened to be a Katie among them who would have the curiosity to turn the key and open the door? That wouldn't do. No, my dear, you may take it as practically certain that there is a way out of this cupboard. Your inquisitive pursuer would open the door and find the cupboard empty, and then the outside key would be highly convincing. Let us investigate."

He stepped into the cupboard which was about four feet deep and of which the back was occupied by five massive but rather narrow shelves, and looked inquisitively around. The whole interior – sides, floor and ceiling – was lined with solid oak boards, and the shelves were occupied by various articles that, to judge by their appearance, had slowly accumulated in the course of years. It was to these shelves that Fittleworth specially directed his attention and that of Katharine.

"You notice," said he, "that all the shelves are more or less filled up with what you call 'clutter,' excepting the second one from the top, which has evidently been cleared, and quite recently, too, as you can see by the dust marks. Also that the back boarding has a hollow space behind it."

By way of demonstrating this, he gave one or two hearty thumps on the hollow-sounding back; but at the third blow he paused and turned excitedly to Katharine.

"We've hit it – literally – Kate. Do you see? This board is beginning to give. It is a hinged flap, of which the joints were hidden by the shelves. We'll soon run Mr Simpson to earth now."

As Katharine craned forward to peer into the cupboard, Fittleworth gave a vigorous shove at the movable board, driving it back several inches. Instantly there followed a loud snap and a thunderous rumbling, and the entire cupboard began to descend rapidly. Fittleworth clutched frantically at the shelf to steady himself, while Katharine, with a little cry of alarm, leaned over the brink of the well-like shaft, looking down, as if petrified, at her vanishing companion.

The cupboard continued to descend for about ten feet. Then it stopped, and, at the same moment, the bottom fell down, swinging like a trap-door on invisible hinges. It was well for Fittleworth that he had kept his grasp of the shelf, for otherwise he must have been precipitated down the shaft that yawned beneath him, a dark, apparently unfathomable, well. As it was, he had nearly been jerked from his none too secure hold, and he now hung by his hands, only his feet kicking in mid-air; an impossible position for more than a bare minute, as he realised at once from the strain on his fingers. However, after some cautious groping with one foot he managed to find the bottom shelf, and when he had got both his feet securely planted on this, the strain on his hands was relieved and he was able to look about him. Glancing up, he saw that only the back half of the cupboard ceiling had come down, so that there was a two-foot space above him, through which he could see the agonised face of Katharine thrust over the brink of the well.

"Can't I do anything, Joe?" she cried in a terrified voice.

"Yes," he replied. "Get that rope of Simpson's and throw one end down to me and tie the other end securely to the leg of the table."

Her face disappeared, and, as the sound of hurried movement came from above, Fittleworth looked over his shoulder at the side of the well that was visible to him; which presented the smooth surface of the chalk through which the shaft had been cut, and at its middle a shallow recess fitted with massive iron rings, and forming a fixed ladder, which apparently gave access to the bottom of the shaft. He looked longingly at those solid rungs, rusty as they were, and considered whether he could reach across and grasp one, but his hold was too insecure to allow of his reaching out with that horrible dark pit, of unknown depth, yawning beneath. There was nothing for it but to cling to the shelf, though his fingers ached with the tension and his muscles were beginning to tremble with the continuous strain. He gazed up at the narrow opening, and listened eagerly for the sounds from above that told him of Katharine's hurried efforts to rescue him; and as he listened, there came to his ears another sound – from beneath – a hollow, sepulchral voice, echoing strangely from the sides of the shaft.

"Is that you, Warren?"

"All right," answered Fittleworth. "We'll get down to you presently. Are you hurt?"

"Yes; broken my ankle, I think. But don't you hurry. Be careful how you come down."

Fittleworth was about to reply, when Katharine's face reappeared at the opening above. "Here's the rope, Joe," said she. "I've tied it quite firmly to the table leg, and I shall keep hold of it as well. Catch."

The rope came rattling down the shaft, and, as Katharine dexterously swung it towards him, Fittleworth caught it with one hand, and hauled on it as well as he could in the hope that the cupboard, partly relieved of his weight, would rise. But the force that he could exert with one hand was not enough for this. Pull as he might, the cupboard remained immovable.

Finding that this was so, and that the repeated efforts were only fatiguing him, he decided to risk grasping the rope with both hands; but the instant he let go his hold on the upper shelf he swung right out over the well, and his feet began to slip from the lower shelf. In another moment he would have been dangling free over the deep chasm – unless the thin rope had broken; but now, as he swung out within reach of the ladder, he made a snatch with one hand at an iron rung. Grasping this firmly, he was able, without difficulty, to spring across on to the ladder, and, as his feet finally left the shelf, the cupboard began, with loud rumblings, to ascend.

Fittleworth stood on the ladder looking up at the receding cupboard and at Katharine's anxious face, and wondering what would happen next. His curiosity was soon satisfied. As the cupboard approached the top of the shaft, the floor began to rise, and would have closed completely but for the rope, on which it jammed, leaving a narrow chink through which came a glimmer of light. It was an awkward predicament, and Fittleworth was doubtful what to do; but, as he was considering, Katharine's voice came through the chink.

"Are you all right, Joe?"

"Yes."

"You had better go down a little farther out of the way. The cupboard is coming down again."

Fittleworth hastily descended a few rungs to avoid a knock on the head and then stopped, wondering how Katharine proposed to send the cupboard down. Before he had reached any conclusion, the rope was partly drawn up, there was a jarring sound above and the cupboard began to descend, but more slowly this time, as if checked in some way. When it had descended a few feet, the floor, not having risen far enough to reach its catch, owing to the rope, began to fall down; and then Fittleworth, looking up, saw to his amazement that Katharine was clinging to the interior. As the cupboard reached the bottom of its run and came to rest, he climbed up the ladder until he was opposite and then looked round anxiously. But Katharine's position was much more secure than his had been, for she was holding firmly with one hand to a massive brass peg that was fixed on the side of the cupboard, and with the other was grasping the rope which she had passed round a stout hook that was fixed near the floor – apparently for that very purpose – and then round the peg; thus she had been able easily to check the descent of the cupboard. These arrangements, however, Fittleworth was not able to see in the dim light which prevailed in the shaft, and remembering his own difficulties, he looked at Katharine in some consternation.

"How on earth are we going to get you up again, Katie?" he asked.

"Why," she replied, "you just run up the ladder and pull at the rope. I've got it firmly fixed to this hook."

Fittleworth crawled up a few rungs and gave a cautious pull at the rope, when the cupboard moved an inch or two upwards, whereupon he began to climb rapidly up the ladder. He was only half-way up, however, when a hollow voice from below echoed appealingly.

"Don't be longer than you can help, Warren."

"Good Heavens!" exclaimed Katharine. "What on earth was that?"

"Hush!" said Fittleworth. "That's our friend Simpson." Then, raising his voice, he called out: "We'll come down to you as soon as we can," and continued his ascent to the top of the ladder.

As soon as he reached the solid floor of the room, he seized the rope and began cautiously to haul on it; and as the tension increased, the great bronze chain which suspended the cupboard began to rumble over its pulley-wheel. In a few seconds the cupboard itself appeared in the opening; as its floor came flush with that of the room it stopped, and a double snap announced that the two catches – the one which supported the cupboard itself and the other which held the floor – had slipped into their places. Then Katharine, having tried the floor with infinite caution, let go the peg and stepped out into the room.

"Well," said Fittleworth as he handed her out, "I'm proud of you, Katie. It was positively heroic of you to come down for me in that way; and how cleverly you managed it, too. It's not for nothing that you are a yachtsman's daughter."

Katharine received these commendations with calm satisfaction, but her mind was evidently running on the unearthly voice that had hailed them from the depths, for she asked anxiously:

"How are we going to get that poor creature up; Joe?"

"We will consider that presently," replied Fittleworth. "Meanwhile, we will just put away the rope and make things ship-shape while we talk matters over."

"But," persisted Katharine, "we can't leave the poor wretch down there in that horrible pit. Can't we get him up now?"

"I think he'll have to stay there until we've settled what to do. We shall want some further appliances, and probably some help. But listen!"

He coiled up the rope quickly and had just replaced it in Simpson's bag, when the door opened and Rachel reappeared.

"If you please, miss," said she, "the two gentlemen, Mr Furse and Mr Tanner, have come to look for Mr Simpson. I told them what had happened, and that you were here. Will you see them, miss? They're in a most awful taking about Mr Simpson."

As she finished speaking, footsteps were heard in the corridor and the two gentlemen entered without further ceremony, upon which Rachel introduced them, somewhat stiffly, and departed. Fittleworth looked at the two strangers curiously and had no difficulty in recognising in them the hautboy player and the water-colour copyist respectively, though it was clear that neither of them recognised him. Both were in a state of great agitation, especially the musician, and it was he who addressed Fittleworth.

"This is a most astonishing and alarming thing, sir. Our friend Simpson appears to have vanished completely."

"Yes," replied Fittleworth; "a most surprising affair. I can't imagine why he should have gone out through the window."

"Are you quite sure that he did?" asked the musician.

"Well," replied Fittleworth, "he's not here, as you see, and he couldn't have got out through the door so he must have left by the window, unless he went up the chimney."

Here Fittleworth caught a reproachful glance from Katharine, and the musician, who had been introduced as Mr Furse, rejoined:

"I can't help thinking that he must be somewhere on the premises. Would you object to our looking round?"

Fittleworth reflected awhile and ultimately ventured on a chance shot.

"I think, perhaps, you may be right, Mr Warren – "

The two men started visibly, and the musician interrupted: "My name, sir, is Furse."

"Very well," said Fittleworth, "Mr Furse, then I think we had better have an explanation, as our activities overlap somewhat. I am acting on behalf of Miss Hyde, the owner of this house."

"But what has that to do with us?" asked Mr Furse.

"I think you will see when I explain my business, which is connected with certain property of Miss Hyde's, to wit, a small gold box, containing certain documents, relating to some of her other property."

For some seconds the two men stared at Fittleworth in speechless amazement; then Furse asked hesitatingly: "But what has this to do with us?"

"Oh, come, come, sir," said Fittleworth impatiently, "it's of no use to try to keep up this pretence. We know that you took the box and that it is in your possession at this moment."

The two men, who appeared completely dumbfounded, glanced quickly at one another, and Furse asked: "Do I understand that this box, of which you are speaking, is the property of this lady?"

"Undoubtedly," replied Fittleworth. "This is Miss Katharine Hyde, the heir and only surviving descendant of Sir Andreas Hyde, whose name will be familiar to you."

"You don't say so!" exclaimed Mr Furse. "I had no idea there were any descendants living. Perhaps you will allow my friend and me to consult together on the matter."

Fittleworth was quite ready to agree to this, but he had no intention of leaving them alone in the room. Accordingly, he suggested the Chancellor's Garden as a retired spot where they could converse at their ease, and proceeded to usher them out by the side door. Returning to the parlour, he found Katharine with the cupboard door open, listening intently for any sounds which might come up through the floor.

"You cold-blooded old wretch, Joe!" she exclaimed, "to sit there calmly discussing that trumpery box, while poor Mr Simpson may be dying at the bottom of that horrible shaft."

"My dear Kate," protested Fittleworth, "we didn't put him there. He shall be got up as soon as possible, but, meanwhile, he's quite a valuable aid to our negotiations."

Katharine was shocked at his callousness and urged an immediate rescue, but Fittleworth, unmoved by her reproaches, calmly watched the two men through the window, as they paced the little green, evidently engaged in anxious discussion. The discussion was, however, quite a brief one, for in about a couple of minutes they turned, with an air of finality, and walked briskly towards the side door.

"They haven't been long," Fittleworth remarked as they passed out of view and the side door was heard to open. "I wonder what they've decided to do? They can't very well say they haven't got the box now."

Fittleworth was right, As soon as the two men entered the room, Mr Furse opened the proceedings in a manner quite frank and business-like.

"We'd like you to tell us, sir," said he, "exactly what you know about this affair and what you wish us to do."

"As to what we know," said Fittleworth, "I may say we know everything. The box, which was sealed with King James' seal and contained an important document, was removed by you – very cleverly, I must admit – from the National Gallery seventeen days ago, and you have come here to search for the property that was deposited by Sir Andreas Hyde. As to what we wish, we simply desire you to restore the box to its owner."

Mr Furse seated himself in a large elbow-chair and, placing his fingertips together, addressed himself to Fittleworth.

"Now, see here," said he. "That box was never in Miss Hyde's possession, and I guess no one knew of its existence, or of the existence of the other property that you mention; and I guess you don't know, now, what that property is or where it's stowed."

"You're wrong there," said Fittleworth, rather casuistically; "we know exactly where it's hidden which is, I think, more than you do; but surely, all this is irrelevant. The property belongs to Miss Hyde and there's an end of the matter. You're not disputing her title, are you?"

"No, sir, we are not. To be perfectly frank with you, our position is this: we lit on the trail of this property by chance, and, being under the impression that it was without an owner, we laid ourselves out to salve it, and I may tell you that we have spent a great deal of time, money and trouble on locating it. Now, it turns out that this is not treasure trove at all; that there is a rightful owner living; and my friend, Tanner, and I have talked the matter over and have decided that we, personally, are prepared to surrender our claim on certain conditions, but of course we can't answer for Mr Simpson, nor can we act without his consent."

"What are your conditions?" asked Fittleworth.

"We should want our expenses refunded, and we want permission to search these premises for our friend."

"That's not unreasonable," said Fittleworth, "and as regards the property of Sir Andreas, I am willing to agree; but I must stipulate that you hand us over immediately the box and its contents. You have them with you, probably."

"No, we haven't," said Furse. "We could produce them, but, first of all, we want to look for Simpson. His case is actually urgent, for the probability is that he has got boxed up in some confounded secret chamber and can't get out."

"You are quite right," said Fittleworth. "I know exactly where he is, and I will make conditions with you. You produce the box and its contents, and I will produce Mr Simpson."

"And supposing we don't agree?" asked Furse.

"Then I am afraid we shall have to retain Mr Simpson as security."

The long, humorous face of Mr Furse wrinkled into a grim smile, as he glanced inquiringly at his companion.

"What do you say to that?" he asked.

Mr Tanner raised his eyebrows. "It seems to me, Warren," said he, "that this gentleman has got us in a cleft stick. I guess we've got to agree." Mr Furse rose and looked at his watch.

"It'll take us well over an hour to produce that box. Say we are back here in an hour and a half?"

"Then," said Fittleworth, "I think we can promise that you shall find Mr Simpson here when you return."

This arrangement having been agreed to, the two gentlemen departed, Fittleworth and Katharine escorting them to the front door. As they disappeared down the drive, the former turned to Katharine:

"Now, my dear, to the work of rescue. I think we shall have to take Rachel into our confidence, as we shall want her assistance."

As a matter of fact, Rachel was lurking in the background, having scented some sort of mystery, and Fittleworth forthwith put her in possession of such of the circumstances as it was necessary for her to know; whereat she was profoundly thrilled and highly gratified.

"There, now," she remarked, "that's what comes of poking and prying about in other people's houses. But how are you going to get him out, sir?"

"He'll have to be hoisted up, I suppose," said Fittleworth. "Do you happen to have such a thing as a length of strong rope?"

He asked the question somewhat hopelessly, stout rope not being a common domestic appliance; but Rachel answered promptly: "There's the well rope, sir, if you could get it off the windlass."

"I think we could manage that," said Fittleworth; "and then we shall want some weights, about two hundredweight altogether."

This presented more difficulty, until Katharine conceived the luminous idea of filling a couple of small sacks with earth, which solved the problem perfectly.

In a few minutes they had collected these appliances and a lantern, and carried them to the Chancellor's Parlour, when, having bolted the door, they fell to work forthwith. First, the door of the cupboard was propped open with a chair; then Fittleworth laid the two small, but heavy, sacks of earth on the bottom shelf, and, the cupboard now being weighted, he set the point of his walking-stick against the movable board at the back, and gave a heavy thrust. Instantly there was a loud snap and the cupboard rumbled away down the shaft, like a primitive lift, and as the great bronze chain ran out, an enormous stone counterpoise was seen to rise at the side. As on the first occasion, the cupboard stopped about ten feet down and the floor dropped like the trap of a gallows. The next proceeding was to light the lantern and attach it to one end of the rope – the other end being secured, as before, to the table – by which Fittleworth lowered it carefully down the shaft until he had paid out some twenty-five feet. Then as its glimmer still showed nothing but the walls of the shaft, and the view was somewhat obstructed by the cupboard, he decided to go down and reconnoitre.

"I suppose that ladder's all right?" said Katharine.

"It seems to be," he answered. "The rungs are rusty, but they seem quite firm and strong, and you may trust me to be mighty careful."

With this, he let himself over the brink and began slowly to descend, watched anxiously by the two women from above, testing each rung cautiously with his foot before throwing his weight on it. As he passed the suspended cupboard the voice of Simpson from below hailed him with the inquiry:

"Is that you, Warren?"

"No," answered Fittleworth, and continued to descend.

"Is it Bell?" asked Simpson.

Fittleworth again replied in the negative, but made a mental note of the name. As he passed the lantern he saw that it had descended to within six or seven feet from the bottom of the shaft, which was covered by a considerable heap of ancient rags and mouldering straw and twigs, thrown down apparently, by some humane person to mitigate the effects of an accidental fall. At one side was a narrow doorway, cut in the chalk, opening upon a short flight of steps, and on the top step a man was sitting, nursing his bare foot.

It was a curious meeting. The light of the lantern reflected from the walls of the narrow cavity, rendered the two men plainly visible to one another, and the recognition was instantaneous. Fittleworth, of course, "placed" his man without difficulty, but the other was evidently at a loss.

"I seem to know your face," he said, looking critically at Fittleworth; "but yet – where have I met you?"

"In the National Gallery," Fittleworth replied; and as the other's face took on an expression of unmistakable alarm, he added: "I've not come with hostile intentions. We will talk over our little business later; for the present we have to consider how to get you out of this hole."

"I'm afraid," said Simpson, "that I can't climb the ladder."

"No, of course you can't," replied Fittleworth, "we shall have to haul you up. But if I fix you in a loop at the end of the rope, you can help us by hauling yourself up with your hands. What do you say?"

Simpson thought the plan would answer admirably, and Fittleworth forthwith set about executing it. First, he called up to Katharine to lower a dozen feet more rope. Then, detaching the lantern from the end of the rope, he made a good-sized bowline knot in the latter, and fitted the loop round Simpson's hips.

"There," said he, "I will go up now and help them to hoist, and, when I give the word, you take hold of the ladder and sit down in the loop of the rope. As we haul, you must help yourself up by the ladder, and be careful that you don't knock that unfortunate foot of yours, which we must have attended to as soon as we get you up."

"It's very good of you," Simpson began; but Fittleworth, considering that this was no time for the exchange of politenesses, began to reascend the ladder. As he stepped out on to the floor of the parlour, he briefly explained the arrangements to his two assistants, and then, having shouted down a warning to the prisoner below, the three began to haul steadily at the rope. It was probably an uncomfortable experience to Simpson, but the plan was highly effective, and in a minute or so the captive appeared at the top of the shaft, and was tenderly helped over the perilous edge.

As he stood on one foot, supported by Fittleworth, he gazed confusedly about the room, and asked: "Where are the others? Warren and Bell, I mean."

"They've gone into Margate," replied Fittleworth "but they'll be back shortly. Meanwhile, if Mistress Rachel can lend us a bedroom, we will see you comfortably settled, and send for a doctor."

"There's a spare bedroom over this," said Rachel "and, as it's all ready, we can take Mr Simpson up at once, and then the boy can go off on his bicycle and fetch Dr Finlay."

"I'm sure," said Simpson, "it's exceedingly charitable of you all to take so much trouble about me. It's more than I deserve, after – " he paused to look doubtfully at Rachel, who, for her part, looked as expressionless as a moderately benevolent graven image, and was equally uncommunicative.

"For the present," said Fittleworth, "we'll confine our attention to your foot. When that has been attended to, and your friends arrive, we can discuss other matters."

As soon as Simpson had been comfortably settled in the cosy, old-fashioned bedroom, with a wet handkerchief applied to his ankle, the party returned to the Chancellor's Parlour.

"Well," asked Katharine, "what is the next thing to be done?"

"The next thing," said Fittleworth, "is to make a little exploration on our own account. There is evidently a chamber or tunnel at the bottom of the shaft, and I propose to go down and see what's in it."

"Then I'm coming down, too," said Katharine.

At this Rachel protested most emphatically. "You'd much better not, miss," she exclaimed. "Supposing you were to fall off the ladder!"

"I'm not going to suppose anything of the kind, Rachel. You'll let me come down, won't you, Joe?" she added wheedlingly.

"I don't see why you shouldn't," replied Fittleworth. "It's quite an easy ladder to climb. But we shall want Rachel to keep guard at the top, as we do not want those two good gentlemen; so the housemaid had better be told that, if they arrive before we have finished our explorations, they are to be shown up to Mr Simpson's room, and are to wait there for us."

The disapproving, but obedient, Rachel received the instructions with resignation, and, having executed them and bolted the door, took her place at the edge of the shaft with an expression of deep foreboding. First, the rope was lowered to its former position, when Fittleworth, steadying himself by it, got on the ladder and descended a few rungs; then Katharine, also grasping the rope and herself frantically grasped by Rachel, essayed the first few perilous steps.

"It's really quite safe and easy, Rachel," she said, as she clung tenaciously to the rusty bars and let herself down cautiously, rung by rung; and, with this assurance, the faithful handmaid was somewhat comforted, though she continued to watch the disappearance of her young mistress into the depths of the shaft with a face of horror and dismay.

The progress down the ladder occupied little more than a minute, and its completion was duly announced for the benefit of the watcher above.

"I suppose," said Katharine, as Fittleworth picked up the lantern, "that you didn't see anything of the mysterious 'it' when you were down here before?"

"No," he replied, "we are going to find 'it' together, Katie; at least, I hope so. Be careful of those steps."

They descended the rudely cut steps, rounded by the damp and slimy with fungous growths, and entered a narrow passage, of which the end was lost in obscurity, and of which the floor descended at a sharp angle. Fittleworth held the lantern aloft, throwing its light on the greenish, sweating walls and the roughly-vaulted roof. There was something weirdly impressive in the aspect of this ancient tunnel, which had probably seen no light for centuries but that which now glimmered from the lantern. The lapse of time was marked not only by that eerie vegetation that clothed the walls, but by little stalactites that drooped from projections on the roof, and sparkling stalagmitic masses which had begun to grow up from the floor. But of traces of visitors there were none, excepting that, in one place, under the mantle of vegetation there could be seen on the wall some indistinct initials with a heart and the date 1594. Slowly the explorers advanced down the sloping tunnel, descending at intervals short flights of steps, which were placed at points where the direction of the tunnel changed, and still there was no sign of any concealed object or of any hiding-place. At length, on descending another short flight of steps, they turned into a straight length of tunnel, at the end of which appeared a bright spot of light, cold and bluish in tone as compared with the yellow glimmer of the lantern – evidently daylight. They hurried forward, and, passing a massive wooden gate, which had fallen back on its decayed hinges, came to a roughly-built wall of chalk masonry which blocked the tunnel. The spot of light corresponded to a space from which one of the stones had fallen or crumbled, and Fittleworth had no difficulty in climbing up and applying his eye to the hole.

"What are you smiling at, Joe?" Katharine asked, as a faint grin appeared on Fittleworth's face.

His reply was to descend and assist her to take his place. It was a very curious scene that she looked upon as she peered through the opening; curious by reason of the contrast that it offered with this grim, old tunnel, wrapt in sepulchral darkness and charged with mystery and memories of a generation long since dead and forgotten. A sea cave with a floor of weed-strewn sand and the shining beach beyond; and near its entrance a pair of very modern lovers, the swain industriously carving their joint initials with a very conspicuous heart, while the maiden stood by and encouraged him with admiring exclamations.

"So," said Fittleworth, as Katharine stepped down, "the world wags pretty much in our days as it did in the year 1594. But, meanwhile, we seem to be at the end of our explorations, and 'it' still remains an unknown quantity. I wish I hadn't been so beastly cocksure with Warren, now."

"But it must be hidden here, somewhere in this tunnel," said Katharine.

"That doesn't follow at all. The purpose of these works is pretty obvious, especially when we consider that the tunnel was cut at least as early as the time of Elizabeth. They form a combined escape and deathtrap. You see that we are looking in near the roof of the cave, and this wall is probably built over a flight of steps. The idea clearly was that a Catholic, or Protestant, as the case might be, could escape down the shaft and out through the cave to a boat. If the pursuers discovered the secret of the cupboard, they would probably be shot down the shaft and killed; and even if they came down the ladder, they could be ambushed at any one of these sharp turns in the tunnel."

"Then," said Katharine, in a tone of disappointment "you think that 'it' may be hidden in some other part of the house?"

"I'm afraid that's what it looks like," replied Fittleworth, "and, as we don't know what 'it' is, or what its size may be, the search for it isn't so very hopeful."

They turned and retraced their steps slowly through the zigzag tunnel and, as they went, they spoke little and apparently thought much. Arrived at the foot of the shaft, Fittleworth, with a reflective air, tied the lantern to the end of the rope, and called out to Rachel to pull it up to the level of the cupboard. Then they began the ascent, Katharine going first.

When they reached the level of the cupboard, Fittleworth paused and looked round.

"Wait a minute, Katie," said he. "I'm going to try a little experiment."

Katharine stopped in her climb and, looking down on him inquisitively, saw him reach across and grasp one of the bags of earth. A good pull dislodged it from the shelf and it fell to the bottom of the shaft with a dull thump.

"Be careful, Joe!" exclaimed Katharine. "You'll have the cupboard going up and shutting us in."

"I want it to go up a little way," he replied; and descending a couple of rungs, he put his hand to the bottom of the cupboard and pushed steadily upwards; when the cupboard, relieved of a portion of its weight, rose three or four feet and again came to rest.

"Eureka!" Fittleworth exclaimed excitedly. "I was right. I thought our secretive friends would not waste such an excellent opportunity."

He followed the cupboard up a few steps and, giving it another shove, sent it up a good six feet. Katharine gave a little cry of delight. In the side of the shaft, at the spot that had been hidden by the suspended cupboard, was a deepish recess, fitted with iron handholds, and pierced by a narrow doorway. Grasping one of the hand-holds, Fittleworth stepped on the ledge of the recess and entered the doorway.

"You're not to go in without me," Katharine commanded, letting herself down in a mighty hurry.

"Very well," said Fittleworth. "Pass me the lantern across, and get a good hold of that handle before you step on the ledge."

He took the lantern from her and, backing into the doorway, watched her anxiously as she crossed to the ledge. The perilous passage accomplished, he backed into the doorway with the lantern, and she followed him into a short passage, and from this, into a small, square chamber. As he turned and held the lantern aloft they both uttered an exclamation of joy; for a single glance around the little cell, showed them that they had found the object of their quest. On the floor, near to one wall, raised from the damp surface on blocks of cut chalk, were three rudely-made chests, clamped with iron bands and guarded by massive locks. Fittleworth threw the light of the lantern on each in succession. All of them were roughly fashioned, as if by a ship's carpenter, and each bore on the lid, incised lettering, the same inscription: "Shipp, *James and Mary*. Stowe in ye lazaret"; and then in dotted lettering, as if marked with an awl or marline-spike, "His M—sty's Portion, W. P."

" 'W. P.,' " mused Fittleworth. "That would be Sir William Phips, whoever he was. Now, the question is, whose property is this? It's His Majesty's portion, but did the king hand it to Sir Andreas as a gift, or only to hold in trust for safe keeping?"

"Does it matter?" inquired Katharine, with feminine disregard for these niceties.

"Yes, it does," replied Fittleworth. "If it belonged to Sir Andreas, it is your property, but if it was the king's, it's treasure trove."

"Rubbish!" exclaimed Katharine. "King James' family is extinct, so there's no question about his heirs; and finding is keeping. Besides, it's in my house and was put here by my ancestor."

"You're a dishonest little baggage!" laughed Fittleworth, whose private opinions, however, on the moral aspects of treasure trove were much the same as those of most other sensible men, "but perhaps the document may give us some further information. At any rate, it is satisfactory to have found 'it' ourselves. And now we had better go up and see if our understudies have arrived yet."

He helped Katharine across to the ladder and, as they emerged from the shaft, to Rachel's unspeakable relief, the front door bell rang.

"That'll be Mr Furse and his friend," remarked Rachel. "The doctor has been and gone away again."

"Then," said Fittleworth, "they had better be shown up to Mr Simpson's room, and, when they are ready to see us, perhaps you will kindly let us know."

He closed the door of the cupboard, and, as Rachel departed on her mission, he drew two chairs up to the table.

"There's one thing I want to say to you," said Katharine. "Of course we have found this property, whatever it is, ourselves, but we should never have found it if it had not been for those three men. They are the real discoverers."

Fittleworth assented somewhat dryly, and Katharine went on: "They've had an awful lot of trouble, Joe and they've been most clever and ingenious, and when we broke in upon them they were on the very point of winning the reward for all their labour."

"They hadn't found the hiding-place," objected Fittleworth.

"No, but I feel sure they would have found it. They are evidently exceedingly clever men – almost as clever as you, Joe."

"Rather more so, I should say," laughed Fittleworth. "They did me in the eye pretty neatly."

"Well, at any rate," said Katharine, ignoring this qualification, "they discovered it by sheer cleverness, and by taking infinite trouble, and it will be an awful disappointment to the poor things to have it snatched from them at the last moment."

"Well," said Fittleworth, as Katharine paused interrogatively.

"Well, don't you think we ought to let them have at least a substantial share of whatever is in those chests?"

Fittleworth smiled grimly. "It's a most irregular business altogether, Katie. In the first place, I, an official of the Gallery, propose to compound a felony by receiving the stolen property, which I fancy we are not going to restore to the owner of the picture."

"Certainly not," said Katharine. "It wasn't his. It's mine."

"And then," continued Fittleworth, "we propose to make a perfectly illegal arrangement with the robbers for disposing of certain treasure trove which is the property of the Crown."

"Oh, stuff, Joe!" exclaimed Katharine. "It's my property, or at least ours, and we're going to keep it, you know we are. Now, how much are we going to give these poor creatures?"

"It's your property, Kate," said Fittleworth, with a grin; "at least, you say it is, so you must decide."

"Very well," said she, "let us consider. There are three chests, one for you, one for me and one for them. What do you say to that?"

Fittleworth, though secretly approving, was disposed to adopt the cantankerous attitude of a trustee or adviser; but Katharine saw through him at once.

"I'm glad you agree with me," she said, ignoring his protests. "We shall enjoy our windfall so much more if we're not greedy. So that's settled. And I think I hear Rachel coming."

A moment later the handmaid entered to announce that Mr Furse and his friends were ready to see them, and they adjourned, forthwith, to the bedroom above.

"I hope," said Katharine, as they entered, "that the doctor has given a favourable report, and that you are in less pain now, Mr Simpson."

"Thank you," was the reply, "I am quite comfortable now. It seems that it was only a severe sprain, after all."

Katharine congratulated him on his escape, and Mr Furse – or Warren – then opened the business with characteristic briskness.

"Now, sir, my friend, Pedley, late Simpson, is quite agreeable to our handing over the box and contents on the terms mentioned, which, however, must include immunity from any proceedings in respect of the picture."

"So far as I am concerned," said Fittleworth, "I agree, although such an agreement is quite illegal, as you know. But the arrangement is between ourselves and need go no farther."

"Quite so," said Warren. "But, does anyone besides Miss Hyde know that you were on our track?"

"No. We acted quite secretly, and as the picture has been restored, no action is likely to be taken by the authorities."

"Then in that case," said Warren, "and as you agree to our terms, I will hand the property to Miss Hyde, and will let you have an account of our expenses later."

With this he produced from his pocket a small paper packet, and, opening it, displayed a small, plain, gold box, somewhat like an exceedingly flat cigar case, which he handed to Katharine.

"The paper," said he, "is inside; and I may say, madam, that I believe you will find it an exceedingly interesting document."

Katharine, having thanked him, opened the little box and took from it a sheet of very thin paper, folded twice, and covered with writing of an antiquated style and very pale and faded. Opening the paper, she ran her eye quickly over the writing, and then handed the document to Fittleworth.

"Perhaps you had better read it aloud," said she.

Fittleworth took the paper and examined it curiously. One side of it was occupied by what seemed to be a list or schedule; the document proper occupied the other, and it was with this that Fittleworth began:

"James, by the Grace of God, King of England, Scotland, France and Ireland, unto our trusty and well-beloved Andreas Hide and all other such persons as may be concerned with these presents. Whereas the saide Andreas Hide hath on sundry occasions contributed divers sums of money for our use and service Now We do convey to the saide Andreas Our portion of the treasure which Captain Sir William Phips of New England did lift from the Spanish wracke at Hispaniola the saide share being of the value of thirty thousand pounds sterling as sett forth in the accompt on the backe hereof to be disposed of in manner following namely the saide treasure to be secured by the saide Andreas Hide in some safe and secret place to be held intact for Our use as occasion may require while the present troubles continue and soe to be held if need bee during Our Life and that of Our Son James Prince of Wales to be faithfully rendered up to Us or to the saide Prince upon Our or his demand as Our or his necessities may require but upon Our death and that of the saide

Prince the saide Treasure to revert absolutely and become the sole property of the saide Andreas Hide or the heirs of his body.

"*Given under Our hand at Our Palace of White Hall on the twentieth day of September in the Year of our Lord God 1688.*

"*James R.*"

As Fittleworth finished reading, he glanced significantly at Katharine, and Mr Warren gave an approving nod.

"So you see, Miss Hyde," said the latter, "there is no question of treasure trove. This is your own lawful property, if you know where to find it. I need not say that if we had known of your existence, we should have notified you. Rather foolishly, we assumed that there were no heirs in existence – that the property was derelict, and, of course, the good old laws of treasure trove don't appeal much to an American."

"Naturally," said Katharine. "May we see what's on the other side?"

Fittleworth turned the paper over and began to read from the inventory on the back:

"*Three chests containing the King's share of Captain Phips' treasure as follows:*

"*The first chest containeth*

"*Twenty-one bars of golde*

"*Two large baggs pieces of eight*

"*Six parcels dust golde*

"*Three baggs coyned golde*

"*One bagg two hundred large pearls*

"*Two baggs unpolished stones (divers).*"

At this point Fittleworth paused. "Is it worthwhile," he asked, "to go right through the list? We shall have to verify the contents of the chests presently, and we know the total value."

"Yes," said Warren, "I guess you'll find enough to pay our little expenses, with a trifle over. And that reminds me that we should like, if possible, to have the sum – which we will put at two hundred pounds – paid in the actual contents of these chests. It has been quite a little romance for us, and we should like some memento of it."

Katharine glanced significantly at Fittleworth, who then said: "I understand that Miss Hyde wishes you to consider yourselves as partners in this enterprise, and to take a substantial share of the treasure – "

"A third," said Katharine, "if you think that's fair."

"Fair!" exclaimed Warren. "It's a great deal more than fair, it's exceedingly handsome; but I really don't – "

"You see," interrupted Katharine, "you are really the discoverers, and it would seem such a tame ending to your little romance if you only took away a few trifles."

Warren was about to protest, but Katharine continued: "We shall be very unhappy if you don't take a fair share. Remember, we should never have known anything about it but for your cleverness, and the daring way in which you borrowed that picture. Come, Mr Warren, I will make a condition; you shall tell us how you did it, and then help us to get the chests out."

To these not very onerous conditions the three Americans agreed after some further protests and consultation between themselves, and Simpson, or rather, Pedley, then asked: "I suppose the chests are stowed in that place at the bottom of the shaft?"

"No, they're not," replied Fittleworth. "They're less than half-way down; but I hope you'll be able to be present when they're lifted, which is the next business that we have to consider, and a rather troublesome business it will be, I expect."

The business, however, turned out to be less troublesome than Fittleworth had anticipated, for the three enterprising American gentlemen, having read the inventory, and knowing the nature of the treasure, had already provided themselves with the appliances necessary for dealing with the ponderous chests.

These appliances, consisting of a powerful tackle, a set of chain slings, some wooden rollers, and one or two crowbars, were stored at their hotel, from whence Warren and Bell proceeded to fetch them without delay. Then Pedley, with his foot in a splint, was carried down to the Chancellor's Parlour, and, the door being bolted, salvage operations began forthwith. The tackle was hooked on to the great bronze chain that suspended the cupboard, and the chests, one by one, secured in the slings, were dragged on rollers to the opening into the shaft, and finally hoisted up to the floor of the parlour.

The old room had doubtless looked on many a strange scene, but on none stranger than that which was revealed by the light of the hanging lamp and the candles that burned in the old silver candlesticks. The three chests, wrenched open, despite their massive locks, by vigorously-wielded crowbars, stood empty in a corner, and the five conspirators, seated round the ancient draw-table, gazed upon a treasure that made even its sturdy legs creak protestingly. Bars of gold – dull, soapy, and worthless in aspect – bags of gold dust, uncut gems and antiquated coins, lay cheek by jowl, with heaps of rings, trinkets, and ornaments of a suspiciously ecclesiastical character. At the head of the table Katharine sat, with the inventory before her, checking the items as they were called out by Fittleworth, with the impressive manner of an auctioneer. It was late at night before the ceremony was concluded; by which time the spoil, divided into three approximately equal portions, had been returned to the chests, of which one, allocated to the three adventurers, was duly marked and secured with the chain slings, ready for removal.

"There is one thing," said Fittleworth, "that I should like to know before we part. I can see pretty well how you got on the track of the treasure, but I do not see how you ascertained which of the stretcher-bars contained the gold box. I noticed that the canvas had been unfastened only at the one end, so you must either have known beforehand, or made a lucky shot."

Warren laughed complacently.

"We Americans are a progressive people," said he, "and we have a way of applying recent scientific knowledge to useful ends. We didn't know beforehand where that gold box was, and we didn't have to make a shot. We just took the picture, in its case, round to an electrical instrument maker's, and got him to pass the X-rays through it, while we looked at it through a fluorescent screen. We couldn't see much of the picture, but we could see the gold box plain enough, so we just made a pencil mark over the spot on the paper in which the case was wrapped. Is there anything more you would like to know?"

"If it wouldn't seem inquisitive," said Fittleworth, "I think we should like to know with whom we have had the pleasure of sharing the plunder."

Warren rubbed his chin, and cast a comical look of inquiry at his two friends; then, having received an assenting nod from each of them, he replied: "We are sharing one or two secrets already, sir, and if I mention that one of us is a Professor of History at a well-known university in the United States and that the other two of us are respectively Professor of European Archæology at the same academic institution and Conservator of a famous Museum, why, then, we shall share one secret more."

Three days later there arrived at the "Captain Digby," where Fittleworth was staying, a letter from the Director asking him to withdraw his resignation. It was a gratifying circumstance, and he hastened to communicate it to Katharine. But in the meantime she had also received a letter – from her tenant, Mrs Matthews – asking to be allowed to determine the tenancy in a month's time. Katharine read her letter to Fittleworth, and then, laying it down, asked somewhat abstractedly:

"Didn't you once say, Joe, that you would like to live in this old house yourself?"

"I did," he replied, "and I repeat it most emphatically."

"Then," said Katharine, "Sir John will have to accept your resignation."

The Bronze Parrot

The Reverend Deodatus Jawley had just sat down to the gate-legged table on which lunch was spread and had knocked his knee, according to his invariable custom, against the sharp corner of the seventh leg.

"I wish you would endeavour to be more careful, Mr Jawley," said the rector's wife. "You nearly upset the mustard-pot and these jars are exceedingly bad for the leg."

"Oh, that's of no consequence, Mrs Bodley," the curate replied cheerfully.

"I don't agree with you at all," was the stiff rejoinder.

"It doesn't matter, you know, so long as the skin isn't broken," Mr Jawley persisted with an ingratiating smile.

"I was referring to the leg of the table," Mrs Bodley corrected, frostily.

"Oh, I beg your pardon!" said the curate; and, blushing like a Dublin Bay prawn, he abandoned himself in silence to the consideration of the numerical ratios suggested by five mutton chops and three prospective consumers. The problem thus presented was one of deep interest to Mr Jawley, who had a remarkably fine appetite for such an exceedingly small man, and he awaited its solution with misgivings born of previous disappointments.

"I hope you are not very hungry, Mr Jawley," said the rector's wife.

"Er – no – er – not unusually so," was the curate's suave and casuistical reply. The fact is that he was always hungry, excepting after the monthly tea-meetings.

"Because," pursued Mrs Bodley, "I see that Walker has only cooked five chops; and yours looks rather a small one."

"Oh, it will be quite sufficient, thank you," Mr Jawley hastened to declare; adding, a little unfortunately, perhaps: "Amply sufficient for any moderate and temperate person."

The Reverend Augustus Bodley emerged from behind the *Church Times* and directed a suspicious glance at his curate; who, becoming suddenly conscious of the ambiguity of his last remark, blushed crimson and cut himself a colossal slice of bread. There was an uncomfortable silence which lasted some minutes, and was eventually broken by Mrs Bodley.

"I want you to go into Dilbury this afternoon, Mr Jawley, and execute a few little commissions."

"Certainly, Mrs Bodley. With pleasure," said the curate.

"I want you to call and see if Miss Gosse has finished my hat. If she has, you had better bring it with you. She is so unreliable and I want to wear it at the Hawley-Jones' garden party tomorrow. If it isn't finished you must wait until it is. Don't come away without it."

"No, Mrs Bodley, I will not. I will be extremely firm."

"Mind you are. Then I want you to go to Minikin's and get two reels of whitey-brown thread, four balls of crochet cotton and eight yards of lace insertion – the same kind as I had last week. And Walker tells me that she has run out of black lead. You had better bring two packets; and mind you don't put them in the same pocket with the lace insertion. Oh, and as you are going to the oil-shop, you may as well bring a jar of mixed pickles. And then you are to go to Dumsole's and order a fresh haddock – perhaps you could bring that with you, too – and then to Barker's and tell them to send four pounds of dessert pears, and be sure they are good ones and not over-ripe. You had better select them and see them weighed yourself."

"I will, I will select them most carefully," said the curate, inwardly resolving not to trust to mere external appearances, which are often deceptive.

"Oh, and by the way, Jawley," said the rector, "as you are going into the town, you might as well take my shooting boots with you, and tell

Crummell to put a small patch on the soles and set up the heels. It won't take him long. Perhaps he can get them done in time for you to bring them back with you. Ask him to try."

"I will, Mr Bodley," said the curate. "I will urge him to make an effort."

"And as you are going to Crummell's," said Mrs Bodley, "I will give you my walking shoes to take to him. They want soling and heeling; and tell him he is to use better leather than he did last time."

Half an hour later Mr Jawley passed through the playground appertaining to the select boarding-academy maintained by the Reverend Augustus Bodley. He carried a large and unshapely newspaper parcel, despite which he walked with the springy gait of a released schoolboy. As he danced across the desert expanse, his attention was arrested by a small crowd of the pupils gathered significantly around two larger boys whose attitudes suggested warlike intentions; indeed, even as he stopped to observe them, one warrior delivered a tremendous blow which expended itself on the air within a foot of the other combatant's nose.

"Oh! Fie!" exclaimed the scandalised curate. "Joblett! Joblett! Do you realise that you nearly struck Byles? That you might actually have hurt him?"

"I meant to hurt him," said Joblett.

"You meant to! Oh, but how wrong! How unkind! Let me beg you – let me entreat you to desist from these discreditable acts of violence."

He stood awhile gazing with an expression of pained disapproval at the combatants, who regarded him with sulky grins. Then, as the hostilities seemed to be – temporarily – suspended, he walked slowly to the gate. He was just pocketing the key when an extremely somnolent pear impinged on the gate-post and sprinkled him with disintegrated fragments. He turned, wiping his coat-skirt with his handkerchief, and addressed the multitude, who all, oddly enough, happened to be looking in the opposite direction.

"That was very naughty of you. *Very* naughty. Someone must have thrown that pear. I won't tempt you to prevarication by asking who? But pears don't fly of themselves — especially sleepy ones."

With this he went out of the gate, followed by an audible snigger which swelled, as he walked away, into a yell of triumph.

The curate tripped blithely down the village street, clasping his parcel and scattering smiles of concentrated amiability broadcast among the villagers. As he approached the stile that guarded the foot-path to Dilbury, his smile intensified from mere amiability to positive affection. A small lady — a very small lady, in fact — was standing by the stile, resting a disproportionate basket on the lower step; and we may as well admit, at once and without circumlocution, that this lady was none other than Miss Dorcas Shipton and the prospective Mrs Jawley.

The curate changed over his parcel to hold out a welcoming hand.

"Dorcas, my dear!" he exclaimed. "What a lucky chance that you should happen to come this way!"

"It isn't chance," the little lady replied. "I heard Mrs Bodley say that she would ask you to go into Dilbury, so I determined to come and speed you on your journey" (the distance to Dilbury was about three and a half miles) "and see that you were properly equipped. Why did not you bring your umbrella?"

Mr Jawley explained that the hat, the boots, the fresh haddock and the mixed pickles would fully occupy his available organs of prehension.

"That is true," said Dorcas. "But I hope you are wearing your chest protector and those cork soles that I gave you."

Mr Jawley assured her that he had taken these necessary precautions.

"And have you rubbed your heels well with soap?"

"Yes," replied the curate. "Thoroughly; most thoroughly. They are a little sticky at present, but I shall feel the benefit as I go on. I have obeyed your instructions to the letter."

"That is right, Deodatus," said Miss Dorcas; "and as you have been so good, you shall have a little reward."

She lifted the lid of the basket and took out a small paper bag, which she handed to him with a fond smile. The curate opened the bag and peered in expectantly.

"Ha!" he exclaimed. "Bull's-eyes! How nice! How good of you, Dorcas! And how discriminating!" (Bull's-eyes were his one dissipation.) "Won't you take one?"

"No, thank you," replied Dorcas. "I mustn't go into the cottages smelling of peppermint."

"Why not?" asked Deodatus. "I often do. I think the poor creatures rather enjoy the aroma, especially the children."

But Dorcas was adamant; and after some further chirping and twittering, the two little people exchanged primly affectionate farewells; and the curate, having popped a bull's eye in his mouth, paddled away along the footpath, sucking joyously.

It is needless to say that Mrs Bodley's hat was not finished. The curate had unwisely executed all his other commissions before calling on the milliner; had ordered the pears, and even tested the quality of one or two samples; had directed the cobbler to send the rector's boots to the hat-shop; and had then collected the lace, black lead, cotton, pickles and the fresh haddock and borne them in triumph to the abode of Miss Gosse. It appeared that the hat would not be ready until seven o'clock in the evening. But it also appeared that tea would be ready in a few minutes. Accordingly, the curate remained to partake of that meal in the workroom, in company with Miss Gosse and her "hands"; and having been fed to bursting-point with French rolls and cake, left his various belongings and went forth to while away the time and paint the town of Dilbury – not exactly red, but a delicate and attenuated pink.

After an hour or so of rambling about the town, the curate's errant footsteps carried him down to the docks, where he was delighted with the spectacle of a military transport, just home from West Africa, discharging her passengers. The khaki-clad warriors trooped down the gangplanks and saluted him with cheerful greetings as he sat on a bollard and watched them. One even inquired if his – Mr Jawley's – mother knew he was out; which the curate thought very kind and attentive of him. But what thrilled him most was the appearance of the chaplain; a fine, portly churchman with an imposing, coppery nose, who was so overjoyed at the sight of his native land that he sang aloud; indeed, his emotion seemed actually to have affected his legs, for his gait was quite unsteady. Mr Jawley was deeply affected.

When the soldiers had gone, he slowly retraced his steps towards the gates; but he had hardly gone twenty yards when his eye was attracted by a small object lying in the thick grass that grew between the irregular paving-stones of the quay. He stooped to pick it up and uttered an exclamation of delight. It was a tiny effigy of a parrot, quaintly wrought in bronze and not more than two and a half inches high including the pedestal on which it stood. A perforation through the eyes had furnished the means of suspension, and a strand of silken thread yet remained to show, by its frayed ends, how the treasure had been lost.

Mr Jawley was charmed. It was such a dear little parrot; so quaint; so naïve. He was a simple man and small things gave him pleasure; and this small thing pleased him especially. The better to examine his find, he seated himself on a nice, clean, white post and proceeded to polish the little effigy with his handkerchief, having previously moistened the latter with his tongue. The polishing improved its appearance wonderfully, and he was inspecting it complacently when his eye lighted on a chalked inscription on the pavement. The writing was upside down as he sat, but he had no difficulty in deciphering the words "Wet Paint."

He rose hastily and examined the flat top of the post. There is no need to go into details. Suffice it to say that anyone looking at that post could have seen that some person had sat on it. Mr Jawley moved away with an angry exclamation. It was very annoying. But that did not justify the expressions that he used, which were not only out of character with his usual mild demeanour, but unsuitable to his cloth, even if that cloth happened to be – but again we say there is no need to go into details. Still frowning irritably, he strode out through the dock gates and up the High Street on his way to Miss Gosse's establishment. As he was passing the fruiterer's shop, Mr Barber, the proprietor, ran out.

"Good evening, Mr Jawley. About those pears that you ordered of my young man. You'd better not have those, sir. Let me send you another kind."

"Why?" asked the curate.

"Well, sir, those pears, to be quite candid, are not very good – "

"I don't care whether they are good or bad," interrupted Mr Jawley. "I am not going to eat them," and he stamped away up the High Street, leaving the fruiterer in a state of stupefaction. But he did not proceed directly to the milliner's. Some errant fancy impelled him to turn up a side street and make his way towards the waterside portion of the town, and it was, in fact, nearly eight o'clock when he approached Miss Gosse's premises (now closed for the night) and rang the bell. The interval, however, had not been entirely uneventful. A blue mark under the left eye and a somewhat battered and dusty condition of hat and clothing seemed reminiscent of recent and thrilling experiences, and the satisfied grin that he bestowed on the astonished caretaker suggested that those experiences, if strenuous, had not been wholly unpleasurable.

The shades of night had fallen on the village of Bobham when Mr Jawley appeared in the one and only street. He carried, balanced somewhat unsteadily on his head, a large cardboard box, but was otherwise unencumbered. The box had originally been of a cubical form, but now presented a slightly irregular outline, and from one corner a thin liquid dripped on Mr Jawley's shoulder, diffusing an aroma of vinegar and onions, with an added savour that was delicate and fish-like. Up the empty street the curate strode with a martial air, and having picked up the box – for the thirteenth time – just outside the gate, entered the rectory, deposited his burden on the drawing room sofa, and went up to his room. He required no supper. For once in a way he was not hungry. He had, in fact, taken a little refreshment in town; and whelks are a very satisfying food, if you only take enough of them.

In his narrow and bumpy bed the curate lay wakeful and wrapped in pleasing meditation. Now his thoughts strayed to the little bronze parrot, which he had placed, after a final polish, on the mantelpiece; and now, in delightful retrospection, he recalled the incidents of his little jaunt. There was, for instance, the slightly intoxicated marine with whom he had enjoyed a playful interview in Mermaid Street. Gleefully he reconstituted the image of that warrior as he had last seen him, sitting in the gutter attending to his features with a reddened handkerchief. And there was the overturned whelk stall and the two blue-jackets outside the "Pope's Head." He grinned at the recollection. And yet there were grumblers who actually complained of the dullness of the clerical life!

Again he recalled the pleasant walk home across the darkening fields; the delightful rest by the wayside (on the cardboard box), and the pleasantries that he had exchanged with a pair of rustic lovers – who had told him that "he ought to be ashamed of himself; a gentleman and a minister of religion, too!" He chuckled aloud as he thought of their bucolic irritation and his own brilliant repartee.

But at this moment his meditations were broken into by a very singular interruption. From the neighbourhood of the mantelpiece, there issued a voice, a very strange voice, deep, buzzing, resonant, chanting a short sentence, framed of yet more strange and unfamiliar words:

"Donköh e didi ma tum. On esse?"

This astounding phrase rang out in the little room with a deep, booming emphasis on the *"tum,"* and an interrogative note on the two final words. There followed an interval of intense silence, and then, from some distance, as it seemed, came the tapping of drums, imitating most curiously the sound and accent of the words – *"tum,"* for instance, being rendered by a large drum of deep, cavernous tone.

Mr Jawley listened with a pleased and interested smile. After a short interval, the chant was repeated; and again, like a far-away echo, the drums performed their curious mimicry of speech. Mr Jawley was deeply interested. After a dozen or so of repetitions, he found himself able to repeat, with a fair accent, the mysterious sentence, and even to imitate the tapping and booming of the drums.

But, after all, you can have too much of a good thing; and when the chant had continued to recur, at intervals of about ten seconds, for a quarter of an hour, Mr Jawley began to feel bored.

"There," said he, "that'll do," and he composed himself for slumber. But the invisible chanter ignoring his remark, continued the performance *da capo* and *ad lib.* – in fact, *ad nauseam.* Then Mr Jawley became annoyed. First he sat up in bed, and made what he considered appropriate comments on the performance, with a few personal references to the performer; and then, as the chant still continued with the relentless persistence of a chapel bell, he sprang out and strode furiously over to the mantelpiece.

"Shut up!" he roared, shaking his fist at the invisible parrot; and, strange to say, both the chant and the drumming ceased forthwith. There are some forms of speech, it would seem, that require no interpreter.

When Mr Jawley entered the breakfast room the following morning, the rector's wife was in the act of helping her husband to a devilled kidney, but she paused in the occupation to greet the curate with a stony stare. Mr Jawley sat down and knocked his knee as usual, but commented on the circumstance in terms which were not at all usual. The rector stared aghast, and Mrs Bodley exclaimed in shrill accents: "Mr Jawley, how dare – "

At this point she paused, having caught the curate's eye. A deathly silence ensued, during which Mr Jawley glared at a solitary boiled egg. Suddenly he snatched up a knife, and with uncanny dexterity decapitated the egg with a single stroke. Then he peered curiously into the disclosed cavity. Now if there was one thing that Mr Jawley hated more than another, it was an underdone egg; and, as his eye encountered a yellow spheroid floating in a clear liquid, he frowned ominously.

"Raw, by gosh!" he exclaimed hoarsely, and, plucking the egg from its calyx, he sent it hurtling across the room. For several seconds the rector stared, silent and open-mouthed, at his curate; then, following his wife's gaze, he stared at the wall, on the chrysanthemum paper of which appeared a new motive uncontemplated by the designer. And, meanwhile, Mr Jawley reached across the table and stuck a fork into the devilled kidney.

When the rector looked round and discovered his loss he essayed some spluttered demands for an explanation. But, since the organs of speech are associated with the act of mastication, the curate was not in a position to answer him. His eyes, however, were disengaged at the moment, and some compelling quality in them caused the rector and his wife to rise from their chairs and back cautiously towards the door. Mr Jawley nodded them out blandly, and being left in possession, proceeded to fill himself a cup of tea and another of coffee, cleared the dish, emptied the toast-rack, and having disposed of these trifles, concluded a Gargantuan repast by crunching up the contents of the sugar basin. Never had he enjoyed such a breakfast, and never had he felt so satisfied and joyous.

Having wiped his smiling lips on the table cloth, he strolled out into the playground, where the boys were waiting to be driven in to lessons. At the moment of his appearance, Messrs Joblett and Byles were in the act of resuming adjourned hostilities. The curate strode through the ring of spectators and beamed on the combatants with ferocious benevolence. His arrival had produced a brief armistice, but as he uttered no protests, the battle was resumed with a tentative prod on the part of Joblett.

The curate grinned savagely. "That isn't the way, Joblett," he exclaimed. "Kick him, man. Kick him in the stomach."

"Beg pardon, sir," said Joblett, regarding his preceptor with saucer eyes. "Did you say kick him?"

"Yes," roared the curate. "In the stomach. Like this!"

He backed a few paces, and fixing a glittering eye on Byles' abdomen, rushed forward, and, flinging his right foot back until it was almost visible over his shoulder, let out a tremendous kick. But Byles' stomach was not there. Neither was Byles – which, of course, follows. The result was that Mr Jawley's foot, meeting with no resistance, flew into space, carrying Mr Jawley's centre of gravity with it.

When the curate scrambled to his feet and glared balefully around, the playground was empty. A frantic crowd surged in through the open house door, while stragglers hurriedly climbed over the walls.

Mr Jawley laughed hoarsely. It was time to open school, but at the moment he was not studiously inclined. Letting himself out by the gate, he strolled forth into the village, and sauntered up the street. And here it was, just opposite the little butcher's shop, that he encountered the village atheist. Now this philosopher who, it is needless to say, was a cobbler by profession, had a standing and perennial joke, which was to greet the curate with the words: "How do, Jawley!" and thereby elicit a gracious "Good morning, Mr Pegg," and a polite touch of the hat. He proceeded this morning to utter the invariable formula, cocking his eye at the expectant butcher. But the anticipated response came not. Instead, the curate turned on him suddenly and growled:

"Say 'sir,' you vermin, when you speak to your betters."

The astounded cobbler was speechless for a moment; but only for a moment.

"What!" he exclaimed, "me say 'sir' to a sneakin' little devil-dodger, what – "

Here Mr Jawley turned and stepped lightly over to the shop. Reaching in through the open front, he lifted a cleaver from its nail, and, swinging it high above his head, rushed with a loud yell at the offending cobbler. But Mr Pegg was not without presence of mind, which, in this case, connoted absence of body. Before you could say "wax," he had darted into his house, bolted the door, and was looking down with bulging eyes from the first floor window on the crown of the curate's hat.

Meanwhile the butcher had emerged angrily from his shop, and approached the curate from behind.

"Here," he exclaimed gruffly, "what are you doing with that chop – " here he paused suddenly as Mr Jawley turned his head, and he continued with infinite suavity:

"Could you, sir, manage to spare that cleaver? If you would be so kind – "

Mr Jawley uttered a sulky growl and thrust the great chopper into its owner's hands; then, as the butcher turned away, he gave a loud laugh, on which the tradesman cleared his threshold at a single bound and slammed the half-door behind him. But a terrified backward glance showed him the curate's face wreathed in smiles, and another glance made him aware of the diminutive figure of Miss Dorcas Shipton approaching up the street.

The curate ran forward to meet her, beaming with affection. But he didn't merely beam. Not at all. The sound of his greeting was audible even to Mr Pegg, who leaned out of window, with eyes that bulged more than ever.

"Really, Deodatus!" exclaimed the scandalised Miss Dorcas. "What can you be thinking about; in such a pub – " Her remonstrances were cut short at this point by fresh demonstrations, which caused the butcher to wipe his mouth with the back of his hand, and Mr Pegg to gasp with fresh amazement.

"Pray, pray remember yourself, Deodatus!" exclaimed the blushing Dorcas, wriggling, at length, out of his too-affectionate grasp. "Besides," she added, with a sudden strategic inspiration, "you surely ought to be in school at this time."

"That is of no consequence, darling," said Jawley, advancing on her with open arms; "old Bod can look after the whelps."

"Oh, but you mustn't neglect your duties, Deodatus," said Miss Dorcas, still backing away. "Won't you go in, just to please me?"

"Certainly, my love, if you wish it," replied Jawley, with an amorous leer. "I'll go at once – but I *must* have just one more," and again the village street rang with a sound as of the popping of a ginger beer cork.

As he approached the school, Mr Jawley became aware of the familiar and distasteful roar of many voices. Standing in the doorway, he heard Mr Bodley declare with angry emphasis that he "would not have this disgraceful noise" and saw him slap the desk with his open hand; whereupon nothing in particular happened excepting an apparently preconcerted chorus as of many goats. Then Mr Jawley entered and looked round; and in a moment the place was wrapped in a silence like that of an Egyptian tomb.

Space does not allow of our recording in detail the history of the next few days. We may, however, say in general terms that there grew up in the village of Bobham a feeling of universal respect for the diminutive curate, not entirely unmixed with superstitious awe. Rustics, hitherto lax in their manners pulled off their hats like clockwork at his approach; Mr Pegg abandoning the village street, cultivated a taste for footpaths, preferably remote, and unobstructed by trees; the butcher fell into the habit of sending gratuitous sweetbreads to the Rectory, addressed to Mr Jawley, and even the blacksmith, when he had recovered from his black eye, adopted a suave and conciliatory demeanour.

The rector's wife, alone, cherished a secret resentment (though outwardly attentive in the matter of devilled kidneys and streaky bacon), and urged the rector to get rid of his fire-eating subordinate; but her plans failed miserably. It is true that the rector did venture tentatively to open the subject to the curate, who listened with a lowering brow and sharpened a lead pencil with a colossal pocket-knife that he had bought at a ship-chandlers in Dilbury. But the conclusion was never reached. Distracted, perhaps, by Mr Jawley's inscrutable manner, the rector became confused and, to his own surprise, found himself urging the curate to accept an additional twenty pounds a year, an offer which Mr Jawley immediately insisted on having in writing.

The only person who did not share the universal awe was Miss Dorcas; for she, like the sundial, "numbered only the sunny hours." But she respected him more than any; and, though dimly surprised at the rumours of his doings, gloried in secret over his prowess.

Thus the days rolled on and Mr Jawley put on flesh visibly. Then came the eventful morning when, on scanning the rector's *Times*, his eye lighted on an advertisement in the Personal Column:

"Ten pounds reward. Lost; a small, bronze effigy of a parrot on a square pedestal; the whole two and a half inches high. The Above Reward will be paid

on behalf of the owner by the Curator of the Ethnographical Department of the British Museum, who has a photograph and description of the object."

Now Mr Jawley had become deeply attached to the parrot. But after all it was only a pretty trifle, and ten pounds was ten pounds. That very afternoon, the Curator found himself confronted by a diminutive clergyman of ferocious aspect, and hurriedly disgorged ten sovereigns after verifying the description; and to this day he is wont to recount, as an instance of the power of money, the remarkable change for the better in the clergyman's manners when the transaction was completed.

It was late in the afternoon when Mr Jawley reappeared in the village of Bobham. He carried a gigantic paper parcel under one arm, and his pockets bulged so that he appeared to suffer from some unclassified deformity. At the stile, he suddenly encountered Mr Pegg, who prepared for instant flight, and was literally stupefied when the curate lifted his hat and graciously wished him "good evening." But Mr Pegg was even more stupefied when a few minutes later, he saw the curate seated on a doorstep with the open parcel on his knees, and a mob of children gathered around him. For Mr Jawley, with the sunniest of smiles, was engaged in distributing dolls, peg-tops, skipping-ropes and little wooden horses, to a running accompaniment of bull's-eyes, brandy balls and other delicacies, which he produced from inexhaustible pockets. He even offered Mr Pegg, himself, a sugar-stick which the philosophic cordwainer accepted with a polite bow and presently threw over a wall. But he pondered deeply on this wonder and is probably pondering still in common with the other inhabitants of Bobham.

But though, from that moment, Mr Jawley became once more the gentlest and most amiable of men, the prestige of his former deeds remained; reverential awe attended his footsteps abroad, devilled kidneys and streaky bacon were his portion at home; until such time as Miss Dorcas Shipton underwent a quieter metamorphosis and became Mrs Deodatus Jawley. And thereafter he walked, not only amidst reverence and awe, but also amidst flowers and sunshine.

P. S. – The curious who would know more about the parrot, may find him on his appropriate shelf in the West African Section, and read the large, descriptive label which sets forth his history:

"Bronze gold-weight in the form of a parrot. This object was formerly the property of the great Ashanti War Chief, Amankwa Tia, whose clan totem was a parrot. It was worn by him, attached to his wrist, as an amulet or charm and, when on a campaign, a larger copy of it, of gilded wood, was carried by the chief herald, who preceded him and chanted his official motto. It may be explained here that each of the Ashanti generals had a distinguishing motto, consisting of a short sentence, which was called out before him by his heralds when on the march, and repeated, with remarkably close mimicry, by the message drums. Thus, when several bodies of troops were marching through the dense forest, their respective identities were made clear to one another by the sound of the chant on the drums. Amankwa Tia's motto was:

" 'Donköh e didi ma tum. On esse?' Which may be translated '(Foreign) Slaves revile me. Why?' A somewhat meaningless sentence, but having, perhaps, a sinister significance."

The Missing Mortgagee

PART I

Early in the afternoon of a warm, humid November day, Thomas Elton sauntered dejectedly along the Margate esplanade, casting an eye now on the slate-coloured sea with its pall of slate-coloured sky, and now on the harbour, where the ebb tide was just beginning to expose the mud. It was a dreary prospect, and Elton varied it by observing the few fishermen and fewer promenaders who walked foot to foot with their distorted reflections in the wet pavement; and thus it was that his eye fell on a smartly-dressed man who had just stepped into a shelter to light a cigar.

A contemporary joker has classified the Scotsmen who abound in South Africa into two groups: those, namely, who hail from Scotland, and those who hail from Palestine. Now, something in the aspect of the broad back that was presented to his view, in that of the curly, black hair and the exuberant raiment, suggested to Elton a Scotsman of the latter type. In fact, there was a suspicion of disagreeable familiarity in the figure which caused him to watch it and slacken his pace. The man backed out of the shelter, diffusing azure clouds, and, drawing an envelope from his pocket, read something that was written on it. Then he turned quickly – and so did Elton, but not quickly enough. For he was a solitary figure on that bald and empty expanse, and the other had seen him at the first glance. Elton walked away slowly, but he had not gone a dozen paces when he felt the anticipated slap on the shoulder and heard the too well-remembered voice.

"Blow me, if I don't believe you were trying to cut me, Tom," it said.

Elton looked round with ill-assumed surprise.

"Hallo, Gordon! Who the deuce would have thought of seeing you here?"

Gordon laughed thickly. "Not you, apparently; and you don't look as pleased as you might now you have seen me. Whereas I'm delighted to see you and especially to see that things are going so well with you."

"What do you mean?" asked Elton.

"Taking your winter holiday by the sea, like a blooming duke."

"I'm not taking a holiday," said Elton. "I was so worn out that I had to have some sort of change; but I've brought my work down with me, and I put in a full seven hours every day."

"That's right," said Gordon. " 'Consider the ant.' Nothing like steady industry. I've brought my work down with me too; a little slip of paper with a stamp on it. You know the article, Tom."

"I know. But it isn't due till tomorrow, is it?"

"Isn't it, by gum! It's due this very day, the twentieth of the month. That's why I'm here. Knowing your little weakness in the matter of dates, and having a small item to collect in Canterbury, I thought I'd just come on, and save you the useless expense that results from forgetfulness."

Elton understood the hint, and his face grew rigid.

"I can't do it, Gordon; I can't really. Haven't got it, and shan't have it until I'm paid for the batch of drawings that I'm working on now."

"Oh, but what a pity!" exclaimed Gordon, taking the cigar from his thick, pouting lips to utter the exclamation. "Here you are, blueing your capital on seaside jaunts and reducing your income at a stroke by a clear four pounds a year."

"How do you make that out?" demanded Elton.

"Tut, tut," protested Gordon, "what an unbusiness-like chap you are! Here's a little matter of twenty pounds – a quarter's interest. If it's paid now, it's twenty. If it isn't, it goes on to the principal, and there's another four pounds a year to be paid. Why don't you try to be more economical, dear boy?"

Elton looked askance at the vampire by his side; at the plump, blue-shaven cheeks, the thick black eyebrows, the drooping nose, and the full, red lips that embraced the cigar, and though he was a mild-tempered man he felt that he could have battered that sensual, complacent face out of all human likeness with something uncommonly like enjoyment. But of these thoughts nothing appeared in his reply, for a man cannot afford to say all he would wish to a creditor who could ruin him with a word.

"You mustn't be too hard on me, Gordon," said he. "Give me a little time. I'm doing all I can, you know. I earn every penny that I am able, and I have kept my insurance paid up regularly. I shall be paid for this work in a week or two and then we can settle up."

Gordon made no immediate reply, and the two men walked slowly eastward, a curiously ill-assorted pair: the one prosperous, jaunty, overdressed; the other pale and dejected, and, with his well-brushed but napless clothes, his patched boots and shiny-brimmed hat, the very type of decent, struggling poverty.

They had just passed the pier, and were coming to the base of the jetty, when Gordon next spoke.

"Can't we get off this beastly wet pavement?" he asked, looking down at his dainty and highly-polished boots. "What's it like down on the sands?"

"Oh, it's very good walking," said Elton, "between here and Foreness, and probably drier than the pavement."

"Then," said Gordon, "I vote we go down"; and accordingly they descended the sloping way beyond the jetty. The stretch of sand left by the retiring tide was as smooth and firm as a sheet of asphalt, and far more pleasant to walk upon.

"We seem to have the place all to ourselves," remarked Gordon, "with the exception of some half-dozen dukes like yourself."

As he spoke, he cast a cunning black eye furtively at the dejected man by his side, considering how much further squeezing was possible, and what would be the probable product of a further squeeze; but he quickly averted his gaze as Elton turned on him a look eloquent of contempt and dislike. There was another pause, for Elton made no reply to the last observation; then Gordon changed over from one arm to the other the heavy fur-lined overcoat that he was carrying. "Needn't have brought this beastly thing," he remarked, "if I'd known it was going to be so warm."

"Shall I carry it for you a little way?" asked the naturally polite Elton.

"If you would, dear boy," replied Gordon. "It's difficult to manage an overcoat, an umbrella and a cigar all at once."

He handed over the coat with a sigh of relief, and having straightened himself and expanded his chest, remarked:

"I suppose you're beginning to do quite well now, Tom?"

Elton shook his head gloomily. "No," he answered, "it's the same old grind."

"But surely they're beginning to recognise your talents by this time," said Gordon, with the persuasive air of a cross-examining counsel.

"That's just the trouble," said Elton. "You see. I haven't any, and they recognised the fact long ago, I'm just a journeyman, and journeyman's work is what I get given to me."

"You mean to say that the editors don't appreciate talent when the see it."

"I don't know about that," said Elton, "but they're most infernally appreciative of the lack of it."

Gordon blew out a great cloud of smoke, and raised his eyebrows reflectively. "Do you think," he said after a brief pause, "you give 'em a fair chance? I've seen some of your stuff. It's blooming prim, you know. Why don't you try something more lively? More skittish, you know, old chap; something with legs, you know, and high-heeled shoes. See what I mean, old chap? High-steppers, with good full calves and not too fat in the ankle. That ought to fetch 'em; don't you think so?"

Elton scowled. "You're thinking of the drawings in 'Hold Me Up,'" he said scornfully, "but you're mistaken. Any fool can draw a champagne bottle upside down with a French shoe at the end of it."

"No doubt, dear boy," said Gordon, "but I expect that sort of fool knows what pays."

"A good many fools seem to know that much," retorted Elton; and then he was sorry he had spoken, for Gordon was not really an amiable man, and the expression of his face suggested that he had read a personal application into the rejoinder. So, once more, the two men walked on in silence.

Presently their footsteps led them to the margin of the weed-covered rocks, and here, from under a high heap of bladder-wrack, a large green shore crab rushed out and menaced them with uplifted claws. Gordon stopped and stared at the creature with Cockney surprise, prodding it with his umbrella, and speculating aloud as to whether it was good to eat. The crab, as if alarmed at the suggestion, suddenly darted away and began to scuttle over the green-clad rocks, finally plunging into a large, deep pool. Gordon pursued it, hobbling awkwardly over the slippery rocks, until he came to the edge of the pool, over which he stooped, raking inquisitively among the weedy fringe with his umbrella. He was so much interested in his quarry that he failed to allow for the slippery surface on which he stood. The result was disastrous. Of a sudden, one foot began to slide forward, and when he tried to recover his balance, was instantly followed by the other. For a moment he struggled frantically to regain his footing, executing a sort of splashing, stamping dance on the margin. Then, the circling sea birds were startled by a yell of terror, an ivory-handled umbrella flew across the rocks, and Mr Solomon Gordon took a complete header into the deepest part of the pool. What the crab thought of it history does not relate. What Mr Gordon thought of it is not suitable for publication; but, as he rose, like an extremely up-to-date merman, he expressed his sentiments with a wealth of adjectives that brought Elton to the verge of hysteria.

"It's a good job you brought your overcoat, after all," Elton remarked for the sake of saying something, and thereby avoiding the risk of exploding into undeniable laughter. The Hebrew made no reply — at least, no reply that lends itself to verbatim report — but staggered towards the hospitable overcoat, holding out his dripping arms. Having inducted him into the garment and buttoned him up, Elton hurried off to recover the umbrella (and, incidentally, to indulge himself in a broad grin), and, having secured it, angled with it for the smart billycock which was floating across the pool.

It was surprising what a change the last minute or two had wrought. The positions of the two men were now quite reversed. Despite his shabby clothing, Elton seemed to walk quite jauntily as compared with his shuddering companion, who trotted by his side with short, miserable steps, shrinking into the uttermost depths of his enveloping coat, like an alarmed winkle into its shell, puffing out his cheeks and anathematising the Universe in general as well as his chattering teeth would let him.

For some time they hurried along towards the slope by the jetty without exchanging any further remarks; then, suddenly, Elton asked: "What are you going to do, Gordon? You can't travel like that."

"Can't you lend me a change?" asked Gordon.

Elton reflected. He had another suit, his best suit which he had been careful to preserve in good condition for use on those occasions when a decent appearance was indispensable. He looked askance at the man by his side and something told him that the treasured suit would probably receive less careful treatment than it was accustomed to. Still the man couldn't be allowed to go about in wet clothes.

"I've got a spare suit," he said. "It isn't quite up to your style, and may not be much of a fit, but I daresay you'll be able to put up with it for an hour or two."

"It'll be dry anyhow," mumbled Gordon, "so we won't trouble about the style. How far is it to your rooms?"

The plural number was superfluous. Elton's room was in a little ancient flint house at the bottom of a narrow close in the old quarter of the town. You reached it without any formal preliminaries of bell or knocker by simply letting yourself in by a street door, crossing a tiny room, opening the door of what looked like a narrow cupboard, and squeezing up a diminutive flight of stairs, which was unexpectedly exposed to view. By following this procedure, the two men reached a small bed-sitting room; that is to say, it was a bedroom, but by sitting down on the bed, you converted it into a sitting room.

Gordon puffed out his cheeks and looked round distastefully.

"You might just ring for some hot water, old chappie," he said.

Elton laughed aloud. "Ring!" he exclaimed. "Ring what? Your clothes are the only things that are likely to get wrung."

"Well, then, sing out for the servant," said Gordon.

Elton laughed again. "My dear fellow," said he, "we don't go in for servants. There is only my landlady and she never comes up here. She's too fat to get up the stairs, and besides, she's got a game leg. I look after my room myself. You'll be all right if you have a good rub down."

Gordon groaned, and emerged reluctantly from the depths of his overcoat, while Elton brought forth from the chest of drawers the promised suit and the necessary undergarments. One of these latter Gordon held up with a sour smile, as he regarded it with extreme disfavour.

"I shouldn't think," said he, "you need have been at the trouble of marking them so plainly. No one's likely to want to run away with them."

The undergarments certainly contrasted very unfavourably with the delicate garments which he was peeling off, excepting in one respect; they were dry; and that had to console him for the ignominious change.

The clothes fitted quite fairly, notwithstanding the difference between the figures of the two men; for while Gordon was a slender man grown fat, Elton was a broad man grown thin; which, in a way, averaged their superficial area.

Elton watched the process of investment and noted the caution with which Gordon smuggled the various articles from his own pockets into those of the borrowed garments without exposing them to view; heard the jingle of money; saw the sumptuous gold watch and massive chain transplanted, and noted with interest the large leather wallet that came forth from the breast pocket of the wet coat.

He got a better view of this from the fact that Gordon himself examined it narrowly, and even opened it to inspect its contents.

"Lucky that wasn't an ordinary pocket-book," he remarked. "If it had been, your receipt would have got wet, and so would one or two other little articles that wouldn't have been improved by salt water. And, talking of the receipt, Tom, shall I hand it over now?"

"You can if you like," said Elton; "but as I told you, I haven't got the money"; on which Gordon muttered:

"Pity, pity," and thrust the wallet into his, or rather, Elton's breast pocket.

A few minutes later, the two men came out together into the gathering darkness, and as they walked slowly up the close, Elton asked: "Are you going up to town tonight, Gordon?"

"How can I?" was the reply. "I can't go without my clothes. No, I shall run over to Broadstairs. A client of mine keeps a boarding house there. He'll have to put me up for the night, and if you can get my clothes cleaned and dried I can come over for them tomorrow."

These arrangements having been settled, the two men adjourned, at Gordon's suggestion, for tea at one of the restaurants on the Front; and after that, again at Gordon's suggestion, they set forth together along the cliff path that leads to Broadstairs by way of Kingsgate.

"You may as well walk with me into Broadstairs," said Gordon; "I'll stand you the fare back by rail"; and to this Elton had agreed, not because he was desirous of the other man's company, but because he still had some lingering hopes of being able to adjust the little difficulty respecting the instalment.

He did not, however, open the subject at once. Profoundly as he loathed and despised the human spider whom necessity made his associate for the moment, he exerted himself to keep up a current of amusing conversation. It was not easy; for Gordon, like most men whose attention is focussed on the mere acquirement of money, looked with a dull eye on the ordinary interests of life. His tastes in art he had already hinted at, and his other tastes lay much in the same direction. Money first, for its own sake, and then those coarser and more primitive gratifications that it was capable of purchasing. This was the horizon that bounded Mr Solomon Gordon's field of vision.

Nevertheless, they were well on their way before Elton alluded to the subject that was uppermost in both their minds.

"Look here, Gordon," he said at length, "can't you manage to give me a bit more time to pay up this instalment? It doesn't seem quite fair to keep sending up the principal like this."

"Well, dear boy," replied Gordon, "its your own fault, you know. If you would only bear the dates in mind, it wouldn't happen."

"But," pleaded Elton, "just consider what I'm paying you. I originally borrowed fifty pounds from you, and I'm now paying you eighty pounds a year in addition to the insurance premium. That's close on a hundred a year; just about half what I manage to earn by slaving like a nigger. If you stick it up any farther you won't leave me enough to keep body and soul together; which really means that I shan't be able to pay you at all."

There was brief pause; then Gordon said dryly:

"You talk about not paying, dear boy, as if you had forgotten about that promissory note."

Elton set his teeth. His temper was rising rapidly. But he restrained himself.

"I should have a pretty poor memory if I had," he replied, "considering the number of reminders you've given me."

"You've needed them, Tom," said the other. "I've never met a slacker man in keeping to his engagements."

At this Elton lost his temper completely.

"That's a damned lie!" he exclaimed, "and you know it, you infernal, dirty, blood-sucking parasite!"

Gordon stopped dead.

"Look here, my friend," said he; "none of that. If I've any of your damned sauce, I'll give you a sound good hammering."

"The deuce you will!" said Elton, whose fingers were itching, not for the first time, to take some recompense for all that he had suffered from the insatiable usurer. "Nothing's preventing you now you know, but I fancy cent. per cent. is more in your line than fighting."

"Give me any more sauce and you'll see," said Gordon.

"Very well," was the quiet rejoinder. "I have great pleasure in informing you that you are a human maw-worm. How does that suit you?"

For reply, Gordon threw down his overcoat and umbrella on the grass at the side of the path, and deliberately slapped Elton on the cheek.

The reply followed instantly in the form of a smart left-hander, which took effect on the bridge of the Hebrew's rather prominent nose. Thus the battle was fairly started, and it proceeded with all the fury of accumulated hatred on the one side and sharp physical pain on the other. What little science there was appertained to Elton, in spite of which, however, he had to give way to his heavier, better nourished and more excitable opponent. Regardless of the punishment he received, the infuriated Jew rushed at him and, by sheer weight of onslaught, drove him backward across the little green.

Suddenly, Elton, who knew the place by daylight, called out in alarm.

"Look out, Gordon! Get back, you fool!"

But Gordon, blind with fury, and taking this as a manœuvre to escape, only pressed him harder. Elton's pugnacity died out instantly in mortal terror. He shouted out another warning and, as Gordon still pressed him, battering furiously, he did the only thing that was possible: he dropped to the ground. And then, in the twinkling of an eye came the catastrophe. Borne forward by his own momentum, Gordon stumbled over Elton's prostrate body, staggered forward a few paces, and fell. Elton heard a muffled groan that faded quickly; and mingled with the sound of falling earth and stones. He sprang to his feet and looked round and saw that he was alone.

For some moments he was dazed by the suddenness of the awful thing that had happened. He crept timorously towards the unseen edge of the cliff, and listened. But there was no sound save the distant surge of the breakers, and the scream of an invisible sea-bird. It was useless to try to look over. Near as he was, he could not, even now, distinguish the edge of the cliff from the dark beach below. Suddenly he bethought him of a narrow cutting that led down from the cliff to the shore. Quickly crossing the green, and mechanically stooping to pick up Gordon's overcoat and umbrella, he made his way to the head of the cutting and ran down the rough chalk roadway. At the bottom he turned to the right and, striding hurriedly over the smooth sand, peered into the darkness at the foot of the cliff.

Soon there loomed up against the murky sky the shadowy form of the little headland on which he and Gordon had stood; and, almost at the same moment, there grew out of the darkness of the beach a darker spot amidst a constellation of smaller spots of white. As he drew nearer the dark spot took shape; a horrid shape with sprawling limbs and a head strangely awry. He stepped forward, trembling, and spoke the name that the thing had borne. He grasped the flabby hand, and laid his fingers on the wrist; but it only told him the same tale as did that strangely misplaced head. The body lay face downwards, and he had not the courage to turn it over; but that his enemy was dead he had not the faintest doubt. He stood up amidst the litter of fallen chalk and earth and looked down at the horrible, motionless thing, wondering numbly and vaguely what he should do. Should he go and seek assistance? The answer to that came in another question. How came that body to be lying on the beach? And what answer should he give to the inevitable questions? And swiftly there grew up in his mind, born of the horror of the thing that was, a yet greater horror of the thing that might be.

A minute later, a panic-stricken man stole with stealthy swiftness up the narrow cutting and set forth towards Margate, stopping anon to listen, and stealing away off the path into the darkness, to enter the town by the inland road.

Little sleep was there that night for Elton in his room in the old flint house. The dead man's clothes, which greeted him on his arrival, hanging limply on the towel-horse where he had left them, haunted him through the night. In the darkness, the sour smell of damp cloth assailed him with an endless reminder of their presence, and after each brief doze, he would start up in alarm and hastily light his candle; only to throw its flickering light on those dank, drowned-looking vestments. His thoughts, half-controlled, as night thoughts are, flitted erratically from the unhappy past to the unstable present, and thence to the incalculable future. Once he lighted the candle specially to look at his watch to see if the tide had yet crept up to that solitary figure on the beach; nor could he rest again until the time of high-water was well past. And all through these wanderings of his thoughts there came, recurring like a horrible refrain, the question, what would happen when the body was found? Could he be connected with it and, if so, would he be charged with murder? At last he fell asleep and slumbered on until the landlady thumped at the staircase door to announce that she had brought his breakfast.

As soon as he was dressed he went out. Not, however, until he had stuffed Gordon's still damp clothes and boots, the cumbrous overcoat and the smart billycock hat into his trunk, and put the umbrella into the darkest corner of the cupboard. Not that anyone ever came up to the room, but that, already, he was possessed with the uneasy secretiveness of the criminal. He went straight down to the beach; with what purpose he could hardly have said, but an irresistible impulse drove him thither to see if it was there. He went down by the jetty and struck out eastward over the smooth sand, looking about him with dreadful expectation for some small crowd or hurrying messenger. From the foot of the cliffs, over the rocks to the distant line of breakers, his eye roved with eager dread, and still he hurried eastward, always drawing nearer to the place that he feared to look on. As he left the town behind, so he left behind the one or two idlers on the beach, and when he turned Foreness Point, he lost sight of the last of them and went forward alone.

It was less than half an hour later that the fatal headland opened out beyond Whiteness. Not a soul had he met along that solitary beach, and though, once or twice, he had started at the sight of some mass of driftwood or heap of seaweed, the dreadful thing that he was seeking had not yet appeared. He passed the opening of the cutting and approached the headland, breathing fast and looking about him fearfully. Already he could see the larger lumps of chalk that had fallen, and looking up, he saw a clean, white patch at the summit of the cliff.

But still there was no sign of the corpse. He walked on more slowly now, considering whether it could have drifted out to sea, or whether he should find it in the next bay. And then, rounding the headland, he came in sight of a black hole at the cliff foot, the entrance to a deep cave. He approached yet more slowly, sweeping his eye round the little bay, and looking apprehensively at the cavity before him. Suppose the thing should have washed in there. It was quite possible. Many things did wash into that cave, for he had once visited it and had been astonished at the quantity of seaweed and jetsam that had accumulated within it. But it was an uncomfortable thought. It would be doubly horrible to meet the awful thing in the dim twilight of the cavern. And yet, the black archway seemed to draw him on, step by step, until he stood at the portal and looked in. It was an eerie place, chilly and damp, the clammy walls and roof stained green and purple and black with encrusting lichens. At one time, Elton had been told, it used to be haunted by smugglers, and then communicated with an underground passage; and the old smuggler's look-out still remained; a narrow tunnel, high up the cliff, looking out into Kingsgate Bay; and even some vestiges of the rude steps that led up to the look-out platform could still be traced, and were not impossible to climb. Indeed, Elton had, at his last visit, climbed to the platform and looked out through the spy-hole. He recalled the circumstance now, as he stood, peering nervously into the darkness, and straining his eyes to see what jetsam the ocean had brought since then.

At first he could see nothing but the smooth sand near the opening; then, as his eyes grew more accustomed to the gloom, he could make out the great heap of seaweed on the floor of the cave. Insensibly, he crept in, with his eyes riveted on the weedy mass and, as he left the daylight behind him, so did the twilight of the cave grow clearer. His feet left the firm sand and trod the springy mass of weed, and in the silence of the cave he could now hear plainly the rain-like patter of the leaping sand-hoppers. He stopped for a moment to listen to the unfamiliar sound, and still the gloom of the cave grew lighter to his more accustomed eyes.

And then, in an instant, he saw it. From a heap of weed, a few paces ahead, projected a boot; his own boot; he recognised the patch on the sole; and at the sight, his heart seemed to stand still. Though he had somehow expected to find it here, its presence seemed to strike him with a greater shock of horror from that very circumstance.

He was standing stock still, gazing with fearful fascination at the boot and the swelling mound of weed when, suddenly, there struck upon his ear the voice of a woman, singing.

He started violently. His first impulse was to run out of the cave. But a moment's reflection told him what madness this would be. And then the voice drew nearer, and there broke out the high, rippling laughter of a child. Elton looked in terror at the bright opening of the cavern's mouth, expecting every moment to see it frame a group of figures. If that happened, he was lost, for he would have been seen actually with the body. Suddenly he bethought him of the spy-hole and the platform, both of which were invisible from the entrance; and turning, he ran quickly over the sodden weed till he came to the remains of the steps. Climbing hurriedly up these, he reached the platform, which was enclosed in a large niche, just as the reverberating sound of voices told him that the strangers were within the mouth of the cave. He strained his ears to catch what they were saying and to make out if they were entering farther. It was a child's voice that he had first heard, and very weird were the hollow echoes of the thin treble that were flung back from the rugged walls. But he could not hear what the child had said. The woman's voice however, was quite distinct, and the words seemed significant in more senses than one.

"No, dear," it said, "you had better not go in. It's cold and damp. Come out into the sunshine."

Elton breathed more freely. But the woman was more right than she knew. It was cold and damp: that thing under the black tangle of weed. Better far to be out in the sunshine. He himself was already longing to escape from the chill and gloom of the cavern. But he could not escape yet. Innocent as he actually was, his position was that of a murderer. He must wait until the coast was clear, and then steal out, to hurry away unobserved.

He crept up cautiously to the short tunnel and peered out through the opening across the bay. And then his heart sank. Below him, on the sunny beach, a small party of visitors had established themselves just within view of the mouth of the cave; and even as he looked, a man approached from the wooden stairway down the cliff, carrying a couple of deck chairs. So, for the present his escape was hopelessly cut off.

He went back to the platform and sat down to wait for his release; and, as he sat, his thoughts went back once more to the thing that lay under the weed. How long would it lie there undiscovered? And what would happen when it was found? What was there to connect him with it? Of course, there was his name on the clothing, but there was nothing incriminating in that, if he had only had the courage to give information at once. But it was too late to think of that now. Besides, it suddenly flashed upon him, there was the receipt in the wallet. That receipt mentioned him by name and referred to a loan. Obviously, its suggestion was most sinister, coupled with his silence. It was a deadly item of evidence against him. But no sooner had he realised the appalling significance of this document than he also realised that it was still within his reach. Why should he leave it there to be brought in evidence – in false evidence, too – against him?

Slowly he rose and, creeping down the tunnel, once more looked out. The people were sitting quietly in their chairs, the man was reading, and the child was digging in the sand. Elton looked across the bay to make sure that no other person was approaching, and then, hastily, climbing down the steps, walked across the great bed of weed, driving an army of sand-hoppers before him. He shuddered at the thought of what he was going to do, and the clammy chill of the cave seemed to settle on him in a cold sweat.

He came to the little mound from which the boot projected, and began, shudderingly and with faltering hand, to lift the slimy, tangled weed. As he drew aside the first bunch, he gave a gasp of horror and quickly replaced it. The body was lying on its back, and, as he lifted the weed he had uncovered – not the face, for the thing had no face. It had struck either the cliff or a stone upon the beach and – but there is no need to go into particulars: it had no face. When he had recovered a little, Elton groped shudderingly among the weed until he found the breast-pocket from which he quickly drew out the wallet, now clammy, sodden and loathsome. He was rising with it in his hand when an apparition, seen through the opening of the cave, arrested his movement as if he had been suddenly turned into stone. A man, apparently a fisherman or sailor, was sauntering past some thirty yards from the mouth of the cave, and, at his heels trotted a mongrel dog. The dog stopped, and, lifting his nose, seemed to sniff the air; and then he began to walk slowly and suspiciously towards the cave. The man sauntered on and soon passed out of view; but the dog still came on towards the cave, stopping now and again with upraised nose.

The catastrophe seemed inevitable. But just at that moment the man's voice rose, loud and angry, evidently calling the dog. The animal hesitated, looking wistfully from his master to the cave; but when the summons was repeated, he turned reluctantly and trotted away.

Elton stood up and took a deep breath. The chilly sweat was running down his face, his heart was thumping and his knees trembled, so that he could hardly get back to the platform. What hideous peril had he escaped and how narrowly! For there he had stood; and had the man entered, he would have been caught in the very act of stealing the incriminating document from the body. For that matter, he was little better off now, with the dead man's property on his person, and he resolved instantly to take out and destroy the receipt and put back the wallet. But this was easier thought of than done. The receipt was soaked with sea water, and refused utterly to light when he applied a match to it. In the end, he tore it up into little fragments and deliberately swallowed them, one by one.

But to restore the wallet was more than he was equal to just now. He would wait until the people had gone home to lunch, and then he would thrust it under the weed as he ran past. So he sat down again and once more took up the endless thread of his thoughts.

The receipt was gone now, and with it the immediate suggestion of motive. There remained only the clothes with their too legible markings. They certainly connected him with the body, but they offered no proof of his presence at the catastrophe. And then, suddenly, another most startling idea occurred to him. Who could identify the body – the body that had no face? There was the wallet, it was true, but he could take that away with him, and there was a ring on the finger, and some articles in the pockets which might be identified. But – a voice seemed to whisper to him – these things were removable, too. And if he removed them, what then? Why, then, the body was that of Thomas Elton, a friendless, poverty-stricken artist, about whom no one would trouble to ask any questions.

He pondered on this new situation profoundly. It offered him a choice of alternatives. Either he might choose the imminent risk of being hanged for a murder that he had not committed, or he might surrender his identity for ever and move away to a new environment.

He smiled faintly. His identity! What might that be worth to barter against his life? Only yesterday he would gladly have surrendered it as the bare price of emancipation from the vampire who had fastened on to him.

He thrust the wallet into his pocket and buttoned his coat. Thomas Elton was dead; and that other man, as yet unnamed, should go forth, as the woman had said, into the sunshine.

PART II

From various causes, the insurance business that passed through Thorndyke's hands had, of late, considerably increased. The number of societies which regularly employed him had grown larger, and, since the remarkable case of Percival Bland, the "Griffin" had made it a routine practice to send all inquest cases to us for report.

It was in reference to one of these latter that Mr Stalker, a senior member of the staff of that office, called on us one afternoon in December; and when he had laid his bag on the table and settled himself comfortably before the fire, he opened the business without preamble.

"I've brought you another inquest case," said he; 'a rather queer one, quite interesting from your point of view. As far as we can see, it has no particular interest for us excepting that it does rather look as if our examining medical officer had been a little casual."

"What is the special interest of the case from our point of view?" asked Thorndyke.

"I'll just give you a sketch of it," said Stalker, "and I think you will agree that it's a case after your own heart.

"On the 24th of last month, some men who were collecting seaweed, to use as manure, discovered in a cave at Kingsgate in the Isle of Thanet, the body of a man, lying under a mass of accumulated weed. As the tide was rising, they put the body into their cart and conveyed it to Margate, where, of course, an inquest was held, and the following facts were elicited. The body was that of a man named Thomas Elton. It was identified by the name-marks on the clothing, by the visiting-cards and a couple of letters which were found in the pockets. From the address on the letters, it was seen that Elton had been staying in Margate, and on inquiry at that address, it was learnt from the old woman who let the lodgings, that he had been missing about four days. The landlady was taken to the mortuary, and at once identified the body as that of her lodger. It remained only to decide how the body came into the cave; and this did not seem to present much difficulty; for the neck had been broken by a tremendous blow, which had practically destroyed the face, and there were distinct evidences of a breaking away of a portion of the top of the cliff, only a few yards from the position of the cave. There was apparently no doubt that Elton had fallen sheer from the top of the overhanging cliff on to the beach. Now, one would suppose with the evidence of this fall of about a hundred and fifty feet, the smashed face and broken neck, there was not much room for doubt as to the cause of death. I think you will agree with me, Dr Jervis?"

"Certainly," I replied; "it must be admitted that a broken neck is a condition that tends to shorten life."

"Quite so," agreed Stalker; "but our friend, the local coroner, is a gentleman who takes nothing for granted – a very Thomas Didymus, who apparently agrees with Dr Thorndyke that if there is no post mortem, there is no inquest. So he ordered a post mortem, which would have appeared to me an absurdly unnecessary proceeding, and I think that even you will agree with me, Dr Thorndyke."

But Thorndyke shook his head.

"Not at all," said he. "It might, for instance, be much more easy to push a drugged or poisoned man over a cliff than to put over the same man in his normal state. The appearance of violent accident is an excellent mask for the less obvious forms of murder."

"That's perfectly true," said Stalker; "and I suppose that is what the coroner thought. At any rate, he had the post mortem made, and the result was most curious; for it was found, on opening the body, that the deceased had suffered from a smallish thoracic aneurism, which had burst. Now, as the aneursim must obviously have burst during life, it leaves the cause of death – so I understand – uncertain; at any rate, the medical witness was unable to say whether the deceased fell over the cliff in consequence of the bursting of the aneurism or burst the aneurism in consequence of falling over the cliff. Of course, it doesn't matter to us which way the thing happened; the only question which interests us is, whether a comparatively recently insured man ought to have had an aneurism at all."

"Have you paid the claim?" asked Thorndyke.

"No, certainly not. We never pay a claim until we have had your report. But, as a matter of fact, there is another circumstance that is causing delay. It seems that Elton had mortgaged his policy to a money-lender, named Gordon, and it is by him that the claim has been made, or rather, by a clerk of his, named Hyams. Now, we have had a good many dealings with this man, Gordon, and hitherto he has always acted in person; and as he is a somewhat slippery gentleman, we have thought it desirable to have the claim actually signed by him. And that is the difficulty. For it seems that Mr Gordon is abroad, and his whereabouts unknown to Hyams; so, as we certainly couldn't take Hyams's receipt for payment, the matter is in abeyance until Hyams can communicate with his principal. And now, I must be running away. I have brought you, as you will see, all the papers, including the policy and the mortgage deed."

As soon as he was gone, Thorndyke gathered up the bundle of papers and sorted them out in what he apparently considered the order of their importance. First he glanced quickly through the proposal form, and then took up the copy of the coroner's depositions.

"The medical evidence," he remarked, "is very full and complete. Both the coroner and the doctor seem to know their business."

"Seeing that the man apparently fell over a cliff," said I, "the medical evidence would not seem to be of first importance. It would seem to be more to the point to ascertain how he came to fall over."

"That's quite true," replied Thorndyke; "and yet, this report contains some rather curious matter. The deceased had an aneurism of the arch; that was probably rather recent. But he also had some slight, old-standing aortic disease, with full compensory hypertrophy. He also had a nearly complete set of false teeth. Now, doesn't it strike you, Jervis, as rather odd that a man who was passed only five years ago as a first-class life, should, in that short interval, have become actually uninsurable?"

"It certainly does look," said I, "as if the fellow had had rather bad luck. What does the proposal form say?"

I took the document up and ran my eyes over it. On Thorndyke's advice, medical examiners for the "Griffin" were instructed to make a somewhat fuller report than is usual in some companies. In this case, the ordinary answers to questions set forth that the heart was perfectly healthy and the teeth rather exceptionally good, and then, in the summary at the end, the examiner remarked: "the proposer seems to be a completely sound and healthy man; he presents no physical defects whatever, with the exception of a bony ankylosis of the first joint of the third finger of the left hand, which he states to have been due to an injury."

Thorndyke looked up quickly. "Which finger, did you say?" he asked.

"The third finger of the left hand," I replied.

Thorndyke looked thoughtfully at the paper that he was reading. "It's very singular," said he, "for I see that the Margate doctor states that the deceased wore a signet ring on the third finger of the left hand. Now, of course, you couldn't get a ring on to a finger with bony ankylosis of the joint."

"He must have mistaken the finger," said I, "or else the insurance examiner did."

"That is quite possible," Thorndyke replied; "but, doesn't it strike you as very singular that, whereas the insurance examiner mentions the ankylosis, which was of no importance from an insurance point of view, the very careful man who made the post mortem should not have mentioned it, though, owing to the unrecognisable condition of the face, it was of vital importance for the purpose of identification?"

I admitted that it was very singular indeed, and we then resumed our study of the respective papers. But presently I noticed that Thorndyke had laid the report upon his knee, and was gazing speculatively into the fire.

"I gather," said I, "that my learned friend finds some matter of interest in this case."

For reply, he handed me the bundle of papers, recommending me to look through them.

"Thank you," said I, rejecting them firmly, "but I think I can trust you to have picked out all the plums."

Thorndyke smiled indulgently. "They're not plums Jervis," said he; "they're only currants, but they make quite a substantial little heap."

I disposed myself in a receptive attitude (somewhat after the fashion of the juvenile pelican) and he continued:

"If we take the small and unimpressive items and add them together, you will see that a quite considerable sum of discrepancy results, thus:

"*In 1903, Thomas Elton, aged thirty-one, had a set of sound teeth. In 1908, at the age of thirty-six, he was more than half toothless.*

"*Again, at the age of thirty-one, his heart was perfectly healthy. At the age of thirty-six, he had old aortic disease, with fully established compensation, and an aneurism that was possibly due to it.*

"*When he was examined he had a noticeable incurable malformation; no such malformation is mentioned in connection with the body.*

"He appears to have fallen over a cliff; and he had also burst an aneurism. Now, the bursting of the aneurism must obviously have occurred during life; but it would occasion practically instantaneous death. Therefore, if the fall was accidental, the rupture must have occurred either, as he stood at the edge of the cliff, as he was in the act of falling, or on striking the beach.

"At the place where he apparently fell, the footpath is some thirty yards distant from the edge of the cliff.

"It is not known how he came to that spot, or whether he was alone at the time.

"Someone is claiming five hundred pounds as the immediate result of his death.

"There, you see, Jervis, are seven propositions, none of them extremely striking, but rather suggestive when taken together."

"You seem," said I, "to suggest a doubt as to the identity of the body."

"I do," he replied. "The identity was not clearly established."

"You don't think the clothing and the visiting-cards conclusive."

"They're not parts of the body," he replied. "Of course, substitution is highly improbable. But it is not impossible."

"And the old woman," I suggested, but he interrupted me.

"My dear Jervis," he exclaimed; "I'm surprised at you. How many times has it happened within our knowledge that women have identified the bodies of total strangers as those of their husbands, fathers or brothers. The thing happens almost every year. As to this old woman, she saw a body with an unrecognisable face, dressed in the clothes of her missing lodger. Of course, it was the clothes that she identified."

"I suppose it was," I agreed; and then I said: "You seem to suggest the possibility of foul play."

"Well," he replied, "if you consider those seven points, you will agree with me that they present a cumulative discrepancy which it is impossible to ignore. The whole significance of the case turns on the question of identity; for, if this was not the body of Thomas Elton, it would appear to have been deliberately prepared to counterfeit that body. And such deliberate preparation would manifestly imply an attempt to conceal the identity of some other body.

"Then," he continued, after a pause, "there is this deed. It looks quite regular and is correctly stamped, but it seems to me, that the surface of the paper is slightly altered in one or two places, and if one holds the document up to the light, the paper looks a little more transparent in those places." He examined the document for a few seconds with his pocket lens, and then passing lens and document to me, said: "Have a look at it, Jervis, and tell me what you think."

I scrutinised the paper closely, taking it over to the window to get a better light; and to me, also, the paper appeared to be changed in certain places.

"Are we agreed as to the position of the altered places?" Thorndyke asked when I announced the fact.

"I only see three patches," I answered. "Two correspond to the name, Thomas Elton, and the third to one of the figures in the policy number."

"Exactly," said Thorndyke, "and the significance is obvious. If the paper has really been altered, it means that some other name has been erased and Elton's substituted; by which arrangement, of course, the correctly dated stamp would be secured. And this – the alteration of an old document – is the only form of forgery that is possible with a dated, impressed stamp."

"Wouldn't it be rather a stroke of luck?" I asked "for a forger to happen to have in his possession a document needing only these two alterations?"

"I see nothing remarkable in it," Thorndyke replied. "A money-lender would have a number of documents of this kind in hand, and you observe that he was not bound down to any particular date. Any date within a year or so of the issue of the policy would answer his purpose. This document is, in fact, dated, as you see, about six months after the issue of the policy."

"I suppose," said I, "that you will draw Stalker's attention to this matter."

"He will have to be informed, of course," Thorndyke replied; "but I think it would be interesting in the first place to call on Mr Hyams. You will have noticed that there are some rather mysterious features in this case, and Mr Hyams's conduct, especially if this document should turn out to be really a forgery, suggests that he may have some special information on the subject." He glanced at his watch and, after a few moments' reflection, added: "I don't see why we shouldn't make our little ceremonial call at once. But it will be a delicate business, for we have mighty little to go upon. Are you coming with me?"

If I had had any doubts, Thorndyke's last remark disposed of them; for the interview promised to be quite a sporting event. Mr Hyams was presumably not quite newly-hatched, and Thorndyke, who utterly despised bluff of any kind, and whose exact mind refused either to act or speak one hair's breadth beyond his knowledge, was admittedly in somewhat of a fog. The meeting promised to be really entertaining.

Mr Hyams was "discovered," as the playwrights have it, in a small office at the top of a high building in Queen Victoria Street. He was a small gentleman, of sallow and greasy aspect, with heavy eyebrows and a still heavier nose.

"Are you Mr Gordon?" Thorndyke suavely inquired as we entered.

Mr Hyams seemed to experience a momentary doubt on the subject, but finally decided that he was not. "But perhaps," he added brightly, "I can do your business for you as well."

"I daresay you can," Thorndyke agreed significantly; on which we were conducted into an inner den, where I noticed Thorndyke's eye rest for an instant on a large iron safe.

"Now," said Mr Hyams, shutting the door ostentatiously, "what can I do for you?"

"I want you," Thorndyke replied, "to answer one or two questions with reference to the claim made by you on the 'Griffin' Office in respect of Thomas Elton."

Mr Hyams's manner underwent a sudden change. He began rapidly to turn over papers, and opened and shut the drawers of his desk, with an air of restless preoccupation.

"Did the 'Griffin' people send you here?" he demanded brusquely.

"They did not specially instruct me to call on you," replied Thorndyke.

"Then," said Hyams, bouncing out of his chair, "I can't let you occupy my time. I'm not here to answer conundrums from Tom, Dick or Harry."

Thorndyke rose from his chair. "Then I am to understand," he said, with unruffled suavity, "that you would prefer me to communicate with the Directors, and leave them to take any necessary action."

This gave Mr Hyams pause. "What action do you refer to?" he asked. "And, who are you?"

Thorndyke produced a card and laid it on the table. Mr Hyams had apparently seen the name before, for he suddenly grew rather pale and very serious.

"What is the nature of the questions that you wished to ask?" he inquired.

"They refer to this claim." replied Thorndyke. "The first question is, where is Mr Gordon?"

"I don't know," said Hyams.

"Where do you think he is?" asked Thorndyke.

"I don't think at all," replied Hyams, turning a shade paler and looking everywhere but at Thorndyke.

"Very well," said the latter, "then the next question is, are you satisfied that this claim is really payable?"

"I shouldn't have made it if I hadn't been," replied Hyams.

"Quite so," said Thorndyke; "and the third question is, are you satisfied that the mortgage deed was executed as it purports to have been?"

"I can't say anything about that," replied Hyams, who was growing every moment paler and more fidgety, "it was done before my time."

"Thank you," said Thorndyke. "You will, of course, understand why I am making these inquiries."

"I don't," said Hyams.

"Then," said Thorndyke, "perhaps I had better explain. We are dealing, you observe, Mr Hyams, with the case of a man who has met with a violent death under somewhat mysterious circumstances. We are dealing, also, with another man who has disappeared, leaving his affairs to take care of themselves; and with a claim, put forward by a third party, on behalf of the one man in respect of the other. When I say that the dead man has been imperfectly identified, and that the document supporting the claim presents certain peculiarities, you will see that the matter calls for further inquiry."

There was an appreciable interval of silence. Mr Hyams had turned a tallowy white, and looked furtively about the room, as if anxious to avoid the stony gaze that my colleague had fixed on him.

"Can you give us no assistance?" Thorndyke inquired, at length. Mr Hyams chewed a pen-holder ravenously, as he considered the question. At length, he burst out in an agitated voice: "Look here, sir, if I tell you what I know, will you treat the information as confidential?"

"I can't agree to that, Mr Hyams," replied Thorndyke. "It might amount to compounding a felony. But you will be wiser to tell me what you know. The document is a side-issue, which my clients may never raise, and my own concern is with the death of this man."

Hyams looked distinctly relieved. "If that's so," said he, "I'll tell you all I know, which is precious little, and which just amounts to this: Two days after Elton was killed, someone came to this office in my absence and opened the safe. I discovered the fact the next morning. Someone had been to the safe and rummaged over all the papers. It wasn't Gordon, because he knew where to find everything; and it wasn't an ordinary thief because no cash or valuables had been taken. In fact, the only thing that I missed was a promissory note, drawn by Elton."

"You didn't miss a mortgage deed?" suggested Thorndyke, and Hyams, having snatched a little further refreshment from the pen-holder, said he did not.

"And the policy," suggested Thorndyke, "was apparently not taken?"

"No," replied Hyams; "but it was looked for. Three bundles of policies had been untied, but this one happened to be in a drawer of my desk and I had the only key."

"And what do you infer from this visit?" Thorndyke asked.

"Well," replied Hyams, "the safe was opened with keys, and they were Gordon's keys — or, at any rate, they weren't mine — and the person who opened it wasn't Gordon; and the things that were taken — at least the thing, I mean — chiefly concerned Elton. Naturally I smelt a rat; and when I read of the finding of the body, I smelt a fox."

"And have you formed any opinion about the body that was found?"

"Yes, I have," he replied. "My opinion is that it was Gordon's body: that Gordon had been putting the screw on Elton, and Elton had just pitched him over the cliff and gone down and changed clothes with the body. Of course, that's only my opinion. I may be wrong; but I don't think I am."

As a matter of fact, Mr Hyams was not wrong. An exhumation, consequent on Thorndyke's challenge of the identity of the deceased, showed that the body was that of Solomon Gordon. A hundred pounds reward was offered for information as to Elton's whereabouts. But no one ever earned it. A letter, bearing the postmark of Marseilles, and addressed by the missing man to Thorndyke, gave a plausible account of Gordon's death; which was represented as having occurred accidentally at the moment when Gordon chanced to be wearing a suit of Elton's clothes.

Of course; this account may have been correct, or again, it may have been false; but whether it was true or false, Elton, from that moment, vanished from our ken and has never since been heard of.

Powder Blue And Hawthorn

PART I

Mr Henry Palmer looked furtively, but critically, at Dr Macmulligan. He had been told that on Friday night he would most probably find the doctor drunk. And so it had turned out. But the question that agitated Mr Palmer was: how drunk was he, and, above all, was he drunk enough?

A delicate and difficult question this. Afflicted persons are apt to spring surprises on one. The nearsighted man, with a squint to boot, who ought to be as blind as a bat, will sometimes develop a disconcerting acuteness of vision; one-legged men astonish us with incredible feats of agility; the uncertainty of the deaf is a matter of daily observation; while as to the drunk, proverbial philosophy has actually devised for them a special directing Providence. So Mr Palmer watched the doctor narrowly and with anxious speculation.

"And how long has this friend of yours been ill?" demanded the latter huskily, and with a slight brogue.

"At intervals, for a week or two," replied Mr Palmer; "but the last attack only came on this morning."

"And I suppose you want me to come this very moment?" said Dr Macmulligan aggressively.

"If you could," replied Palmer. "He's in a very critical state."

"I know," growled Macmulligan. "It is the old story. Put off sending for the doctor till the patient's at the last gasp, and then drag him away from his dinner or out of his bed."

"I'm sorry," said Palmer; "but may I take it that you'll come?"

"I suppose ye may," replied the doctor. "Juty is juty, though 'tis devilish unpleasant. Give me the name and address, and I'll be with you in a jiffy."

He opened a manuscript book, and, dipping his pen in an open jar of cough lozenges, stared interrogatively at Mr Palmer. The latter noticed the circumstance approvingly, and decided that Dr Macmulligan would do.

Sheerness Harbour, that is the wide estuary of the Medway, at nine o'clock on an autumn night, with a brisk sou'-wester and driving rain, is no ideal sailing ground. Dr Macmulligan, hunched up in the stern sheets of the boat, swore continuously, with exacerbations as the spray slapped his face and trickled down the collar of his mackintosh.

"It's a disagreeable journey that I've brought you," Palmer said apologetically; "beastly cold, too. May I offer you a little refresher to keep the weather out?" and here he produced from a locker a large flat bottle and a tumbler.

" 'Dade! but you may," the doctor replied with alacrity; "'tis cold enough to freeze a brass monkey." He took the flat bottle, and, with unexpected steadiness, poured out half a tumblerful, and, having sniffed at it approvingly, took a quick gulp and drew a deep breath.

"'Tis a fine whisky that," he remarked, with another gulp in verification. "I'd like to know your wine merchant, sir."

Palmer laughed. "So I suspect," said he, "would some of the gentlemen at the Custom House."

The suggestion contained in that last remark so gratified the doctor that he could do no less than pledge the wine merchant anew; and, in fact, by the time the boat's fore-foot grated on the little hard on the Isle of Grain, the flat bottle contained nothing but convivial memories. Nevertheless, as they fought their way through wind and rain, the doctor's comparative steadiness of gait filled his conductor with surprise and secret uneasiness. But the thing had to be carried through now, and bracing himself for the final scene, he rapped softly on the door of a lonely house on the marshes.

In a few moments the door was unfastened, and its opening revealed a man, holding a candle in one hand, and, in the other, a handkerchief with which he mopped his eyes. He blinked inquiringly at the new-comers, and asked dejectedly:

"Is that the doctor, Henry?"

"Yes," replied Palmer, "I hope – "

Here he paused, and the other shook his head sadly.

"Come in," said he; and, as they followed him into the dismal room, on the table of which another flat bottle and three tumblers were set out, he continued: "It happened less than an hour after you left, Henry. I suppose the doctor may as well see him?"

"And phwat for?" demanded the doctor, adding somewhat obscurely: "D'ye take me for Lazarus?"

To this the dejected man made no reply, but, taking up the candle, stole out of the room on tiptoe and began to ascend the stairs, followed by Palmer and the protesting doctor. Silently they crept up – excepting the doctor, who missed a step half-way up, and commented hoarsely on the circumstance – to a door on the first floor, which their conductor noiselessly opened and beckoned them to enter.

The room was in total darkness save for the light of the candle, which showed a large bed by the wall, and lying on it, on the farther side, a motionless figure covered by a sheet. The man with the candle tiptoed to the bed, and reverently drawing back the sheet, let the flickering light fall on the uncovered face. And a ghastly face it was with its dead-white skin, its bandaged jaws, and the two pennies resting on the eyelids, and looking, in the dim light, like the dark shadows of empty sockets.

Palmer and his friend gazed sadly at the still figure and sighed deeply. But the doctor was less affected. After a single glance at the bed, he turned away with a grunt, remarking: "We've had our trip in the wet for nothing. 'Twas an undertaker ye wanted," and with this he proceeded cautiously to descend the stairs to the more cheerful room below, whither the other two men shortly followed.

"I suppose, said Palmer, as he mixed the doctor a glass of toddy, "we shall want a certificate?" Macmulligan nodded.

"You couldn't write it now and save a journey?"

"No; I don't carry the forms about with me," the doctor replied, adding with a bibulous twinkle, "Ye see, me patients are usually alive – to begin with, at anny rate. But ye'll have to put me across in the boat, so ye can come to the surgery and get the certificate. And ye can call on the undertaker and fix up the funeral, too. 'Tis best to get these affairs settled quickly. Ye don't want a corpse in the house longer than ye can help."

Having delivered this advice gratis, the medicus emptied his tumbler, and rose. Palmer buttoned his oilskin coat, and the three men went out to the door. The rain had now ceased, but as the two voyagers stepped forth into the night a chilly wind swept across the marshes and the low murmur of breaking waves came up from the shore. The man who was left behind watched the two figures as they receded down the rough path, and, as they disappeared, he stepped into the sitting room, and, taking a pair of marine glasses from a shelf, went out and followed the other two stealthily down the path. Through the glasses he watched them get into the boat, saw them push off and hoist the sail, and then, as the dim shape of the latter faded into the darkness, he returned to the house and shut the door.

Having replaced the binoculars, he once more took the candle and ascended the stairs. But not on tiptoe this time. Taking the stairs two at a time, he walked briskly into the chamber of death, and set the candle on a chest of drawers.

"It's all clear, Joe," said he. "I've seen 'em start across."

On this the figure on the bed pushed back the sheet and sat up, and having adroitly caught the two pennies as they dropped, spun them in the air, and began to untie the jaw bandage.

"Yah!" he exclaimed, wagging his chin up and down. "What a relief it is to get that beastly thing off! Chuck us my dressing gown, Tom, and a towel to wipe off this powder."

He stood up, stretching himself, and, having donned the dressing gown and wiped his face briskly, descended with his companion to the lower room.

"So much for act one," he remarked, pouring himself out a "tot" of whisky. "We're safe for the certificate, I suppose, Barratt?"

"Yes," replied Barratt, "and for the burial order. We've got over the main difficulty. All the rest is plain sailing."

"It may be," rejoined the other, "but it's deuced complicated. Just run over the programme again, and see if I can get it into my thick head."

Barratt took up a position on the hearthrug with an expository air, and proceeded to explain. "It's really quite simple," said he, "so far as getting the stuff is concerned. The difficulty was to find a safe place to stow it until the hue and cry was over, and we've done that. The programme now is: First, we've got to get the local undertaker to make us a coffin to measurements that Palmer will give him, and deliver it to Palmer, who will bring it across in the boat; and there'll have to be a lead coffin inside, which he'll have to leave open for us to solder down. I think Palmer will be able to manage that. Then, when we have got the coffin, Palmer takes the boat up to East Haven Creek by Canvey Island, and leaves her there. Next, he and I call at the premises – properly made-up, of course – with your duplicate keys, and some dummy specimens in cases and ask the caretaker for a receipt for them. While he is unpacking the cases, we grab him from behind and run him down to the strong room and lock him in. Then we open the door for you and you show us where the most classy articles are kept. While we are packing them in the cases, you go and give Jim Baker the tip, and he brings his car round – with the wrong number plate on it. We carry the cases out –they will be quite small ones – and stow them in the car, get in ourselves, and away we go. It's all quite simple and straightforward, broad daylight, nothing suspicious about it, cases always going in and out there. Well; Jimmy runs us down near to the creek. It will be dark by then. We get out and carry the case across the marshes to the boat, drop down with the tide and sail across here. Meanwhile, Jimmy slithers away, and when he gets to a quiet place at a safe distance changes his number plate. Then off he scoots to Norwich. They can suspect him if they please, but they won't find any of the stuff about him, because it will be safely screwed down in the late William Brunton's coffin."

"Then, are you going to send the coffin to Gravelham by rail?"

"No; too much fuss and too many papers and records in the company's books. I shall send the burial order to Allen, the undertaker, and tell him the coffin is coming by barge. Then he will collect it and make all the arrangements for the funeral; and I shall stipulate that the remains are to be deposited in the catacombs, not in a grave or vault. That's why we've got to have a lead coffin."

"You say you've got a key of the catacombs?"

"Not a key; a squeeze. I got it about the time I first thought of this, little jaunt, when you were taking the squeeze from the keys of your late employer, like a faithful and trustworthy private secretary – "

"Oh, chuck that!" interrupted the other irritably. "You needn't jeer after having egged me on to do it."

"Right-o, Murray, old man," said Barratt with a cynical grin, "we'll get back to the business. Mr Allen will arrange a nice quiet funeral, and when we have followed our dear departed brother to his last resting place – for the present – we can take a little holiday and let things settle down. Do you follow the process?"

"I think so," replied Murray, "and it seems quite a neat plan."

"Neat!" exclaimed Barratt; "it's positively masterly. Just consider! Here we've got a bulky swag that we can't melt and we can't break up, and which, if it were all together, would give us away instantly; and yet which is quite negotiable piece by piece. All we want is a safe hiding-place, and, by Jove! we've got it. These catacombs are better than any bank or safe deposit. When we want to raise the wind, all we've got to do is to call on the late lamented, and hook out one or two pieces. The Yankee collector will do the rest."

"But are the catacombs quite accessible?"

"Bless you!" laughed Barratt, "they seem to have been built for the very purpose. The cemetery is outside the town, and all you've got to do is to get over the wall; you can bring a ladder if you like, there's no one to interfere. I tell you, Murray, this little investment will yield us an income for years."

"So it ought," growled Murray. "It will take something substantial to recompense me for all that I've gone through."

On which Barratt grinned once more, and cut off the end of a cigar.

PART II

Mr Edward Allen, Furnisher and Undertaker, stood in his little office, rubbing his hands softly and sympathetically, as four bereaved gentlemen, in correct, but unostentatious mourning, were ushered in. The names by which he knew then are not material to this history; to us they are known respectively as Thomas Barratt, Henry Palmer, Joseph Murray, and Jimmy Baker.

"I am deeply concerned, gentlemen," said Mr Allen, giving his hands an extra rub, "to inform you that the coffin has not yet arrived. The weather, as you know, has been somewhat boisterous, and doubtless the barge has been delayed by the exigencies of navigation."

The four men looked at one another uneasily, and Mr Allen continued: "We may expect it at any moment. My conveyance is waiting at the wharf, and the mourning carriage is in readiness to start the instant the coffin arrives."

At these unwelcome tidings the countenances of the four mourners assumed an expression admirably in keeping with the business on hand, though, during the temporary absence of the undertaker, they exchanged remarks which might have sounded slightly out of character. However, there was nothing for it but to wait on the vagaries of wind and tide; and this they did, with outward calm and inward tumult of spirit.

As some three-quarters of an hour passed, their nervous tension progressively increased. And then came a dramatic interruption. At the door of the office the undertaker appeared in a state of manifest agitation, accompanied by a seafaring man, whom Barratt instantly recognised as the skipper of the barge.

"Gentlemen," the undertaker said, in impressive tones, "I deeply regret to announce that a most dreadful thing has happened. It appears that the coffin has been – er – temporarily mislaid."

The four men with one accord, sprang to their feet.

"Mislaid!" they exclaimed with one voice, and Jimmy Baker added: "What the blazes do you mean by 'mislaid'?"

The undertaker indicated the skipper with a silent wave of the hand, and the skipper stared sulkily at the sou'-wester that he held.

"Overboard," he remarked stolidly.

"What!" shrieked Barratt.

"Overboard it is," the skipper persisted doggedly.

"But, how did it happen?" demanded Palmer.

"Why, d'ye see," replied the skipper, in even, unimpassioned tones, "'twas like this here: we set that there coffin across the fo'ksl scuttle, to be out o' the way like, 'cos my mate, he didn't like a-havin' of it aboard. Said as how it'd bring trouble on us; and right he were, sure enough. We hadn't fair got out through the Jenkin afore it began. Up comes a bloomin' collier a-hootin' like blazes and nearly wipes the paint off our quarter; then up we bumps agin the Yantlet Buoy, and I reckon that started the bloomin' corfin a-travellin', though we didn't twig it. Then up comes a regular squall from west'ard, and lays us right over to leeward – nearly capsized us, that there squall did, and I reckon the lurch we took give that corfin another lift. But we never noticed nothin' cos, just then, a steam trawler an' a collier an' a Rooshian timber boat all comes on top of us together a-bellerin' like bulls o' Bashan. Thought we was bound for the cellar that time, I did, and so did my mate. But we jest managed to get 'er about afore the timber boat 'it us, and, as we come up, we takes a sea right over the 'ead. That's what done it, I reckon, but we didn't spot it, you understand. Well, when we was clear o' them blighters, I says to my mate, I says: 'Bill,' I says, 'jest run forrard and take a turn of a rope's end round that there corfin.' So he 'ooks it forrard, and then I 'ears 'im' oller out 'Joe,' he says, 'there ain't no bloomin' corfin 'ere,' 'e says. 'What!' I says. 'No,' he says, 'corfin's gone overboard,' 'e says, an' that's how it happened. I puts up me 'elm, and we cruised about there for nigh upon a hower, but nary a sign o' that there corfin did we see. Three times we was within a inch o' bein' run down, an' we nearly smashed ourselves on the Middle Blyth buoy, an' then we lost our tide, an' 'ad to bring up in Hole Haven. So now yer know about it."

As the skipper finished his narrative, he surveyed his hearers with a defiant stare, noting with some surprise the consternation that appeared on the countenances of the four mourners. To his nautical mind it seemed that the obsequies had been very satisfactorily concluded, and the needless expense of a shore funeral saved. Even the undertaker viewed his clients' emotion with secret wonder, and thought they must have been exceedingly attached to the deceased.

"Well, Mr Allen," said Barratt gloomily, when the skipper had departed; "what's going to happen, and what is to be done?"

Mr Allen was doubtful, but opined that the coffin would probably turn up somewhere. "But," he added, "I don't suppose you want an inquest."

His clients certainly did not, and said so with much emphasis. Then Mr Allen developed the luminous idea of having some bills printed, or advertising in the papers; and he had begun drafting an advertisement beginning: "Lost, a coffin with contents," when Barratt interrupted him:

"The coffin was addressed to you, Mr Allen," said he. "For security, I painted the direction on the wood with Stockholm tar, so it won't have washed off."

Mr Allen was secretly shocked, but outwardly approving.

"A very wise precaution," said he, "and most fortunate under the circumstances." Here he was called away for a short time, and during his absence the four conspirators debated anxiously whether they should scatter and watch the developments from afar, deputing the undertaker to conduct the funeral, or whether they should take the risk of waiting for tidings of the lost sheep. They had not reached any conclusion when Mr Allen returned, and, having decided to continue the discussion later, they solemnly adjourned the proceedings and prepared to depart.

Just as they reached the outer door of the premises, a seafaring man of truculent aspect entered, and stared around; and, looking out, they were aware of four other mariners approaching up the street, bearing a large, elongated object wrapped in a tarpaulin.

"Are you Mr Allen?" the ship-man inquired, fixing a fierce blue eye on the undertaker; and when the undertaker admitted his identity, the seaman continued: "I'm the master of the tug *Peacock*. Name of Swivells. I've got a coffin consigned to you. Picked her up derelict off Yantlet Creek. Will ye 'ave 'er? If you say yes, you've got to pay salvage; if not, I delivers 'er to the Receiver of Wrecks."

Mr Allen began cautiously to inquire as to the amount of the salvage dues, when Barratt interrupted:

"We won't haggle for a sovereign or so, Mr Allen. I'll settle with the captain, if you will arrange to have the funeral carried out without delay."

Mr Allen bowed and hurried away, and so faithfully did he carry out his instructions that when the five mariners came forth from the saloon bar of "The Privateer," four singularly cheerful-looking mourners were in the very act of scrambling into the mourning carriage.

Decency will not allow us to follow the proceedings further. On the ears of the less callous Murray, the solemn and beautiful words of the Burial Service jarred painfully, whereas, to Barratt, we have with regret to admit that the references to the Resurrection merely associated themselves with the projected liberation of the swag. And thus the curtain fell on the obsequies of the late William Brunton, and thereafter the funeral baked meats were consumed without tears or lamentation — quite the contrary, in fact — in the festive neighbourhood of Piccadilly Circus.

PART III

Nearly six months had passed. The memory of the mysterious and successful robbery, by which the famous Harland collection of Chinese porcelain was plundered of its choicest gems, had faded from the minds of all but professed collectors; and the funeral of the late William Brunton had become to Mr Allen and his friends as a tale that is told – and told pretty frequently.

It was a dark night. The Parish Church clock had just struck half-past eleven; the heavy goods train had just rumbled through the station, and belated steamers were hooting on the river, when four men approached the cemetery of Gravelham by a deserted footpath, and gathered under the black shadow of the wall.

"Your show, Barratt," said a voice, resembling that of Mr Jimmy Baker. "I'll hoist you up while you fix the contraption."

In response, Barratt produced from his overcoat pocket a small rope ladder of thin, tough line, with two iron hooks at the top. Being hoisted up by the accommodating Jimmy, he fixed the hooks to the coping, got astride the wall, and dropped down inside. The others quickly followed, and the last one, having been hoisted up for the purpose, detached and pulled over the ladder and refixed it on the inside. Then, leaving it hanging, they stole off along the path towards the catacombs.

"This is a ghoulish sort of job," grumbled Murray, as they descended the steps and stood in the well-like cavity before the grisly black doors. It was certainly an eerie place. Even in the darkness they could see the crumbling tablets on the moss-grown jambs, seeming to whisper of dissolution and decay. A strange mouldy smell seemed to hang about that grim portal, and as they waited while Barratt oiled the great key, the wind stirred the big black doors until it sounded as if someone within were stealthily groping for some means of escape.

At length the great key was inserted, the bolt shot back with a hollow clang, and the gloomy door swung inwards with a long-drawn sepulchral groan.

"Poof!" exclaimed Murray, breathing the musty air distastefully; "let's have a light, Barratt, for God's sake!"

"Wait till I've shut the door and stopped up the keyhole," was the reply; and Murray heard with an uncomfortable thrill the heavy door pushed to and the key turned from the inside. Then Barratt composedly produced a reading lantern and, having lit the candle, threw its light along a massive shelf and on the square ends of the row of coffins.

"Fourth from the end, I think," said Palmer, "but I'd better hop up and have a squint"; and as he climbed up, Murray asked:

"How many are you going to take, Barratt?"

"Only three," was the reply; "two Powder Blues and a Red Hawthorn. It's no use taking more than we've negotiated. Have you got him, Palmer?"

"Yes," replied Palmer, "it's all right. Stand by to catch hold when I shove," and, stooping to grasp the end, he gave a heave that slid the coffin well out beyond the edge of the shelf. His companions caught it, and with some difficulty lifted it to the ground. Then Barratt produced from his pocket a ratchet screwdriver of most approved design, and began skilfully to extract the screws.

"Now," he said, as he picked out the last, and his companions each drew a jemmy from his pocket, "stand by to hoist all together."

The jemmies were duly inserted into the well-pitched crack; Barratt gave the words "One, two, three," and as he uttered the word "three" there was a bursting sound, the lid tilted and slid off, and the four men sprang back with astonished gasps. Barratt snatched up the lantern and threw its light into the coffin, and from the four men came simultaneously muffled cries of amazement.

There was a brief interval of silence, during which the conspirators stood motionless as statues, staring with incredulous horror at the coffin. At length Barratt spoke:

"You idiot, Palmer; you've sent us down the wrong coffin!"

Palmer stumbled round, and, lifting the lid, held it up to the light of the lantern, which shone inexorably on the name-plate of the mythical William Brunton, and on the tar-written inscription which had so shocked the susceptibilities of the undertaker.

"It's our coffin right enough," said Palmer; "there's no doubt of that."

"Isn't there?" shouted Baker wrathfully. "Then perhaps you will tell me how that old woman got into it, and what's become of our swag?"

"That's what we should like somebody to tell us," said Barratt, staring gloomily at the coffin, and holding his handkerchief over his nose. "Someone has butted in and upset our apple cart. Someone who'd got a superfluous corpse."

"You're right, Barratt," said Murray. "Very superfluous, indeed. Look here," and he advanced cautiously to the coffin and pointed to a ragged hole in the throat of the repulsive figure within it.

"Yes," agreed Barratt, "there's no mistake about it. That old woman has been 'done in.' Our coffin must have come in mighty handy for somebody who was in a tight place. And by that same token, we're in a pretty tight place ourselves. The sooner we get that coffin lid on again and clear out, the healthier it will be for our necks."

The justice of these remarks was obvious. Willing and rather shaky hands replaced the lid. The screws were run rapidly into their holes, and the coffin replaced on its shelf. Once more the lock clanged, the gloomy door swung open with a groan and closed forever on the tragedy of the late William Brunton. A couple of minutes later, four dejected men trailed along the dark footpath on a circuitous route to the station, and for a while none of them spoke. It was Mr Jimmy Baker who broke the silence in a tone of deep exasperation:

"Well," he exclaimed, "you are a pretty lot of blighters! Just see what you've done. You've blued about three hundred pounds of good money, and what have you got for it? You've provided a free funeral for some old Jude who wasn't wanted, and you've made one of her pals a present of fifty thousand pounds worth of stuff. And where do I come in!"

"You don't come in at all," growled Barratt; "you go out – with the rest of us; and devilish thankful you ought to be!"

PART IV

It was about a month later that the *Morning Telegraph* published under conspicuous headlines the following announcement:

"Strange Discovery of the Harland Treasures

"The mystery which enshrouded the remarkable robbery from Mr Harland's collection of priceless Chinese porcelain has been resolved into an even greater mystery. Yesterday morning, the Rector of Stoke, in the Hundred of Hoo, walking down to the Blyth Sand to bathe, and looking round to observe the effects of the recent gale, noticed with surprise the necks of a number of blue jars standing up out of the sand. Picking one up, he saw at once that it was a porcelain vessel of great beauty, and proceeded with extreme care to disinter the remainder. Having some knowledge of porcelain, he immediately recognised the pieces as Chinese vases and jars of the kind known as Powder Blue and Hawthorn; and, recalling the late robbery, he carefully conveyed them to his house and communicated with the police. They have since been identified by Mr Harland as his property, and he is to be congratulated on the fact that the discovery was made by so cultivated and conscientious a person."

The above paragraph was read with very different feelings by different readers. To the four conspirators, and to the public at large, it only made the mystery more profound. One man alone read in it nothing more than the final closing of a painful chapter. Laying down the paper, that man – a simple, white-haired bargeman – closed his eyes, and recalled the tragic incidents of a stormy night some seven months ago. He saw himself on his little barge, breasting the waters of the dark estuary, alone with his turbulent, drunken wife. He saw her, in a fit of wild passion, rush down to the cabin for the old-fashioned service revolver that he had foolishly kept there. He saw her struggle out of the little hatch, gibbering and threatening. He saw the flash and heard the loud report as she fell sprawling on the deck, and recalled his stony horror as he stood looking down at her corpse. And then, that marvellous interposition of Providence! The mysterious bumping and tapping against the barge's side; the floating coffin, so weirdly opportune; and then that great wonder when, having painfully hauled it on deck and unscrewed the lid, his knife, ripping open the lead case, had revealed no corpse, but a mere collection of crockery! He recalled the dreadful exchange, the hollow splash as the coffin went once more adrift; the secret landing on the Blyth Sand; the careful interment of the china at high-water mark, and the tremulously-spoken, though casuistically true report which he had circulated next day that his old woman had slipped overboard in the darkness. He recalled it all clearly with a sigh that was not wholly regretful; then he opened his eyes, folded the newspaper and closed the chapter for ever.

Percival Bland's Proxy

PART I

Mr Percival Bland was a somewhat uncommon type of criminal. In the first place he really had an appreciable amount of common sense. If he had only had a little more, he would not have been a criminal at all. As it was, he had just sufficient judgment to perceive that the consequences of unlawful acts accumulate as the acts are repeated; to realise that the criminal's position must, at length, become untenable; and to take what he considered fair precautions against the inevitable catastrophe.

But in spite of these estimable traits of character and the precautions aforesaid, Mr Bland found himself in rather a tight place and with a prospect of increasing tightness. The causes of this uncomfortable tension do not concern us, and may be dismissed with the remark, that, if one perseveringly distributes flash Bank of England notes among the money-changers of the Continent, there will come a day of reckoning when those notes are tendered to the exceedingly knowing old lady who lives in Threadneedle Street.

Mr Bland considered uneasily the approaching storm cloud as he raked over the "miscellaneous property" in the Salerooms of Messrs Plimpton. He was a confirmed frequenter of auctions, as was not unnatural; for the criminal is essentially a gambler. And criminal and auction-frequenter have one quality in common; each hopes to get something of value without paying the market price for it.

So Percival turned over the dusty oddments and his own difficulties at one and the same time. The vital questions were: When would the storm burst? And would it pass by the harbour of refuge that he had been at such pains to construct? Let us inspect that harbour of refuge.

A quiet flat in the pleasant neighbourhood of Battersea bore a name-plate inscribed, Mr Robert Lindsay; and the tenant was known to the porter and the charwoman who attended to the flat, as a fair-haired gentleman who was engaged in the book trade as a travelling agent, and was consequently a good deal away from home. Now Mr Robert Lindsay bore a distinct resemblance to Percival Bland; which was not surprising seeing that they were first cousins (or, at any rate, they said they were; and we may presume that they knew). But they were not very much alike. Mr Lindsay had flaxen, or rather sandy, hair; Mr Bland's hair was black. Mr Bland had a mole under his left eye; Mr Lindsay had no mole under his eye − but carried one in a small box in his waistcoat pocket.

At somewhat rare intervals the cousins called on one another; but they had the very worst of luck, for neither of them ever seemed to find the other at home. And what was even more odd was that whenever Mr Bland spent an evening at home in his lodgings over the oil shop in Bloomsbury, Mr Lindsay's flat was empty; and as sure as Mr Lindsay was at home in his flat so surely were Mr Bland's lodgings vacant for the time being. It was a queer coincidence, if anyone had noticed it; but nobody ever did.

However, if Percival saw little of his cousin, it was not a case of "out of sight, out of mind." On the contrary; so great was his solicitude for the latter's welfare that he not only had made a will constituting him his executor and sole legatee, but he had actually insured his life for no less a sum than three thousand pounds; and this will, together with the insurance policy, investment securities and other necessary documents, he had placed in the custody of a highly respectable solicitor. All of which did him great credit. It isn't every man who is willing to take so much trouble for a mere cousin.

Mr Bland continued his perambulations, pawing over the miscellaneous raffle from sheer force of habit, reflecting on the coming crisis in his own affairs, and on the provisions that he had made for his cousin, Robert. As for the latter, they were excellent as far as they went, but they lacked definiteness and perfect completeness. There was the contingency of a "stretch," for instance; say fourteen years penal servitude. The insurance policy did not cover that. And, meanwhile, what was to become of the estimable Robert?

He had bruised his thumb somewhat severely in a screw-cutting lathe, and had abstractedly turned the handle of a bird-organ until politely requested by an attendant to desist, when he came upon a series of boxes containing, according to the catalogue, "a collection of surgical instruments the property of a lately deceased practitioner." To judge by the appearance of the instruments, the practitioner must have commenced practice in his early youth and died at a very advanced age. They were an uncouth set of tools, of no value whatever excepting as testimonials to the amazing tenacity of life of our ancestors; but Percival fingered them over according to his wont, working the handle of a complicated brass syringe and ejecting a drop of greenish fluid on to the shirtfront of a dressy Hebrew (who requested him to "point the dam thing at thomeone elth necht time"), opening musty leather cases, clicking off spring scarifiers and feeling the edges of strange, crooked-bladed knives. Then he came upon a largish black box, which, when he raised the lid, breathed out an ancient and fish-like aroma and exhibited a collection of bones, yellow, greasy-looking and spotted in places with mildew. The catalogue described them as "a complete set of human osteology"; but they were not an ordinary "student's set," for the bones of the hands and feet, instead of being strung together on cat-gut, were united by their original ligaments and were of an unsavoury brown colour.

"I thay, misther," expostulated the Hebrew, "shut that bocth. Thmellth like a blooming inquetht."

But the contents of the black box seemed to have a fascination for Percival. He looked in at those greasy remnants of mortality, at the brown and mouldy hands and feet and the skull that peeped forth eerily from the folds of a flannel wrapping; and they breathed out something more than that stale and musty odour. A suggestion – vague and general at first, but rapidly crystallising into distinct shape – seemed to steal out of the black box into his consciousness; a suggestion that somehow seemed to connect itself with his estimable cousin Robert.

For upwards of a minute he stood motionless, as one immersed in reverie, the lid poised in his hand and a dreamy eye fixed on the half-uncovered skull. A stir in the room roused him. The sale was about to begin. The members of the knock-out and other habitués seated themselves on benches around a long, baize-covered table; the attendants took possession of the first lots and opened their catalogues as if about to sing an introductory chorus; and a gentleman with a waxed moustache and a striking resemblance to his late Majesty, the third Napoleon, having ascended to the rostrum bespoke the attention of the assembly by a premonitory tap with his hammer.

How odd are some of the effects of a guilty conscience! With what absurd self-consciousness do we read into the minds of others our own undeclared intentions, when those intentions are unlawful! Had Percival Bland wanted a set of human bones for any legitimate purpose – such as anatomical study – he would have bought it openly and unembarrassed. Now, he found himself earnestly debating whether he should not bid for some of the surgical instruments, just for the sake of appearances; and there being little time in which to make up his mind – for the deceased practitioner's effects came first in the catalogue – he was already the richer by a set of cupping-glasses, a tooth-key, and an instrument of unknown use and diabolical aspect, before the fateful lot was called.

At length the black box was laid on the table, an object of obscene mirth to the knockers-out, and the auctioneer read the entry:

"Lot seventeen; a complete set of human osteology. A very useful and valuable set of specimens, gentlemen."

He looked round at the assembly majestically, oblivious of sundry inquiries as to the identity of the deceased and the verdict of the coroner's jury, and finally suggested five shillings.

"Six," said Percival.

An attendant held the box open, and, chanting the mystic word "Loddlemen!" (which, being interpreted, meant "Lot, gentlemen"), thrust it under the rather bulbous nose of the smart Hebrew; who remarked that "they 'ummed a bit too much to thoot him" and pushed it away.

"Going at six shillings," said the auctioneer, reproachfully; and as nobody contradicted him, he smote the rostrum with his hammer and the box was delivered into the hands of Percival on the payment of that modest sum.

Having crammed the cupping-glasses, the tooth key and the unknown instrument into the box, Percival obtained from one of the attendants a length of cord, with which he secured the lid. Then he carried his treasure out into the street, and, chartering a four-wheeler, directed the driver to proceed to Charing Cross Station. At the station he booked the box in the cloakroom (in the name of Simpson) and left it for a couple of hours; at the expiration of which he returned, and, employing a different porter, had it conveyed to a hansom, in which it was borne to his lodgings over the oil-shop in Bloomsbury. There he, himself, carried it, unobserved, up the stairs, and, depositing it in a large cupboard, locked the door and pocketed the key.

And thus was the curtain rung down on the first act.

The second act opened only a couple of days later, the office of call-boy – to pursue the metaphor to the bitter end – being discharged by a Belgian police official who emerged from the main entrance to the Bank of England. What should have led Percival Bland into so unsafe a neighbourhood it is difficult to imagine, unless it was that strange fascination that seems so frequently to lure the criminal to places associated with his crime. But there he was within a dozen paces of the entrance when the officer came forth, and mutual recognition was instantaneous. Almost equally instantaneous was the self-possessed Percival's decision to cross the road.

It is not a nice road to cross. The old-fashioned horse-driver would condescend to shout a warning to the indiscreet wayfarer. Not so the modern chauffeur, who looks stonily before him and leaves you to get out of the way of Juggernaut. He knows his "exonerating" coroner's jury. At the moment, however, the procession of Juggernauts was at rest; but Percival had seen the presiding policeman turn to move away and he darted across the fronts of the vehicles even as they started. The foreign officer followed. But in that moment the whole procession had got in motion. A motor omnibus thundered past in front of him; another was bearing down on him relentlessly. He hesitated, and sprang back; and then a taxicab, darting out from behind, butted him heavily, sending him sprawling in the road, whence he scrambled as best he could back on to the pavement.

Percival, meanwhile, had swung himself lightly on to the footboard of the first omnibus just as it was gathering speed. A few seconds saw him safely across at the Mansion House, and in a few more, he was whirling down Queen Victoria Street. The danger was practically over, though he took the precaution to alight at St Paul's, and, crossing to Newgate Street, board another west-bound omnibus.

That night he sat in his lodgings turning over his late experience. It had been a narrow shave. That sort of thing mustn't happen again. In fact, seeing that the law was undoubtedly about to be set in motion, it was high time that certain little plans of his should be set in motion, too. Only, there was a difficulty; a serious difficulty. And as Percival thought round and round that difficulty his brows wrinkled and he hummed a soft refrain.

"Then is the time for disappearing.
Take a header – down you go –."

A tap at the door cut his song short. It was his landlady, Mrs Brattle; a civil woman, and particularly civil just now. For she had a little request to make.

"It was about Christmas Night, Mr Bland," said Mrs Brattle. "My husband and me thought of spending the evening with his brother at Hornsey, and we were going to let the maid go home to her mother's for the night, if it wouldn't put you out."

"Wouldn't put me out in the least, Mrs Brattle," said Percival.

"You needn't sit up for us, you see," pursued Mrs Brattle, "if you'd just leave the side door unbolted. We shan't be home before two or three; but we'll come in quiet not to disturb you."

"You won't disturb me," Percival replied with a genial laugh. "I'm a sober man in general; but 'Christmas comes but once a year.' When once I'm tucked up in bed, I shall take a bit of waking on Christmas Night."

Mrs Brattle smiled indulgently. "And you won't feel lonely, all alone in the house?"

"Lonely!" exclaimed Percival. "Lonely! With a roaring fire, a jolly book, a box of good cigars and a bottle of sound port –ah, and a second bottle if need be. Not I."

Mrs Brattle shook her head. "Ah," said she, "you bachelors! Well, well. It's a good thing to be independent," and with this profound reflection she smiled herself out of the room and descended the stairs.

As her footsteps died away Percival sprang from his chair and began excitedly to pace the room. His eyes sparkled and his face was wreathed with smiles. Presently he halted before the fireplace, and, gazing into the embers, laughed aloud.

"Damn funny!" said he. "Deuced rich! Neat! Very neat! Ha! Ha!" And here he resumed his interrupted song:

"When the sky above is clearing,
When the sky above is clearing,
Bob up serenely, bob up serenely,
Bob up serenely from below!"

Which may be regarded as closing the first scene of the second act.

During the few days that intervened before Christmas, Percival went abroad but little; and yet he was a busy man. He did a little surreptitious shopping, venturing out as far as Charing Cross Road; and his purchases were decidedly miscellaneous. A porridge saucepan, a second-hand copy of "Gray's Anatomy," a rabbit skin, a large supply of glue and upwards of ten pounds of shin of beef seems a rather odd assortment; and it was a mercy that the weather was frosty, for otherwise Percival's bedroom, in which these delicacies were deposited under lock and key, would have yielded odorous traces of its wealth.

But it was in the long evenings that his industry was most conspicuous; and then it was that the big cupboard with the excellent lever lock, which he himself had fixed on, began to fill up with the fruits of his labours. In those evenings the porridge saucepan would simmer on the hob with a rich lading of good Scotch glue, the black box of the deceased practitioner would be hauled forth from its hiding-place, and the well-thumbed "Gray" laid open on the table.

It was an arduous business though; a stiffer task than he had bargained for. The right and left bones were so confoundedly alike, and the bones that joined were so difficult to fit together. However, the plates in "Gray," were large and very clear, so it was only a question of taking enough trouble.

His method of work was simple and practical. Having fished a bone out of the box, he would compare it with the illustrations in the book until he had identified it beyond all doubt, when he would tie on it a paper label with its name and side – right or left. Then he would search for the adjoining bone, and, having fitted the two together, would secure them with a good daub of glue and lay them in the fender to dry. It was a crude and horrible method of articulation that would have made a museum curator shudder. But it seemed to answer Percival's purpose – whatever that may have been – for gradually the loose "items" came together into recognisable members such as arms and legs, the vertebræ – which were, fortunately, strung in their order on a thick cord – were joined up into a solid backbone, and even the ribs, which were the toughest job of all, fixed on in some semblance of a thorax. It was a wretched performance. The bones were plastered with gouts of glue and yet would have broken apart at a touch. But, as we have said, Percival seemed satisfied, and as he was the only person concerned, there was nothing more to be said.

In due course, Christmas Day arrived. Percival dined with the Brattles at two, dozed after dinner, woke up for tea, and then, as Mrs Brattle, in purple and fine raiment, came in to remove the tea-tray, he spread out on the table the materials for the night's carouse. A quarter of an hour later, the side-door slammed, and, peering out of the window, he saw the shopkeeper and his wife hurrying away up the gas-lit street towards the nearest omnibus route.

Then Mr Percival Bland began his evening's entertainment; and a most remarkable entertainment it was, even for a solitary bachelor, left alone in a house on Christmas Night. First, he took off his clothing and dressed himself in a fresh suit. Then, from the cupboard, he brought forth the reconstituted "set of osteology," and, laying the various members on the table, returned to the bedroom, whence he presently reappeared with a large, unsavoury parcel which he had disinterred from a trunk. The parcel, being opened, revealed his accumulated purchases in the matter of shin of beef.

With a large knife, providently sharpened beforehand, he cut the beef into large, thin slices which he proceeded to wrap around the various bones that formed the "complete set"; whereby their nakedness was certainly mitigated though their attractiveness was by no means increased. Having thus "clothed the dry bones," he gathered up the scraps of offal that were left, to be placed presently inside the trunk. It was an extraordinary proceeding, but the next was more extraordinary still.

Taking up the newly clothed members one by one, he began very carefully to insinuate them into the garments that he had recently shed. It was a ticklish business, for the glued joints were as brittle as glass. Very cautiously the legs were separately inducted, first into underclothing and then into trousers, the skeleton feet were fitted with the cast-off socks and delicately persuaded into the boots. The arms, in like manner, were gingerly pressed into their various sleeves and through the arm-holes of the waistcoat; and then came the most difficult task of all – to fit the garments on the trunk. For the skull and ribs, secured to the backbone with mere spots of glue, were ready to drop off at a shake; and yet the garments had to be drawn over them with the arms enclosed in the sleeves. But Percival managed it at last by resting his "restoration" in the big, padded armchair and easing the garments on inch by inch.

It now remained only to give the finishing touch; which was done by cutting the rabbit-skin to the requisite shape and affixing it to the skull with a thin coat of stiff glue; and when the skull had thus been finished with a sort of crude, makeshift wig, its appearance was so appalling as even to disturb the nerves of the matter-of-fact Percival. However, this was no occasion for cherishing sentiment. A skull in an extemporised wig or false scalp might be, and in fact was, a highly unpleasant object; but so was a Belgian police officer.

Having finished the "restoration," Percival fetched the water-jug from his bedroom, and, descending to the shop, the door of which had been left unlocked, tried the taps of the various drums and barrels until he came to the one which contained methylated spirit; and from this he filled his jug and returned to the bedroom. Pouring the spirit out into the basin, he tucked a towel round his neck and filling his sponge with spirit, proceeded very vigorously to wash his hair and eyebrows and as, by degrees, the spirit in the basin grew dark and turbid, so did his hair and eyebrows grow lighter in colour until, after a final energetic rub with a towel, they had acquired a golden or sandy hue indistinguishable from that of the hair of his cousin Robert. Even the mole under his eye was susceptible to the changing conditions, for when he had wetted it thoroughly with spirit, he was able with the blade of a penknife, to peel it off as neatly as if it had been stuck on with spirit-gum. Having done which, he deposited it in a tiny box which he carried in his waistcoat pocket.

The proceedings which followed were unmistakable as to their object. First he carried the basin of spirit through into the sitting room and deliberately poured its contents on to the floor by the arm-chair. Then, having returned the basin to the bedroom, he again went down to the shop, where he selected a couple of galvanised buckets from the stock, filled them with paraffin oil from one of the great drums and carried them upstairs. The oil from one bucket he poured over the armchair and its repulsive occupant; the other bucket he simply emptied on the carpet, and then went down to the shop for a fresh supply.

When this proceeding had been repeated once or twice the entire floor and all the furniture were saturated, and such a reek of paraffin filled the air of the room that Percival thought it wise to turn out the gas. Returning to the shop, he poured a bucketful of oil over the stack of bundles of firewood, another over the counter and floor and a third over the loose articles on the walls and hanging from the ceiling. Looking up at the latter he now perceived a number of greasy patches where the oil had soaked through from the floor above, and some of these were beginning to drip on to the shop floor.

He now made his final preparations. Taking a bundle of "Wheel" firelighters, he made a small pile against the stack of fire-wood. In the midst of the firelighters he placed a ball of string saturated in paraffin; and in the central hole of the ball he stuck a half-dozen diminutive Christmas candles. This mine was now ready. Providing himself with a stock of firelighters, a few balls of paraffined string and a dozen or so of the little candles, he went upstairs to the sitting room, which was immediately above the shop. Here, by the glow of the fire, he built up one or two piles of firelighters around and, partly under the arm-chair, placed the balls of string on the piles and stuck two or three bundles in each ball. Everything was now ready. Stepping into the bedroom, he took from the cupboard a spare overcoat, a new hat and a new umbrella — for he must leave his old hats, coat and umbrella in the hall. He put on the coat and hat, and, with the umbrella in his hand, returned to the sitting room.

Opposite the armchair he stood awhile, irresolute, and a pang of horror shot through him. It was a terrible thing that he was going to do; a thing the consequences of which no one could foresee. He glanced furtively at the awful shape that sat huddled in the chair, its horrible head all awry and its rigid limbs sprawling in hideous grotesque deformity. It was but a dummy, a mere scarecrow; but yet, in the dim firelight, the grisly face under that horrid wig seemed to leer intelligently, to watch him with secret malice out of its shadowy eye-sockets, until he looked away with clammy skin and a shiver of half-superstitious terror.

But this would never do. The evening had run out, consumed by these engrossing labours; it was nearly eleven o'clock, and high time for him to be gone. For if the Brattles should return prematurely he was lost. Pulling himself together with an effort, he struck a match and lit the little candles one after the other. In a quarter of an hour or so, they would have burned down to the balls of string, and then –

He walked quickly out of the room; but, at the door, he paused for a moment to look back at the ghastly figure, seated rigidly in the chair with the lighted candles at its feet, like some foul fiend appeased by votive fires. The unsteady flames threw flickering shadows on its face that made it seem to mow and gibber and grin in mockery of all his care and caution. So he turned and tremblingly ran down the stairs – opening the staircase window as he went. Running into the shop, he lit the candles there and ran out again, shutting the door after him.

Secretly and guiltily he crept down the hall, and opening the door a few inches peered out. A blast of icy wind poured in with a light powdering of dry snow. He opened his umbrella, flung open the door, looked up and down the empty street, stepped out, closed the door softly and strode away over the whitening pavement.

PART II

It was one of the axioms of medico-legal practice laid down by my colleague, John Thorndyke, that the investigator should be constantly on his guard against the effect of suggestion. Not only must all prejudices and preconceptions be avoided, but when information is received from outside, the actual, undeniable facts must be carefully sifted from the inferences which usually accompany them. Of the necessity for this precaution our insurance practice furnished an excellent instance in the case of the fire at Mr Brattle's oil-shop.

The case was brought to our notice by Mr Stalker of the "Griffin" Fire and Life Insurance Society a few days after Christmas. He dropped in, ostensibly to wish us a Happy New Year, but a discreet pause in the conversation on Thorndyke's part elicited a further purpose.

"Did you see the account of that fire in Bloomsbury?" Mr Stalker asked.

"The oil-shop? Yes. But I didn't note any details, excepting that a man was apparently burnt to death and that the affair happened on the twenty-fifth of December."

"Yes, I know," said Mr Stalker. "It seems uncharitable, but one can't help looking a little askance at these quarter-day fires. And the date isn't the only doubtful feature in this one; the Divisional Officer of the Fire Brigade, who has looked over the ruins, tells me that there are some appearances suggesting that the fire broke out in two different places – the shop and the first-floor room over it. Mind you, he doesn't say that it actually did. The place is so thoroughly gutted that very little is to be learned from it; but that is his impression; and it occurred to me that if you were to take a look at the ruins, your radiographic eye might detect something that he had overlooked."

"It isn't very likely," said Thorndyke. "Every man to his trade. The Divisional Officer looks at a burnt house with an expert eye, which I do not. My evidence would not carry much weight if you were contesting the claim."

"Perhaps not," replied Mr Stalker, "and we are not anxious to contest the claim unless there is manifest fraud. Arson is a serious matter."

"It is wilful murder in this case," remarked Thorndyke.

"I know," said Stalker. "And that reminds me that the man who was burnt happens to have been insured in our office, too. So we stand a double loss."

"How much?" asked Thorndyke.

"The dead man, Percival Bland, had insured his life for three thousand pounds."

Thorndyke became thoughtful. The last statement had apparently made more impression on him than the former ones.

"If you want me to look into the case for you," said he, "you had better let me have all the papers connected with it, including the proposal forms."

Mr Stalker smiled. "I thought you would say that – know you of old, you see – so I slipped the papers in my pocket before coming here."

He laid the documents on the table and asked: "Is there anything that you want to know about the case?"

"Yes," replied Thorndyke. "I want to know all that you can tell me."

"Which is mighty little," said Stalker; "but such as it is, you shall have it.

"The oil-shop man's name is Brattle and the dead man, Bland, was his lodger. Bland appears to have been a perfectly steady, sober man in general; but it seems that he had announced his intention of spending a jovial Christmas Night and giving himself a little extra indulgence. He was last seen by Mrs Brattle at about half-past six, sitting by a blazing fire, with a couple of unopened bottles of port on the table and a box of cigars. He had a book in his hand and two or three newspapers lay on the floor by his chair. Shortly after this, Mr and Mrs Brattle went out on a visit to Hornsey, leaving him alone in the house."

"Was there no servant?" asked Thorndyke.

"The servant had the day and night off duty to go to her mother's. That, by the way, looks a trifle fishy. However, to return to the Brattles; they spent the evening at Hornsey and did not get home until past three in the morning, by which time their house was a heap of smoking ruins. Mrs Brattle's idea is that Bland must have drunk himself sleepy, and dropped one of the newspapers into the fender, where a chance cinder may have started the blaze. Which may or may not be the true explanation. Of course, a habitually sober man can get pretty mimsey on two bottles of port."

"What time did the fire break out?" asked Thorndyke.

"It was noticed about half-past eleven that flames were issuing from one of the chimneys, and the alarm was given at once. The first engine arrived ten minutes later, but, by that time, the place was roaring like a furnace. Then the water-plugs were found to be frozen hard, which caused some delay; in fact, before the engines were able to get to work the roof had fallen in, and the place was a mere shell. You know what an oil-shop is, when once it gets a fair start."

"And Mr Bland's body was found in the ruins, I suppose?"

"Body!" exclaimed Mr Stalker; "there wasn't much body! Just a few charred bones, which they dug out of the ashes next day."

"And the question of identity?"

"We shall leave that to the coroner. But there really isn't any question. To begin with, there was no one else in the house; and then the remains were found mixed up with the springs and castors of the chair that Bland was sitting in when he was last seen. Moreover, there were found, with the bones, a pocket-knife, a bunch of keys and a set of steel waistcoat buttons, all identified by Mrs Brattle as belonging to Bland. She noticed the cut steel buttons on his waistcoat when she wished him 'good night.' "

"By the way," said Thorndyke, "was Bland reading by the light of an oil lamp?"

"No," replied Stalker. "There was a two-branch gasalier with a porcelain shade to one burner, and he had that burner alight when Mrs Brattle left.'

Thorndyke reflectively picked up the proposal form, and, having glanced through it, remarked: "I see that Bland is described as unmarried. Do you know why he insured his life for this large amount?"

"No; we assumed that it was probably in connection with some loan that he had raised. I learn from the solicitor who notified us of the death, that the whole of Bland's property is left to a cousin – a Mr Lindsay, I think. So the probability is that this cousin had lent him money. But it is not the life claim that is interesting us. We must pay that in any case. It is the fire claim that we want you to look into."

"Very well," said Thorndyke; "I will go round presently and look over the ruins, and see if I can detect any substantial evidence of fraud."

"If you would," said Mr Stalker, rising to take his departure, "we should be very much obliged. Not that we shall probably contest the claim in any case."

When he had gone, my colleague and I glanced through the papers, and I ventured to remark: "It seems to me that Stalker doesn't quite appreciate the possibilities of this case."

"No," Thorndyke agreed. "But, of course, it is an insurance company's business to pay, and not to boggle at anything short of glaring fraud. And we specialists, too," he added with a smile, "must beware of seeing too much. I suppose that, to a rhinologist, there is hardly such a thing as a healthy nose – unless it is his own – and the uric acid specialist is very apt to find the firmament studded with dumb-bell crystals. We mustn't forget that normal cases do exist, after all."

"That is true," said I; "but, on the other hand, the rhinologist's business is with the unhealthy nose, and our concern is with abnormal cases."

Thorndyke laughed. " 'A Daniel come to judgment,' " said he. "But my learned friend is quite right. Our function is to pick holes. So let us pocket the documents and wend Bloomsbury way. We can talk the case over as we go."

We walked at an easy pace, for there was no hurry, and a little preliminary thought was useful. After a while, as Thorndyke made no remark, I reopened the subject.

"How does the case present itself to you?" I asked.

"Much as it does to you, I expect," he replied. "The circumstances invite inquiry, and I do not find myself connecting them with the shopkeeper. It is true that the fire occurred on quarter-day; but there is nothing to show that the insurance will do more than cover the loss of stock, chattels and the profits of trade. The other circumstances are much more suggestive. Here is a house burned down and a man killed. That man was insured for three thousand pounds, and, consequently, some person stands to gain by his death to that amount. The whole set of circumstances is highly favourable to the idea of homicide. The man was alone in the house when he died; and the total destruction of both the body and its surroundings seems to render investigation impossible. The cause of death can only be inferred; it cannot be proved; and the most glaring evidence of a crime will have vanished utterly. I think that there is a quite strong *prima facie* suggestion of murder. Under the known conditions, the perpetration of a murder would have been easy, it would have been safe from detection, and there is an adequate motive.

"On the other hand, suicide is not impossible. The man might have set fire to the house and then killed himself by poison or otherwise. But it is intrinsically less probable that a man should kill himself for another person's benefit than that he should kill another man for his own benefit.

"Finally, there is the possibility that the fire and the man's death were the result of accident; against which is the official opinion that the fire started in two places. If this opinion is correct, it establishes, in my opinion, a strong presumption of murder against some person who may have obtained access to the house."

This point in the discussion brought us to the ruined house, which stood at the corner of two small streets. One of the firemen in charge admitted us, when we had shown our credentials, through a temporary door and down a ladder into the basement, where we found a number of men treading gingerly, ankle deep in white ash, among a litter of charred woodwork, fused glass, warped and broken china, and more or less recognisable metal objects.

"The coroner and the jury," the fireman explained; "come to view the scene of the disaster." He introduced us to the former, who bowed stiffly and continued his investigations.

"These," said the other fireman, "are the springs of the chair that the deceased was sitting in. We found the body – or rather the bones – lying among them under a heap of hot ashes; and we found the buttons of his clothes and the things from his pockets among the ashes, too. You'll see them in the mortuary with the remains."

"It must have been a terrific blaze," one of the jurymen remarked. "Just look at this, sir," and he handed to Thorndyke what looked like part of a gas-fitting, of which the greater part was melted into shapeless lumps and the remainder encrusted into fused porcelain.

"That," said the fireman, "was the gasalier of the first-floor room, where Mr Bland was sitting. Ah! you won't turn that tap, sir; nobody'll ever turn that tap again."

Thorndyke held the twisted mass of brass towards me in silence, and, glancing up the blackened walls, remarked: "I think we shall have to come here again with the Divisional Officer, but meanwhile, we had better see the remains of the body. It is just possible that we may learn something from them."

He applied to the coroner for the necessary authority to make the inspection, and, having obtained a rather ungracious and grudging permission to examine the remains when the jury had "viewed" them, began to ascend the ladder.

"Our friend would have liked to refuse permission," he remarked when we had emerged into the street, "but he knew that I could and should have insisted."

"So I gathered from his manner," said I. "But what is he doing here? This isn't his district."

"No; he is acting for Bettsford, who is laid up just now; and a very poor substitute he is. A non-medical coroner is an absurdity in any case, and a coroner who is hostile to the medical profession is a public scandal. By the way, that gas-tap offers a curious problem. You noticed that it was turned off?"

"Yes."

"And consequently that the deceased was sitting in the dark when the fire broke out. I don't see the bearing of the fact, but it is certainly rather odd. Here is the mortuary. We had better wait and let the jury go in first."

We had not long to wait. In a couple of minutes or so the "twelve good men and true" made their appearance with a small attendant crowd of ragamuffins. We let them enter first, and then we followed. The mortuary was a good-sized room, well lighted by a glass roof, and having at its centre a long table on which lay the shell containing the remains. There was also a sheet of paper on which had been laid out a set of blackened steel waistcoat buttons, a bunch of keys, a steel-handled pocket-knife, a steel-cased watch on a partly-fused rolled-gold chain and a pocket corkscrew. The coroner drew the attention of the jury to these objects, and then took possession of them, that they might be identified by witnesses. And meanwhile the jurymen gathered round the shell and stared shudderingly at its gruesome contents.

"I am sorry, gentlemen," said the coroner, "to have to subject you to this painful ordeal. But duty is duty. We must hope, as I think we may, that this poor creature met a painless, if in some respects a rather terrible death."

At this point, Thorndyke, who had drawn near to the table, cast a long and steady glance down into the shell; and, immediately his ordinarily rather impassive face seemed to congeal; all expression faded from it, leaving it as immovable and uncommunicative as the granite face of an Egyptian statue. I knew the symptom of old and began to speculate on its present significance.

"Are you taking any medical evidence?" he asked.

"Medical evidence!" the coroner repeated, scornfully. "Certainly not, sir! I do not waste the public money by employing so-called experts to tell the jury what each of them can see quite plainly for himself. I imagine," he added, turning to the foreman, "that you will not require a learned doctor to explain to you how that poor fellow mortal met his death?" And the foreman, glancing askance at the skull, replied, with a pallid and sickly smile, that "he thought not."

"Do you, sir," the coroner continued, with a dramatic wave of the hand towards the plain coffin, "suppose that we shall find any difficulty in determining how that man came by his death?"

"I imagine," replied Thorndyke, without moving a muscle, or, indeed, appearing to have any muscles to move, "I imagine you will find no difficulty whatever."

"So do I," said the coroner.

"Then," retorted Thorndyke, with a faint, inscrutable smile, "we are, for once, in complete agreement."

As the coroner and jury retired, leaving my colleague and me alone in the mortuary, Thorndyke remarked:

"I suppose this kind of farce will be repeated periodically so long as these highly technical medical inquiries continue to be conducted by lay persons."

I made no reply, for I had taken a long look into the shell, and was lost in astonishment.

"But my dear Thorndyke!" I exclaimed; "what on earth does it mean? Are we to suppose that a woman can have palmed herself off as a man on the examining medical officer of a London Life Assurance Society?"

Thorndyke shook his head. "I think not," said he. "Our friend, Mr Bland, may conceivably have been a woman in disguise, but he certainly was not a negress."

"A negress!" I gasped. "By Jove! So it is. I hadn't looked at the skull. But that only makes the mystery more mysterious. Because, you remember, the body was certainly dressed in Bland's clothes."

"Yes, there seems to be no doubt about that. And you may have noticed, as I did," Thorndyke continued dryly, "the remarkably fire-proof character of the waistcoat buttons, watch-case, knife-handle, and other identifiable objects."

"But what a horrible affair!" I exclaimed. "The brute must have gone out and enticed some poor devil of a negress into the house, have murdered her in cold blood, and then deliberately dressed the corpse in his own clothes! It is perfectly frightful!"

Again Thorndyke shook his head. "It wasn't as bad as that, Jervis," said he, "though I must confess that I feel strongly tempted to let your hypothesis stand. It would be quite amusing to put Mr Bland on trial for the murder of an unknown negress, and let him explain the facts himself. But our reputation is at stake. Look at the bones again and a little more critically. You very probably looked for the sex first; then you looked for racial characters. Now carry your investigations a step further."

"There is the stature," said I. "But that is of no importance, as these are not Bland's bones. The only other point that I notice is that the fire seems to have acted very unequally on the different parts of the body."

"Yes," agreed Thorndyke, "and that is *the* point. Some parts are more burnt than others; and the parts which are burnt most are the wrong parts. Look at the backbone, for instance. The vertebræ are as white as chalk. They are mere masses of bone ash. But, of all parts of the skeleton, there is none so completely protected from fire as the backbone, with the great dorsal muscles behind, and the whole mass of the viscera in front. Then look at the skull. Its appearance is quite inconsistent with the suggested facts. The bones of the face are bare and calcined and the orbits contain not a trace of the eyes or other structures; and yet there is a charred mass of what may or may not be scalp adhering to the crown. But the scalp, as the most exposed and the thinnest covering, would be the first to be destroyed, while the last to be consumed would be the structures about the jaws and the base, of which, you see, not a vestige is left."

Here he lifted the skull carefully from the shell, and, peering in through the great foramen at the base, handed it to me.

"Look in," he said, "through the Foramen Magnum – you will see better if you hold the orbits towards the skylight – and notice an even more extreme inconsistency with the supposed conditions. The brain and membranes have vanished without leaving a trace. The inside of the skull is as clean as if it had been macerated. But this is impossible. The brain is not only protected from the fire; it is also protected from contact with the air. But without access of oxygen, although it might become carbonised, it could not be consumed. No, Jervis; it won't do."

I replaced the skull in the coffin and looked at him in surprise.

"What is it that you are suggesting?" I asked.

"I suggest that this was not a body at all, but merely a dry skeleton."

"But," I objected, "what about those masses of what looks like charred muscle adhering to the bones?"

"Yes," he replied, "I have been noticing them. They do, as you say, look like masses of charred muscle. But they are quite shapeless and structureless; I cannot identify a single muscle or muscular group; and there is not a vestige of any of the tendons. Moreover, the distribution is false. For instance, will you tell me what muscle you think that is?"

He pointed to a thick, charred mass on the inner surface of the left tibia or shin bone. "Now this portion of the bone – as many a hockey-player has had reason to realise – has no muscular covering at all. It lies immediately under the skin."

"I think you are right, Thorndyke," said I. "That lump of muscle in the wrong place gives the whole fraud away. But it was really a rather smart dodge. This fellow Bland must be an ingenious rascal."

"Yes," agreed Thorndyke; "but an unscrupulous villain too. He might have burned down half the street and killed a score of people. He'll have to pay the piper for this little frolic."

"What shall you do now? Are you going to notify the coroner?"

"No; that is not my business. I think we will verify our conclusions and then inform our clients and the police. We must measure the skull as well as we can without callipers, but it is, fortunately, quite typical. The short, broad, flat nasal bones, with the 'Simian groove,' and those large, strong teeth, worn flat by hard and gritty food, are highly characteristic." He, once more, lifted out the skull, and, with a spring tape, made a few measurements, while I noted the lengths of the principal long bones and the width across the hips.

"I make the cranial-nasal index 55.1," said he, as he replaced the skull, "and the cranial index about 72, which are quite representative numbers; and, as I see that your notes show the usual disproportionate length of arm and the characteristic curve of the tibia, we may be satisfied. But it is fortunate that the specimen is so typical. To the experienced eye, racial types have a physiognomy which is unmistakable on mere inspection. But you cannot transfer the experienced eye. You can only express personal conviction and back it up with measurements.

"And now we will go and look in on Stalker, and inform him that his office has saved three thousand pounds by employing us. After which it will be Westward Ho! for Scotland Yard, to prepare an unpleasant little surprise for Mr Percival Bland."

There was joy among the journalists on the following day. Each of the morning papers devoted an entire column to an unusually detailed account of the inquest on the late Percival Bland – who, it appeared, met his death by misadventure – and a verbatim report of the coroner's eloquent remarks on the danger of solitary, fireside tippling, and the stupefying effects of port wine. An adjacent column contained an equally detailed account of the appearance of the deceased at Bow Street Police Court to answer complicated charges of arson, fraud and forgery; while a third collated the two accounts with gleeful commentaries.

Mr Percival Bland, *alias* Robert Lindsay, now resides on the breezy uplands of Dartmoor, where, in his abundant leisure, he, no doubt, regrets his misdirected ingenuity. But he has not laboured in vain. To the Lord Chancellor he has furnished an admirable illustration of the danger of appointing lay coroners; and to me an unforgettable warning against the effects of suggestion.

The Attorney's Conscience

I suppose if I were a sensitive man I should not be writing this history; or, at any rate, should not contemplate its perusal by strangers. For no man cares to be written down a liar; and many will conceal an incredible truth rather than run the risk. However, of these hyper-sensitive folk I am not one. For a good many years now I have practised at the bar; and, if that fact offers no guarantee of unimpeachable veracity it at least furnishes presumptive evidence of a fairly robust moral epidermis. I may not be believed; but the frankest scepticism will leave me undisturbed and unabashed.

My connection with the surprising events that I am about to record, began at the moment of my entering the shop of Mr Reuben Solomon in Booksellers' Row. The "Row" has been swept away some years by a progressive County Council, and sorrowful ratepayers may look in through the palings and see very expensive wild flowers blooming – but not paying rates – upon its site. But in those days it was still standing, a happy hunting-ground for the bibliophile and a perennial joy to the urban artist; and Mr Solomon's shop still gladdened the bookish eye with colossal black-letter folios, antique volumes in rusty calf and dainty, vellum-bound Elzivirs.

I found Mr Solomon alone at the back of the shop dusting a range of shelves with a feather brush, and at once noticed a departure from his usual sprightly, genial manner. The worthy bookseller looked in decidedly low spirits.

"Good morning, Mr Solomon," I said cheerfully; "I hope I find you well this beautiful weather."

"Then you don't," he replied sourly.

"Indeed! I am sorry for that. What's the matter?"

He laid down the feather brush and looked at me gloomily.

"Balmy," said he.

"Balmy?" I repeated.

"Yes, sir," he rejoined. "Balmy." And then, as I stared at him in astonishment, he added by way of elucidation: "on the crumpet."

I was exceedingly surprised. Solomon was a cultivated man – I might say a learned man – and was not addicted to these coarse colloquialisms. But, of course, I did not take him seriously. The diagnosis of insanity is not usually made by the lunatic himself.

"You're out of spirits this morning, Mr Solomon," I said.

"Spirits be blowed!" said he. "If I'm not going off my blooming onion I'll – but there! it's no concern of yours, Mr Mitchell. You've come to see those books that I wrote to you about. I've made them up into a parcel, as I thought you would like to take them home to look at at your leisure. There are five of them – "

He broke off abruptly, and, to my amazement, began to retreat down the shop in a most singular, stealthy manner, flattening himself against the wall as if he were squeezing past some bulky obstacle, and watching suspiciously the opposite range of bookshelves. When he was half-way down the shop, he turned and almost ran out; and on following him into the street, I found him earnestly examining the stock-in-trade of another bookseller some three doors farther up.

"You were saying, Mr Solomon – " I began.

"Yes, about that parcel of books. It is on the shelf over the fireplace. Your name is written on it. Perhaps you wouldn't mind going in and taking it. I find the shop rather stuffy just at present."

This was certainly very queer behaviour and most unlike Solomon, who was in general the very pink of politeness. I was greatly puzzled; but, as I was somewhat pressed for time, I went into the shop, found my parcel and bustled off with it after a few hasty words to the bookseller.

As I had to call at the chambers of another barrister, I took the opportunity to run up to my own and leave the parcel there; and, as the books were of some value and were not mine, at present, I bestowed them in the upper part of my bureau, and, according to my invariable habit, turned the key. Then I went about my business.

From my friend's chambers I went across to the Appeal Court, in which I was that day engaged. I lunched with the QC with whom I was associated, and when the court rose I went home with him to dine and talk over the case.

I remained with him until past eleven o'clock. When I emerged from his chambers in Paper Buildings, I perceived three persons – two men and a woman – sauntering slowly up towards Crown Office Row and looking about them with the leisurely air of sightseers. One of the men, who carried a violin-case, was apparently acting as showman, and, as I overtook them, I recognised him as a crony of mine, a law student named Leyland. I would have passed with a flourish of the hat, but he hailed me to stop.

"I say, Mitchell, can you tell us where it was that Lamb lived with his sister? Wasn't it Crown Office Row?"

"No; he was born in Crown Office Row, but the chambers where he and Mary Lamb lived were in Mitre Court Buildings."

"Then," said Leyland, addressing the lady, "you will have to come and see the place by daylight. The gate is shut now. We must get Mr Mitchell to show us round the old place some day; he knows every stone of it and who lived in every house from the time of the Knights Templars downward. You wouldn't mind, Mitchell, would you? Miss Bonnington is rabid on historic associations."

"I should be proud and delighted," said I.

"It is a dear old place," said Miss Bonnington; "so peaceful and monastic. How I should love to live here! But I suppose there are no Eves in this Paradise."

"No," I answered. "It is given up to Adam and the serpent; especially the serpent."

Miss Bonnington laughed: and a very pretty, musical laugh it was, and very pleasant to listen to. Indeed, she impressed me as a very charming young lady; sweet-faced and soft-spoken, though quite self-possessed.

"I didn't know you played the fiddle, Leyland," said I, glancing at the case in his hand.

"I don't," he replied. "This is Miss Bonnington's. I groan aloud on the 'cello, and Mr Bonnington hammers the 'well-tempered clavier.' We've been having a little revival meeting in my chambers."

Thus we chatted as we strolled quietly up the untenanted walk. My appointment as future cicerone seemed to have served as an informal introduction, and when we came to the corner of Fig Tree Court, we halted to gossip awhile before saying goodnight.

"What a very extraordinary old gentleman that was!" Miss Bonnington said suddenly. "And how inquisitively he looked at us."

We all turned to follow her gaze, but the old gentleman had already passed into the gloom of the narrow court and was little more than a bulky shadow.

"He's a deuce of a size," said Leyland. "Looks like a turtle walking upright."

"Yes," said Miss Bonnington, "but did you see how oddly he was dressed? He seemed to have a cocked hat and gaiters like a bishop's. Would he be a judge, do you think?"

I laughed at the idea of one of Her Majesty's judges going abroad in a cocked hat and gaiters, and delicately suggested an optical illusion.

"Well," said Leyland, "you'll be able to see for yourself, presently. He has turned into your entry. I expect he has come to offer you a brief."

"Then," said I, "I mustn't keep him waiting. Remember, that whenever you are disposed for a historic prowl round the Temple, I am at your service."

I shook hands with my newly-made friends and Leyland and betook myself to number 21, Fig Tree Court, on the second floor of which my chambers were situated. Slowly ascending the stone stairs, I speculated on the unknown visitor of quaint aspect, until I at length reached my own landing. But there was nobody waiting for me. Evidently Leyland had mistaken the entry, for mine were the only residential chambers in the building.

I let myself in with my key, shut the heavy "oak," and was about to take off my overcoat when my attention was arrested by a very strange circumstance.

There was a light in my sitting room.

It was very singular and rather disturbing. I stood in the tiny lobby gazing at the streak of light – the door stood slightly ajar – and wondering if it could possibly be a burglar, though burglary was practically unknown in the Temple, and listening intently. There were no sounds of movement or, indeed, of any kind except a faint, continuous creak, curiously like the squeak of a quill pen. I stepped forward on tiptoe, softly pushed open the door, and looked into the room.

What I saw astonished me beyond words. Seated at my open bureau, writing rapidly with one of the quill pens which I, with an old-fashioned lawyer's conservatism, still use, was a man, apparently a stranger. As his back was turned to me I could not see what he was like, excepting that he was excessively bulky, and that he wore a grey wig. This latter fact puzzled me greatly. It is not customary for counsel to wear their wigs in chambers at midnight, and I could see, moreover, that he was not in his gown. It was very remarkable.

I watched him for a while in speechless astonishment, a huge, unreal silhouette against the light of the single wax candle that I always keep in the antique silver candlestick on my bureau. He wrote on steadily with a loud chirping of the quill, turned the paper over, continued on the other side, and finally signed his name with an elaborate flourish, as I gathered from a series of more vehement squeaks. Then he laid the pen in the rack and helped himself to a pinch of snuff.

At this point I thought it expedient to attract his attention, and, to that end, coughed gently. But he took no notice. I coughed again a little louder, but still he appeared unaware of my presence. And then suddenly it flashed upon me that I must have got into the wrong chambers. I do not know why I thought this, for there was my own bureau with my own candlestick on it, there was the parcel of books at the stranger's elbow, and there was the high back of my Queen Anne chair cutting across the tail of his wig. But the misgiving was so strong that I must needs steal back into the lobby and softly open the outer door to satisfy myself.

No; there was no mistake. There was my own name "Mr James Mitchell" painted legibly above the lintel. Having ascertained this, I re-entered, closed the door rather noisily and strode across the lobby. But now another surprise awaited me.

The room was in darkness.

I stopped short expecting my visitor to come out. But he did not; nor was there any sound of movement from within. Rather nervously I struck a wax match and once more entered; and, as I looked round I uttered a gasp of amazement.

The room was empty.

I stood for some seconds staring with dropped jaw into the dim vacancy until the match burned my finger; when I dropped it and lit another in a mighty hurry. For the idea suddenly occurred to me that this unwieldy stranger must be a lunatic, and was perhaps at this moment lurking under the table. Very hastily I lit the gas and stepped back to the door. But a moment's investigation showed me that there was no one in hiding. The room was undeniably empty; and yet there was no exit save by the door at which I had entered. The affair was incomprehensible and beyond belief. Not only was the room empty; there was no sign of its having been entered. The bureau was shut, and when I stepped over to it and tried the flap, I found it locked as I had left it.

Needless to say, I searched the entire "set." I lit the gas in the lobby, the bedroom, the office and the little kitchen. I looked under the bed, into the wardrobe, and opened cupboards that would hardly have hidden a baby, much less the leviathan who had so amazingly vanished. And when I had proved beyond all doubt that there was no one in the chambers but myself, I went back to the sitting room and gazed uncomfortably at the bureau. Of course there could be only one explanation. The fat man was an illusion; a figment of my own brain. There had really never been anyone in the place at all.

This was all very well as an explanation, but it was not particularly satisfactory. Hallucinations are awkward things. The brain that generates non-existent fat men is not a sound brain. And the circumstantiality of the illusion only made it worse. For I could recall the fat man perfectly as he sat with the candlelight filtering through the edge of his wig; and now that I came to reflect on it, that wig was a very peculiar one. It was not a barrister's wig at all, nor a judge's, in fact it was not a horse-hair wig of any kind. It was softer and closer as if made of actual human hair.

Reflection on the subject was so disquieting that I determined to dismiss it from my mind; and, to that end, set about composing a letter which I had to send off to a solicitor in the morning. Unlocking and opening the flap of the bureau, I lit the candle, and, seating myself, took a sheet of paper from the stationery drawer and picked up a pen from the rack. As I turned over the opening paragraph of my proposed letter, and before I had raised the lid of the ink-stand, I tried the point of the pen, as is my habit, on my thumb-nail. How can I express my astonishment when, on glancing at my nail after doing so, I perceived on it a little spot of wet ink!

I was thunderstruck. Here, at any rate, was a tangible fact; and what made it more conclusive was the circumstance that I had, that very morning, placed a new pen in the rack and thrown the old one away. This pen, therefore, now charged with wet ink, had never been used by me. It was an amazing affair. I sat for a quite considerable time reflecting on it, and might have reflected much longer, but that, happening to glance at the pen in my hand, I perceived that it was perfectly clean and unused. There was not a sign of ink on it, either wet or dry. Instinctively I held up my thumb-nail and looked at it. But the spot of ink had vanished; or, at least, there was no spot there, and, of course, there had never been any spot. The wet ink, like the fat man, was an illusion; the product of some disordered state of my own brain.

It was excessively disturbing, but it was useless to puzzle over it and fret about it. No doubt the condition would pass, and meanwhile it were wiser to ignore it, and quietly attend to my health. Thus reflecting, I addressed myself to my letter, dipped my pen, wrote "Dear Sir," and plunged forthwith into the matter. I wrote on with the easy fluency of a man who is committing to paper that which is already in his mind, reached the bottom of the page, turned over, finished the letter in a couple more lines, and signed my name. Then I rose and fetched the letter-book from my copying-press.

I had opened the book, and was about to take the brush from the water pot when my eye chanced to fall on the letter that I had just written; whereupon I fairly cried out with astonishment. For the name that I had signed was not my own name, nor was it even in my own handwriting; and, if anything could make the affair more astonishing, it was that I had written down a name that was entirely strange to me – Phineas Desborough. Who on earth was Phineas Desborough? and what was his confounded name doing at the foot of my letter?

I don't mind admitting that I was now considerably alarmed, and that the hand with which I picked up the precious document was far from a steady one. So completely was I overpowered that I was sensible of no further surprise on finding the matter of the epistle as strange as the signature, or on seeing the purple copying ink fade before my eyes into a spectral brown. My capacity for astonishment was exhausted. However, I reflected grimly, there could be no breach of confidence in reading my own letter, and accordingly I reseated myself and proceeded to run my eye, with far from pleasurable curiosity, over the faded writing to ascertain what I had been saying. I read the letter through with close attention and now quote its contents with a clear memory. They were as follows:

"16, Field Court, Gray's Inn,
"11th April, 1785.

"Madam, – Your esteemed Letter of the 20th ultimo was duly received by me with profound gratification. Pray permit me respectfully to acknowledge the gracious condescension of your language towards one who has wrought much mischief and who now makes restitution only on the verge of the grave. It were better, I conceive, since your guardian must on no account be privy to our meeting, that you should not be seen at my chambers. You say that you will arrive in London on the evening of the 22nd instant, and will be free from the observation of your guardian on the following afternoon. That being so, I venture to give you the following directions: Walk from your lodging at the Saracen up Fleet Street on the south side and so through that arch of Temple Bar that abuts on Mr Child's Bank. In that arch I shall take my stand at three of the clock punctually, and since the arch encloses but a strait passage, and my person (by reason of my habit of body and the dropsy with which it hath pleased God most justly to afflict me) will occupy the greater part thereof, you

must needs pass me so close that I may readily place the book in your hands without being observed.

"Conceal the book most carefully ('tis but a small one), and when you are quite private and secure from observation, carry a sharp pen-knife round the line that I have marked within the cover so as to cut fairly through the lining.

"I shall say no more, save that I have devised my entire property by will to your brother Jonathan, and that I entreat you to advise me when you have accomplished my directions and have the writing safely in your custody.

> *"I am, Madam,*
> *"Your Most obedient humble Servant,*
> *"Phineas Desborough.*
> *"To Mrs Susan Pierpoint."*

I laid the letter down and took a few turns up and down the room. Here, at least, was no illusion. The circumstantial detail and the names of the persons, entirely unknown to me, seemed to put that quite out of the question. The thing that troubled me most was the ink, the change in which admitted of no reasonable explanation. And, now that I came to think of it, the paper itself had seemed to undergo some kind of metamorphosis; a change that I had, as it were, noted subconsciously and passed over at the moment. To make sure that this was actually the case, I stepped over to the bureau and again took up the letter. And then I stood like a graven image with the sheet of paper in my hand and my eyes riveted on the opening words:

> *"19, Fig Tree Court,*
> *"Inner Temple,*
> *"18th May, 1901.*

> *"Dear Sir,*
> *"Bayste v. Jarvie,*
> *"Referring to our conversation of the 16th instant –"*

I turned the page and looked on my signature "James Mitchell," of which the ink was still fresh and purple. So Phineas Desborough's letter, like the ink-spot and the fat man, was after all an illusion.

But what an illusion! Even as I glanced over my own missive, couched in the characterless phraseology of today, the more rounded periods of the antique letter came fresh and word-perfect to my memory. There was something out of the common here. Either some outside agency had by some means gained access to my consciousness, or I was (to borrow Mr Solomon's graceful euphemism) "going balmy on the crumpet." And neither alternative was an agreeable one to contemplate.

I placed my letter in an envelope, which I addressed but left open that I might examine it in the morning and make sure that it had undergone no fresh metamorphoses. Then I went to bed, to lie awake a full hour meditating on Phineas Desborough and Mistress Susan Pierpoint and wondering if there had been such persons or if they were merely the products of a disordered brain.

Among my acquaintances in the Temple at this period was, as I have already mentioned, a law student named Frank Leyland. I had a great regard for Leyland. In the first place, he was a fine handsome young fellow, and I have a partiality for good-looking people. Then he was fairly bursting with health and good spirits, qualities which, also, I appreciate highly. For your happy man is a benefactor to his species. Just as one may gather knowledge from the wise, so, by contact with the happy, may one improve one's spirits; a truth deserving of consideration by the middle-aged.

It was on the following Sunday night that I encountered Leyland, emerging with the other worshippers from the Temple Church, and — I regret to say — yawning prodigiously.

"Why do you go to church if it makes you yawn?" I asked.

"Free lesson in elocution," he replied. "There's no model like a good-class parson. Actor's no good; too florid. Lawyer's too prosy. But a parson's the happy mean; a good style not hampered by matter. Are you going home?"

"Yes, I was going home; to Fig Tree Court, that is to say."

"Why not come and smoke a cigar with me?" Leyland suggested.

Why not? I was not specially yearning for a solitude which was apt to be disturbed by reminiscences of the late (or never) Phineas Desborough and suspicions of crumpetic unsoundness.

"I've just bought a Wheatley's Pepys," said Leyland; and that settled it. A minute later we were in his rather expensively appointed chambers in Tanfield Court with a pile of his newly-purchased books on the table.

We overhauled the treasures one by one, dipping into them and sampling passages, criticising illustrations and appraising bindings, until, at the bottom of the pile, we came on Goodeve's "Real Property."

"I am glad to see you are not neglecting your studies," I said, nodding at the forbidding volume, but not essaying to sample its contents.

"Oh, it's not professional enthusiasm," said Leyland. "I have a personal interest in property law at the moment. That's why I bought Goodeve; but now that I've got you here, I don't see why I shouldn't take counsel's opinion instead of muddling it out myself."

"Neither do I. It will probably save time. Pass the tobacco-jar and propound your riddle."

He pushed over the jar and a box of cigars. "The question is," said he, "what is the position of a man who threatens to cut his only son off with a shilling?"

"Well," I replied, "in my limited experience as a playgoer, his position is usually in the middle of the hearth-rug, with his legs a-straddle, and his hands under his coat-tails."

Leyland grinned cheerfully. "I mean his legal position," said he. "Can he do it?"

"That is a very vague question to come from a half-fledged barrister. The question turns on the manner in which the property is held. If a man holds his property absolutely, he can dispose of it absolutely; if he holds it subject to conditions, he can only dispose of it in accordance with those conditions. But why do you want to know?"

"Because my respected governor has expressed his intention – contingently – of putting the process into operation on me."

"Indeed! Would it be indiscreet to ask why?"

"Oh, the usual thing. My matrimonial projects are not acceptable."

"Your father objects to the lady, you mean?"

"No; he has never seen her. But he jibs at her father. You see, my governor is an old-fashioned country gentleman and he's nuts on his family. God knows why. There seem to have been untold generations of country bumpkins bearing our name, and, for some reason, he is proud of the fact, and considers us the salt of the earth. Now, the lady's father is a musician; he plays the organ and teaches music. Also he is not a millionaire. But the organ is the real trouble. My governor says he's not going to have his son marrying the daughter of a damned organ-grinder. So there you are."

"It's not delicately put," I remarked.

"No, the gov's a rude old man when he's put out. But it's such confounded nonsense. The musician's is a noble profession, and, as to the organ, why it's the Zeus of the instrumental Olympus. Think of all the great men who have played the organ. There's Mozart and Bach, and Handel himself – "

"And Johnny Morgan," I interrupted; but by Leyland's feeble smile I saw that he had never heard the old song, and so missed the point of the joke.

"Well, the upshot of it is," Leyland concluded, "that the governor refuses his consent. He says if I marry the daughter I can apprentice myself to her father, and he will furnish me with one shilling sterling, and the price of a monkey."

"Why a monkey?" I asked.

"Oh, he seems to think that a monkey is an indispensable adjunct to organ playing. He's not musical, you know."

"Don't you think he will give way if he is treated judiciously?"

"No, I don't He's as obstinate as a mule. And what's worse, he has snookered me for the time being by explaining his intentions by letter to my proposed papa-in-law. The result being that I am at present a rejected suitor."

"But, if you are rejected, your legal position is pointless."

"Oh, is it, by Jove!" said Leyland. "You don't think I agree to the rejection, do you? Because I don't. I tell you, Mitchell, I'm going to marry Kate Bonnington," and Leyland stuck out his chin with a distinct reminiscence of the parental mulishness.

"So I gathered from your manner the other evening; and I can't pretend to disapprove after seeing Miss Bonnington. But you say that relations between you are broken off for the present."

"Oh, no, they're not," said Leyland. "We are perfectly good friends still. You see, I am taking lessons on the organ from Papa Bonnington."

"That savours of mere low cunning on your part. But go on."

"Well, Bonnington is quite willing, in the abstract, for me to marry his daughter, and Miss Kate is also agreeable – in the abstract – but they both refuse to be the cause of my being disinherited."

"And, of course," I added, "you couldn't cut much of a figure as a married man on one shilling sterling and the price of a monkey."

"Exactly. But if the old man can't disinherit me, I think matters could be arranged. I might, for instance, borrow enough on my expectations to start myself in some sort of business. Hence my inquiry as to the governor's powers."

"Which brings us back to the original question; does your father hold the property absolutely or conditionally?"

"I'm hanged if I know," said Leyland. "I suppose I must try to find out. What I do know is that there seems to be a strong suspicion of some sort of flaw in the title."

"Indeed! That sounds unpleasant; but it is also rather vague."

"It's quite vague," said Leyland. "But I'd better tell you what I know about it, which is uncommonly little. The story is connected with an ancestor of ours named Anthony Leyland, who lived in the time of George the Second. Anthony seems to have been mixed up in some Jacobite foolery, and, when that game fizzled out after the '45, he retired to the continent. The man who then held the Leyland property was a Whig and a loyalist, so, I suppose Anthony reckoned that if he kept out of sight, his peccadilloes would be forgotten by the time he was due to succeed to the estate. But, as a matter of fact, he never did succeed to it. He lived at Louvain, and died there before his innings was due. It seems that at Louvain he carried on some sort of business in partnership with a man named Bonnington.

"Bonnington!" I exclaimed.

"Yes," laughed Leyland; "Bonnington. That is the cream of the joke, and that is what, I suspect, makes the old man so bitter. You'll hear why presently.

"Well, at the time of his death, Anthony was a widower with two children, a daughter named Susan, ten years old, who lived in England with an aunt, and a son, Jonathan, who had been born in Louvain, and who was only two years old. Of this son and also of the daughter he made Bonnington the guardian; but it seems he also made some arrangements with the family lawyer, for this gentleman – whose name I forget – passed through Louvain a few days before Anthony's death, and had an interview with him. Also it is known that this lawyer subsequently acted for Anthony's son.

"Six months after Anthony's death the property fell in, and Bonnington, with the aid of the lawyer, managed to put Jonathan Leyland in possession, the management of affairs devolving on him (Bonnington) during Jonathan's minority. Well, it was all plain sailing so far. Jonathan was duly placed in possession, and in the course of time grew up to manhood or, at least, to the adult state, for he was never more than about half a man."

"What do you mean by that?" I asked.

"Well, in the first place, he was a dwarf, and in the second, his left arm and leg were withered – apparently from his infancy. There is a portrait of him at home that shows a hideous little goblin with a lop-sided face and a big crutch. He seems to have been a rare old cough-drop – a regular terror to the neighbourhood, with a pleasant habit of rousing up the servants with the end of his crutch. He was a malignant, ill-conditioned little devil. He used to beat his wife and harry his sister, and generally raise Cain in the house. The only person he could get on with was Bonnington; but Bonnington's son, Walter, who was about his own age, seems to have been a special mark for his malice; and when he reached his majority, he hoofed out the unlucky Walter to fend for himself."

"How do you know all this?" I asked.

"His sister, Susan, kept a sort of diary and family chronicle which we have at home with a number of old letters. She married quite young, but became a widow a couple of years later, and came back to live under the fraternal roof. And a gay old time she seems to have had."

"But what about the flaw in the title?" I asked.

"I'm just coming to that. It seems that one fine day, Mistress Susan received a very queer letter from the lawyer – I can't remember the fellow's name, but it doesn't matter – hinting to her that there had been some hocus-pocus about the property, and that both Bonnington and he were concerned in the fraud, whatever it was. I've seen the letter, and deuced vague it is; but he goes on to say that he has committed the facts for safe keeping to a volume of Horace or Virgil or some other Latin writer – I forget which – in his possession, and that he wants to hand the volume to her to be used in evidence after his death. The letter is endorsed on the back by Mistress Susan to this effect; that she did write to Mr – whatever his name was – proposing to come to London and call on him, but he has never replied, or, which I rather suspect, he has answered, and his letter has been intercepted by my guardian (as I still call him) Mr Bonnington. And there the matter ends. There's something queer, but we don't know what it is. We only know that Bonnington was in it; and that's what makes my governor so mad. He's frightfully sick to think that his title is shaky, and he loathes the name Bonnington."

"But," I said, "it is only a chance similarity of name, I suppose?"

"Is it, by Jove?" said Leyland. "Not a bit. Kate's father is the direct descendant of the much-abused Walter. We know that, because the families have always kept more or less in touch. The enmity is my governor's personal hobby."

"Well, Leyland," I said, after a reflective pause, "it seems to me that your cue is to imitate the wisdom of the late Anthony. Lie low and don't stir up mud. You don't want to upset the title to your own property."

A distinct recrudescence of the ancestral mulishness appeared in Leyland's face, "I daresay you're right," he said, "but, all the same, I'd like to know what that old lawyer had to tell. By the way, what do you suppose he meant by 'committing the facts' to what seems to have been a printed book?"

"Who can say? He may have written a statement on the fly-leaf, or, more probably, have attached a cipher connected with the text. However, as I have said, you had better leave the title alone and try more persuasive methods with your father. Introduce him to Miss Bonnington, for instance. That would probably settle the matter."

Leyland's face brightened at my appreciation of the maiden of his choice, and, dismissing the legal question, he said: "Speaking of Kate, you promised to take her and her father on a personally-conducted tour round the Temple. When can I ask them to come? Sunday's no good, you know, to an organist."

I considered my engagements for the week, and then replied: "Wednesday would do for me. Let them come early, and, when we have seen everything and traced the historical connections from Adam downwards, we will all repair to my chambers and drink tea. How will that do?"

Leyland thought it would do excellently, and, subject to his friends' agreement, the arrangement was made.

Need I hesitate to confess that my chambers in Fig Tree Court broke out, about this time, into unwonted sprightliness? Or to tell how the brief bag that I brought home on Wednesday received its lading at the pastrycook's? Or how an iced cake was smuggled into the Temple in a wig-box? Or how the ancient silver teapot was secretly polished with a silk handkerchief and sundry "collector's pieces" came forth of a cabinet to grace the tea-table? Why not? I am but a musty bachelor to whose lair the visitations of fair maids are in good truth as angel's visits. And angels must be suitably entertained. To pretty Kate Bonnington I had taken an instant liking, and my friend Leyland's little romance engaged my warmest sympathy. Such a romance might have been my own but for – however, that is another story.

We met the tourists in state at the main entrance and carried them in procession through the ancient precincts. We talked of the Wars of the Roses, of the Knights Templars and of Twelfth Night. We raised the shades of Johnson and Goldsmith, of Burke and Sheridan. In Mitre Court Buildings we saw poor Charles and Mary Lamb go forth weeping, hand in hand, to the dreaded madhouse, and waited for them to "come again with rejoicing." We threw crumbs for the sparrows by the fountain and talked of Martin Chuzzlewit and Ruth Pinch (and here methought the fair Kate looked a shade conscious), and we looked into the church and to Mr Bonnington's joy heard Father Smith's organ play. It was all very pleasant. The sky was sunny, the plane trees were golden, and when we turned into Fig Tree Court the shade and coolness were very grateful.

Under the influence of tea the historic and literary reminiscences revived. Then Leyland, who was something of a bibliophile, strolled over to my shelves, tea cup in hand, to browse among my books and terrify me for the safety of my precious wedgwood. Suddenly he turned – and nearly upset the cup.

"I saw Solomon this morning – the bookseller, I mean, not the other chap. He was asking after you. Said he'd sent you some books to look over."

"God bless me!" I exclaimed, "so he did, and I have never opened the parcel."

"Let's open it now and see what they are," said Leyland.

I produced the parcel, and, cutting the string, displayed the treasures: a "Treacle Bible," an ancient treatise on alchemy and magic, a couple of recent historical works and a chubby, vellum-bound duodecimo.

"What a dear little book!" Miss Bonnington exclaimed, pouncing on the latter, to our undissembled amusement. "So dainty and small and genteel. Oh, why can't people print and bind books like this now?"

Her question passed unanswered, for Leyland was already deep in the "Treacle Bible" – a mere curiosity which I, certainly, had no intention of keeping – and expounding its peculiarities to Mr Bonnington. From the bible we passed on to the book of magic, over which we discussed the quaint beliefs of our ancestors. Suddenly Mr Bonnington looked at his daughter and asked:

"What is the matter, Kate?"

At the question, I looked up from the book. Miss Bonnington was sitting rigidly still with the little volume, clasped in both hands, resting in her lap. Her eyes were wide open and fixed, apparently, on the opposite wall.

"What is it Kate?" her father repeated; and, as she still appeared unconscious of the question, he leaned forward and lightly touched her hand; whereupon she started violently and gazed around her like a suddenly-awakened sleeper.

"What an extraordinary thing!" she exclaimed.

"What is an extraordinary thing, my dear?" demanded Mr Bonnington.

"Is it possible to dream without going to sleep?" she asked.

"If you have been dreaming and you haven't been to sleep, it must be," her father answered. "Have you?"

"It is astonishing," she said. "It must have been a dream, and yet it was so real, so vivid."

"What was, my dear? What was? Hey? Hm?" and in his impatience Mr Bonnington leaned forward and tapped her knuckles.

"Be patient and I'll tell you. The dream began quite suddenly. This place vanished, and I was in a street, a crowded street filled with people in curious dresses such as one sees in old engravings. There was no pavement; only a row of posts between the road and the footway on which I was walking. The shops had funny little small-paned windows, like the shops in a country village, and each one had a sign hanging above the window or door. I walked quickly, and had the feeling of going somewhere for a definite purpose, and presently, when a kind of arched gateway came in sight, I seemed to have expected it. This gateway – I seem, even now, to recognise it; perhaps from having seen it in some picture – had three arches, a large one over the road, and two small ones for foot-passengers, and a large window over the middle arch. As I approached the gate to pass through I saw a man standing under the left-hand arch as if waiting for someone. He was an elderly man, very fat and very pale; and now that I come to think of him, he reminds me of that old gentleman who passed us that night in Fig Tree Court. I walked towards him with a very curious feeling of having expected to find him there, and, as I passed through the arch, brushing closely against him because he took up so much of the space, he put something into my hand. I remember taking what he gave me as if I had expected it; and then you woke me up."

"Can't you recall what it was that he gave you?" Mr Bonnington asked.

"I have a sort of feeling that it was a book; but I expect that it is only because I was holding this book when I woke," and she held up the little duodecimo and laid it on the table.

As Kate Bonnington told her story, I listened with growing wonder, and, when she had finished, I fell into a reverie in which the eager questionings of her father and Frank Leyland came to me as sounds from an infinite distance. I roused only when Leyland, taking the little book carelessly from the table, glanced at it and addressed me.

"You remember, Mitchell, I was telling you about a book to which that old lawyer had committed certain facts. I thought it was Horace or Virgil. It wasn't, it was Sallust. This reminded me."

He held the little book towards me, and I read on the label "Sallustii Opera."

For a few moments I looked vacantly at the book; then, with eager expectation I took it from his hand and opened it; and somehow, it seemed in no wise strange, but perfectly natural and in order, that I should find on the fly-leaf, traced in faded, brown ink in a hand which I recognised, "Phineas Desborough, 1756."

I say that it seemed quite natural, but I must, nevertheless, have been really astounded for I presently became aware that my three friends were regarding me with uncommon curiosity.

"What is the matter, Mitchell?" asked Leyland. "You look as if you had seen a ghost too."

"Perhaps I have," was my reply; and I returned to the examination of the mysterious little volume. The fly-leaf bore no mark other than the name and date, but when I turned to the back cover I at once perceived – and again it seemed quite natural and reasonable – a thin, pale line of brown ruled round the margin of what my bookish eye instantly detected as a false end-paper. Without a word, I produced my penknife, and, opening it, laid the little book on the table. As I brought the point of the keen blade on to the faded line, Leyland sprang up and exclaimed: "Good Lord! What is the man going to do now?"

I made no reply, but carried the blade steadily along the line until it had traversed the four sides, separating a little panel of the end-paper. I lifted this off, and then, turning the book over, shook out two little sheets of very thin yellowish paper, each covered with pale brown, very minute writing.

"By Jove!" exclaimed Leyland. "Hidden banknotes, hey!" He picked up one of the little leaves, glanced at it, and then stood staring at me, as if thunderstruck.

"Good God, Mitchell," he said in a low voice. "Do you see what this is?"

He handed the little leaf to me, and I then saw that he had been looking at the back of the document, on which was written in ordinary-sized handwriting:

"The statement of Anthony Leyland, Gent, received by me from his hand on the 16th day of August, 1753, in a sealed packet which I afterwards opened.

"Phineas Desborough."

"This is a confidential document, Leyland," I said. "It concerns you, and may contain important family secrets."

"Secrets be hanged!" he replied. "There are no secrets between us. Read it out. Let us hear what Anthony Leyland had to say in 1753."

My legal instincts rose in revolt at the proposal, though I was devoured by curiosity. But Leyland was immovable, and, after a few ineffectual protests, I put on my spectacles and addressed myself to the decipherment of the microscopic script.

"Louvain,
"August the 3rd, 1753.

"My dearest Child, – I am writing these words (with a crow's-quill-pen), lying on the bed whence I shall presently be borne to an alien grave, trusting that, by the Christian charity of some stranger, they shall come safely to your hand. I am dying in a strange land, with no friend near me, and no fellow-countryman save my partner, James Bonnington; to whose care, therefore, I must needs commit my little son, your brother Jonathan. But this I do with much misgiving, for I trust not Mr Bonnington, who is a shrewd and worldly

man; and who hath been most willing and even eager to undertake the duty, which makes me mistrust him the more. To be plain, I fear he may practise some fraud. For you are to know that this Bonnington is a widower (his wife died in the late sickness which carried off your dear mother), and hath one little son but a month or two older than your brother; a poor, mis-shapen wretch, having one arm and leg withered from his birth, on whom his father doteth — though I blame him not for that. But my fear is that he shall set this poor bantling in your brother's place; which he may readily do since he is your brother's guardian, and no one knoweth the children. Perchance I misjudge him; and God grant that it be so. Yet, for safety, I tell you this. That your brother is a lusty child, well-shapen and fair like his mother. That he hath a mole on his left cheek, and on his right breast a mother-mark of a red colour, about the bigness of a groat. By these you shall know the child; for Bonnington's son is sallow and black, and, as I have said, maimed from birth.

"Should that happen which I fear, and this letter reach you safely, keep it till you are of age, and then seek counsel of some wise and honest man.

"I commend you, dear child, to the good God: and so farewell.

"From your loving Father,

"Anthony Leyland."

"To Mistress Susan Leyland."

"August the 15*th*. Mr Desborough, the attorney, is now in Louvain, and comes to me tomorrow, when I shall deliver this to his keeping to convey to you.

"A. L."

There was profound silence for a while after I had finished reading. Then Leyland asked:

"What is the other paper, Mitchell?"

I picked up the paper, and, glancing at it, replied:

"It is Desborough's statement. Shall I read it?"

"Certainly," said Leyland, and accordingly I read aloud:

"I, Phineas Desborough, of 16, Field Court, Gray's Inn, Attorney at Law, do affirm and declare as follows: 'That I received the attached statement from Anthony Leyland, Gent. in a sealed packet: that I opened the packet and withheld the letter from Susan Leyland to whom I had promised to deliver it:

that I did afterwards conspire with James Bonnington to substitute his son Walter for Jonathan the son of the said Anthony: that with my connivance and assistance the said Walter did enter into possession of the estate real and personal to which the said Jonathan was entitled which estate he doth continue to hold; that the said Walter did and still doth pass under the name and style of Jonathan Leyland and that the said Jonathan was and still is unlawfully and fraudulently caused to believe that his name is Walter Bonnington and that he is the son of the said James Bonnington.

"Given under my hand this 29th day of March, 1785.

"Phineas Desborough."

"Signed in my presence,

"William Horrell, of 6 Hand Court, Holborn, Clerk."

I laid down the paper, and looked at my three friends, but for some time none of us spoke. Leyland was the first to break the silence; and his first words framed the inevitable question.

"How did you know those papers were in that book, Mitchell?"

There was no occasion for secrecy or reticence. My audience was not likely to be sceptical. In a few words, I told the story of my midnight visitor and the mysterious letter. And when the wonder of this had a little subsided, there came the further and equally inevitable question.

"By the light of those two statements, Mitchell, what do you say is the present position? It seems that my governor is playing cuckoo."

"The position is," said I, "that you are Frank Bonnington, and that Miss Kate here is Kate Leyland."

"And would those papers be good evidence in a court of law?"

"Probably. But I must point out that after the lapse of a hundred and fifty years, it might prove very difficult to oust a tenant from possession. And your father has the sinews of war, and would probably fight to the last ditch."

"Now there you are quite wrong," said Leyland. "The governor is as obstinate as the devil, but he's an honest man, and generous, too. If you show him those papers and give him all the facts, I'll undertake that he'll march out, bag and baggage, without any action at law at all."

Here Mr Bonnington rose and reached out for the papers. "If that is the case," said he, "I think we had better pop those two statements in the grate, and put a match to them." And he would have done it but that I, with a lawyer's solicitude for documents, whisked them out of his reach and, clapping them in my pocket-book, buttoned my coat.

"Quite right, Mitchell," said Leyland. "I am sure you agree with me that justice must be done."

"I do. I agree most emphatically. But I must insist on its being done in a reasonable manner."

"As for instance – "

"Well, I understand that Mr Bonnington, as I will still call him, has no son and only one daughter. Now supposing he enters an action against your father, and succeeds in ousting him; what is the result? The result is that Miss Kate Bonnington becomes transformed into Kate Leyland. But surely, my dear boy, the same result could be reached by a much shorter and less costly process."

Leyland stared at me for a few moments and then his face broke out into an appreciative grin. "By Jove, Mitchell," said he, "you ought to be Lord Chief Justice. Of course, that's the plan." He turned his gaze on Miss Kate (whose complexion had suddenly assimilated itself to that of the peony), and added: "That is to say, if Miss Leyland would condescend to marry a poor, penniless devil like Frank Bonnington."

That weighty question they subsequently settled to their mutual satisfaction and everyone else's. For the "governor" justified his son's estimate of his character by "climbing down" with the agility of an opossum. Thus, by a short and inexpensive procedure, Kate Bonnington became Kate Leyland – it happened the very day after I took silk – and thus, after a century and a half, did Phineas Desborough make restitution.

The Luck of Barnabas Mudge

Barnabas Mudge was a man whose intellect was above his station in life; which is not necessarily to rate him with Aristotle or Herbert Spencer. For his station was only that of a jobbing bricklayer. Still, there are bricklayers and bricklayers; and Barnabas was of the brainy variety, which is by no means the most common.

Hitherto, however, his mental gifts had not materially advanced him along the road to prosperity. Possibly luck had been against him, or it may have been that the village of Baconsfield offered but a limited scope for the working of his philosophic mind. At any rate, when we make his acquaintance on a sweltering day in June, we find him occupied in the unworthy task of demolishing a ruinous, isolated cottage on the extreme outskirts of the village.

It was a roasting day. As Barnabas stood on the summit of the wall, sulkily pecking at the solid old brickwork, the sweat ran down his face and arms and even wetted the haft of his pick. To make matters worse, old Joe Gammet was depositing a liberal dressing of fish manure on the adjacent field. The deceased fish were presently to be sown evenly over the ground, not with the design – as the unagricultural reader might suppose – of producing a crop of mackerel, but for the purpose of enriching the soil; but at present the enrichment was more diffused, for the fish, set out in symmetrical heaps, lay under the broiling sun, "wasting their sweetness on the desert air."

"Paw!" exclaimed Barnabas, driving his pick viciously into a joint of the hard old brickwork, "them fish do stink. Talk about the plagues of Egypt! Frogs is nothin' to it. And here comes that old swine with another load."

He glanced sourly at the approaching cart and, taking aim at a spot lower down the wall, struck with the energy of exasperation. But here he encountered mortar of a somewhat different quality. The pick buried itself in a crumbling joint, and, as he wrenched at the haft, a considerable mass of brickwork detached itself and fell to the ground.

"Hallo!" said Barnabas. And well he might. For the falling bricks had disclosed a small, cubical chamber in the wall; which chamber, as he could see by craning forward, was occupied by a covered, earthenware jar. This was highly interesting. It was also just a trifle inopportune; for old Gammet had now approached to within a hundred yards and was smiling with ominous geniality.

Barnabas clambered down and began hastily to repair the effects of his last vigorous stroke, fitting the dislodged bricks back in their places as well as he could in the short time at his disposal. Then he climbed up to his former perch and began to work furiously on another part of the wall with his back to the approaching cart. But this aloofness of manner availed him nothing; for Joe Gammet, having arrived opposite the cottage, halted his cart, and, displaying a miscellaneous assortment of variegated teeth, hailed his acquaintance in a fine, resonant agricultural voice.

"Wot O! Barney!"

Barnabas looked round, with a red handkerchief applied to his nose.

"Here, I say, Joe!" he gasped. "Just you move on with that there perfumery of your'n. It's a-makin' me giddy."

Old Gammet chuckled and expectorated skilfully through a convenient aperture in the teeth. "You needn't be so delicut," said he. "Nice, 'ealthy country smell, I calls it. Nourishin' too. Wot's good for the land is good for them wot lives on the land." He took up a reposeful posture in the dismantled doorway and continued reflectively: "Rare tough job you've got there, Barney. Them old coves could build, they could. Used the right sort of stuff, they did. But there's a patch there that don't look much class of work. Why, I could pull it down with my 'ands!"

He fixed a filmy eye on the piece of wall that Barnabas had just reconstituted and made as if to enter the cottage.

"'Ere, don't you come inside," roared Barnabas. "It ain't safe." In illustration of this, he adroitly dislodged a few bricks just over the threshold, causing the aged Gammet to hop out through the doorway with quite surprising agility.

"Couldn't yer see me a-standin' underneath?" the old labourer demanded indignantly.

"I can't see nothin'," said Barnabas. "I can only smell. Would you mind movin' them wallflowers o' yourn a bit further off?"

Old Gammet growled an unintelligible reply, and, sulkily grabbing his horse's bridle, moved away in the direction of the cart track that led into the field. Barnabas watched him impatiently, and, when the cart had fairly entered the field, he looked up and down the lane to satisfy himself that no further interruption threatened, and, once more, scrambled down.

He removed the bricks more carefully this time, with a view to subsequent rebuilding, if necessary, and, thrusting his head into the mysterious cavity in the wall, took off the cover of the jar.

"My eye!" he exclaimed as he applied the organ thus apostrophised to the mouth of the jar. And perfectly natural the exclamation was; for the jar was full to the brim of glistening golden coins.

For a few seconds he stood petrified with incredulous joy. Then he put forth a tremulous hand and picked out half a dozen or so; and his joy was yet further intensified. He had expected to find some ancient unmarketable coinage that shouted "Treasure Trove" from every worn line of its obsolete device. But nothing of the kind. The quantity of gold that passed through his hands was as a rule, inconsiderable. But he knew a sovereign when he saw it. And he saw it now. Yea, not one, but several hundreds.

"Immortal scissors!" ejaculated Barnabas; and once more I repeat that the exclamation was justified by the circumstances.

Now, to the pellucid intellect of Barnabas Mudge certain facts were at once obvious. Here, for instance, was a negotiable property of some hundreds of pounds – wealth beyond the dreams of avarice. That property, it is true, was not strictly speaking his; but Barnabas was a practical man to whom the pedantic subtleties of the law made no appeal. A more immediate problem was how to secure this heaven-sent windfall; and to this he gave his earnest attention as, having replaced the coins and the jar cover, he once more carefully built up the opening of the hiding-place.

Hitherto, luck had persistently been against him. All the village knew him to be a poor man; and if now he should suddenly blossom out into unexplained wealth, curiosity would be aroused and probably suspicion too. Yet it was useless to be rich if one had to live in the appearance of poverty; and hoarding money was folly as this forgotten treasure plainly demonstrated. However, the final management of this undreamed of wealth could be considered later. The immediate problem was how to get it safely conveyed to his own house unobserved by prying eyes. As his truck, small as it was, could not be pulled in through the doorway, the precious jar would have to be carried out to the road, which might be safe enough if it were previously wrapped in a sack. But the magnitude of the stake was affecting his nerves to the extent of developing a perfectly unreasonable degree of caution and secretiveness.

At present old Gammet was the insuperable obstacle. It was impossible to reopen the hiding-place and bring out the jar until he was gone; for he had seen the loose brickwork, and, being a crafty old rascal, might smell a rat. Thus reasoned Barnabas with absurdly exaggerated wariness – for conscience doth make cowards of us all – and as he pecked listlessly at the wall he kept an anxious eye on the old labourer, cursing his dilatory movements and his ridiculous care for appearances. For Joe Gammet, if his olfactory sense was not very discriminating, had a fastidious eye, and was evidently bent on disposing his unsavoury commodity in something like a symmetrical pattern; in fact, Barnabas could actually see him carefully counting the already deposited heaps and pacing out the distance to the site for the next one.

"Now, there's a fat-headed old blighter for you!" Barnabas growled angrily as he watched. "Why can't he dump the stuff down and hook it?" In his exasperation he found himself counting the heaps, too, and calculating how many more the cart-load would produce. There were at present two complete rows, each of thirty-one heaps, and old Gammet was now engaged in depositing the twenty-sixth heap in the third row; and such is the power of suggestion that Barnabas paused in his labours to see if the dwindling contents of the cart would furnish out the five more heaps that were needed to complete the third row.

As a matter of fact the "perfumery" petered out, at the twenty-ninth heap, to Gammet's evident regret for, having deposited it, he solemnly and with extended arm, counted the whole collection over again. And then, at last, he climbed into the empty cart and disconsolately drove away.

"Now for the oof," said Barnabas as the cart disappeared up the lane. He climbed down from his perch, and, placing in readiness a sack that he had brought with him, began to remove the loose bricks. But at this moment there smote on his ears the sound of wheels approaching from the opposite direction to that which Gammet had taken.

"Drat it!" he exclaimed, hastily replacing the bricks and creeping to a small side window that commanded a view down the lane. "Who is it now? Why it's Mother Mooney and that slut of a gel of hern. Now what might they be up to?"

At present they were up to speering about in an inquisitive and highly suspicious manner, and meanwhile, Mrs Mooney was mooring to a fence rail a donkey which was harnessed to a primitive cart. Then, from the latter, the two women extracted each a sack and bustled into the field lately occupied by Mr Gammet. Barnabas watched them with absolute stupefaction as they bore down on the heaps of fish with unmistakable intentions.

"Well, I'm blowed!" exclaimed Barnabas. "If they ain't come to pinch the myrrh and frankincense! So that's the way you runs a market garden. But I don't see what they wants a-countin' of 'em for; that there donkey cart won't hold the whole bilin'."

The object of this mysterious proceeding, however, became evident presently, for it appeared that the two marauders, having noted Mr Gammet's symmetrical arrangement, had decided not to disturb it and thereby draw attention to their unlawful proceedings. They accordingly began operations on number twenty-nine, and, having stowed it in their sacks, carried these to the donkey cart, and returning with two empty ones, renewed the assault on Gammet's property at the last heap on the next row.

"There now!" exclaimed Barnabas admiringly, "there's a artful old baggage for yer! Thinks old Gammet won't miss 'em; and more he won't neither if she don't take too many."

His good opinion of her was justified in this also, for the discreet Mrs Mooney contented herself with the removal of the three terminal heaps, leaving Mr Gammet's symmetrical pattern apparently unchanged, and cleanly picking up even the minutest incriminating fragments.

Barnabas patiently awaited the retreat of the two raiders, and as the donkey cart at length disappeared down the lane, he took another last look round and then once more uncovered the treasure chamber. The jar, though of no great size, was uncommonly heavy, and its introduction to the sack under the agitating circumstances was a matter of some difficulty. When it was safely accomplished and he had staggered out with his prize to the truck and there buried it under a heap of tools, sash-frames, rafters and other debris from the cottage, there followed several agonised minutes, during which he feverishly built up the opening of the chamber – for it would obviously have been madness to leave that cavity exposed to the inquisitive eyes of the villagers. But fortunately no one passed down the lane while he was thus occupied, nor was there anyone in sight when at length he stole forth guiltily and, taking up the pole of the truck, set out homewards at a pace, and with a degree of anxious care, suggestive of a rural funeral. We need not describe that journey in detail; let it suffice to say that at the end of it, Barnabas felt several years older and found himself deeply impressed alike with the surprising populousness of Baconsfield and his own hitherto unsuspected popularity. At length, with a sigh of relief, he trundled his cart into the tiny backyard of the cottage in which he lived all alone; a few moments more and he had borne his treasure in through the back door and shot the bolt; and thus was the first, and most essential, step taken on the road to fortune.

It is needless to say that Mr Mudge's first proceeding was to ascertain the extent of his wealth; to which end he tenderly bore the jar up the tiny staircase to the room above, where he tipped out its contents, in a glorious shining heap, on the bed, and began, with trembling fingers, to count the coins into smaller heaps in the manner of a glorified Gammet.

The total was no less than six hundred and thirteen golden sovereigns, a sum, the bare contemplation of which produced symptoms of vertigo, and as he knelt by the narrow pallet, running an ecstatic eye over the unbelievable collection, his intellect began once more to occupy itself with the problem of an unsuspicious transition from poverty to affluence. No miser was Barnabas, who might find pleasure in mere gloating over a hoard of unnegotiable riches; but he was too wary to plunge into such sudden self-indulgence as might set the villagers whispering into the ear of the rural constable. What was necessary was some plausible explanation of the change in his financial condition; an explanation that was rendered necessary, not only by the amount of the windfall, but by a very curious circumstance which he had noticed while counting the coins; namely, that the sovereigns all bore the same date. That was, in fact, very odd indeed, and caused Barnabas to speculate in some surprise whether the identity of date was due to a miser's freak, or whether perchance, the hoard was the product of some forgotten bank robbery. Of course, that was no business of his excepting as to its result; which was that he would need to use some extra caution in introducing that large family of twins to a censorious world.

He turned the problem over again and again as he replaced the coins in the jar and deposited the latter in a recess up the bedroom chimney; but he reached no conclusion. He cogitated on it profoundly as he boiled the kettle and made his tea, but still without result; and when, later in the evening, he locked up the house and directed his accustomed steps towards the Black Bull Inn, he was still without the vestige of a plan. And yet the change in his circumstances had not been without some slight and subtle influence; for, yielding to an impulse of which he was hardly conscious, he had, just before starting, transferred, from the oaken chest in his bedroom, in which he kept his little savings, no less a sum than fifteen shillings to the pocket of his mole-skin trousers.

He was not the first to arrive in the tap-room of the "Black Bull." By no means. Over a dozen rustics had already arrived, and were at the moment recreating themselves by throwing darts at a cork target on the wall, and backing their respective abilities by small wagers. As Barnabas entered, old Joe Gammet was in the very act of taking aim; not a particularly good aim it seemed, for the dart ultimately found a billet in the corner of an adjacent picture frame.

"I'll 'ave that shot over again," the wily old rustic affirmed, with great presence of mind. "This 'ere Barney a-baulked me a-comin' in so sudden-like"; and, regardless of the protests of his disconcerted comrades, he stolidly pulled the dart out of the frame, returned to his station, and forthwith made a bull's-eye.

In the inevitable dispute that followed as to the payment of the wager, Barnabas found himself implicated by the ingenious Gammet, who sought thus to divert the attention of the losers. But Barnabas was no gambler, and with equal adroitness, he proceeded to excuse himself.

"My 'and ain't steady enough, Joe," said he. "Tain't recovered yet from that there fish of yourn."

Old Gammet snorted disdainfully. "You makes a rare outcry, you do," said he, "about a few 'eaps o' nice, fresh fish."

"A few!" exclaimed Barnabas. "Dunno what you call a few. There was upwards of eighty 'eaps of 'em."

"Upwards o' ninety, Barney," corrected Gammet. Barnabas shook his head. "Upwards of eighty, I should say," said he. The actual number had escaped him for the moment, and his rejoinder was dictated by the mere habit of contradiction inherent in the British rustic. But Gammet took him up sharply. "I tell yer there was over ninety o' them 'eaps," he said dogmatically.

The definiteness of the statement aroused Mr Mudge's attention, and, rapidly recalling the actual numbers, with the little subtraction sum worked by Mrs Money, he said in a dogged tone:

"Not ninety, Joe, over eighty. I looked at them 'eaps carefully and I've got a educated eye."

"Look 'ere!" exclaimed Gammet, in suppressed excitement, "you ain't the only cove wot's got a educated eye. I got one, too, and I tell yer there's over ninety o' them 'eaps, and I'll bet yer a shullin' I'm right."

Barnabas smiled a discreet smile. "I never bets, Joe," said he, "and you knows it. But, all the same, there worn't ninety o' them 'eaps," and with this he strolled through into the bar to obtain the refreshment necessary for the continuance of the discussion, and also to reflect at leisure on the situation. When he returned with his tankard of ale, he was aware of a certain ill-concealed expectancy in the aspect of his rustic acquaintances, strongly suggestive, to his mind of a secret understanding; and his agile intellect instantly framed an appropriate course of action.

"Uncommon sudden this 'ot weather's set in," he remarked to the company in general.

"Remarkable," agreed Gammet, "but to return to this 'ere fish – "

"Not me," said Barnabas, "I've had enough o' that there fish. 'Twixt eighty and ninety 'eaps of 'em – "

"Over ninety," interrupted Gammet.

"Not over," retorted Barnabas. "Under ninety, I say, and I reckon I can trust my eye to a dozen or so."

"There's more'n ninety," said Gammet; and, as Barnabas shook his head once more, old Gammet continued eagerly:

"Why don't yer back yer opinion if yer'e so bloomin' cocksure?"

"'Twouldn't be fair," said Barnabas. "I ain't never wrong in a matter o' numbers."

A howl of derision from the assembled company greeted this boastful statement, and Barnabas was so earnestly invited by the assembled rustics to pouch old Gammet's "shullin'," that he, at length, and with much show of reluctance, accepted the wager. But no sooner were the preliminaries arranged, than Bob Chalmers, the miller, came forward and said he'd have a shullin's worth, too, and his example being followed, one after the other, by the rest of the company, Barnabas found himself committed to the extent of twelve shillings; which sum was duly carried in procession by the rustic sportsmen into the bar and deposited with the counterstakes in the custody of the landlord; who, in his turn becoming inoculated, invested a shilling himself. Then the whole twenty-six shillings in assorted coinage having been lodged in an empty Toby jug, and the bar being placed in the care of the landlord's wife, the whole company of gamesters set forth together to inspect the deceased leviathans.

"Now then," said old Gammet, as the party halted at the entrance to the field, and several numbers furtively produced pocket handkerchiefs, "let's be clear about this 'ere bet. I say there's over ninety o' them 'eaps and you say there's under ninety. Ain't that right?"

"Under ninety it is," agreed Barnabas, and with this the procession entered the field.

The procedure was deliberate and exhaustively thorough. Sam Pullet's new ash sapling, that he had cut that very day, was adopted as a tally-stick, and as the procession halted opposite each malodorous heap it was registered by a notch cut on the stick. The process took time, especially as there was a tendency to periodic misunderstandings as to which heap the last notch referred to; but at length, after four false starts had been made and corrected by beginning again *de novo*, the entire round was completed, and all that remained was to count the notches.

This task was assigned to the landlord, and as that sportsman reached the last notch, and falteringly pronounced the word, "eighty-eight," he turned a reproachful eye on Joe Gammet.

"You've made a mistake, Tom," exclaimed the chap-fallen Joseph, who had, however, already detected the discrepancy, but despairingly strove to temporise. He took the stick from the landlord, and, running his fingers down the notches, continued, with ill-feigned triumph: "There, I told yer so, ninety-one it is, ninety-one, I makes it."

"Then you makes it wrong," said Barnabas; and the stick being solemnly passed round, elicited the unanimous verdict of eighty-eight, and a general lowering of the sportsmen's visages. Three times more did that melancholy procession slowly perambulate that marine necropolis, and each time the same depressing result emerged. At the end of the third perambulation there was a deathly silence, and then Bob Chalmers broke into open reproaches.

"Look 'ere, Joe Gammet!" he exclaimed, gloomily, "what's the meanin' o' this 'ere? You told us as how you'd counted 'em yerself. It's my belief as it's a put-up job."

"Nothun o' the kind," retorted Gammet. "Ninety-one 'eaps I counted afore I come away. Somebody 'as bin and stole three of 'em," and here he fixed a suspicious eye on Barnabas, who retorted sarcastically by offering to turn out his pockets.

"Stole yer grandmother, Joe," the landlord growled somewhat obscurely. "Who's a-goin' to steal rotten fish?"

Joe Gammet was about to make an angry rejoinder, possibly resenting the singular ancestry ascribed to him by the landlord's last remark, when Barnabas blandly interposed with the suggestion that they should return and refresh on the proceeds of the gamble; on which there were signs of reviving cheerfulness, especially on the part of the landlord.

The company which left the "Black Bull" that evening was hilarious beyond all precedent, but none of the roisterers staggered homewards in a more joyous frame than did Barnabas Mudge. For he had found a solution to his problem, By this chance, foolish incident he had found a way to that appearance of modest affluence that he had justly considered necessary to his safety. With characteristic energy and judgment he followed out the policy thus suggested by chance. A judicious measurement, privately taken, of the sundial on the church porch, with another of the tap-room table, served with due diplomacy to evolve another wager; secret inspections of the weather forecasts in the papers at the village library not only made him an authority on meteorology, but enriched him to the extent of four and threepence. After a few such demonstrations of his infallibility, the cautious rustics began to decline his invitations to back their opinions; but although his actual activities thus necessarily came to an end, a general vague belief grew up, and was fostered by him, that his unerring judgment and never-failing luck were furnishing him with a handsome increase of income.

It was about this time that Barnabas Mudge embarked on the one and only real gamble of his life. It came about in this wise; returning homeward by a footpath across the fields, he suddenly perceived a smart-looking gig, drawn by a handsome, mettlesome horse, careering wildly down an adjacent cart track. From the fact that the gig was empty, Barnabas naturally inferred that the horse had bolted, and as he knew that the track led direct to the steep edge of a gravel pit, he perceived that a disaster was imminent. Now Mr Mudge was not only a man of intellect; he was also a man of action. The galloping horse was yet some distance away, and there was still time for some effort to avert the catastrophe. Accordingly, he ran across the field, and, lurking behind a bush that bordered the cart track, awaited the approach of the runaway until the latter had advanced to within some thirty or forty yards, when he darted out, cap in hand, and proceeded to execute a sort of fandango with much flourishing of arms and encouraging exhortations; as a result of which the astonished horse stopped dead to observe this amazing apparition, and before he could recover his wits, Barnabas had swooped down on him and grabbed him by the bridle. A few seconds later, while Barnabas was still soothing his captive's troubled spirit by equine blandishments, a small man appeared on the cart track, running as fast as two extremely spindly and slightly bandy legs would propel him, and, approaching breathlessly, introduced himself as the proprietor of the horse.

"You've had a narrow squeak, you have," said Barnabas. "Another hundred yards, and he'd have been in the gravel pit."

"I know," said the new-comer. "I thought of that pit as soon as the beggar started. You're a trump, that's what you are, my lad," and his hand strayed towards his breeches pocket.

And here, once again, we perceive the subtle effect of the invaluable jar of gold. A month ago, Barnabas would have pocketed gleefully the two sovereigns that were exhibited in the stranger's palm. But now he was a man of means and could afford to indulge in the expensive luxury of pride.

"No, thank you," he said, magnanimously waving the sovereigns away. "I'm glad to have been able to help you, but I reckon you'd have done the same for me."

The horsey gentleman returned the coins to his pocket, somewhat reluctantly. "Don't see that you need be so blooming proud," he said, as he relieved Barnabas of his charge; "however, if you won't take a tip in hard cash, perhaps you'll take a tip of another kind; only, mind you," he added impressively, "what I'm going to tell you mustn't go any farther. Is that agreed?"

Barnabas gave the required assurance, and the other resumed:

"Now, listen to me. I'm a trainer – name of Bates; you may have heard of me. Well now, I've got a regular soft thing on, and I'm going to take you into it, only, you mustn't let on to a living soul. You know the Imperial Cup's going to be run for next week at Newmarket." Barnabas nodded. "Well now, there are two outsiders entered for the first two races; King Tom and Columbine. There'll be long odds against them both. Now, if you take those odds, you'll have as near as may be a dead cert. That's a tip that's worth money, and I tell you again to keep it to yourself."

With this and a touch of the hat, he started forward with the mollified horse, leaving Barnabas to return to the footpath.

Now, Mr Mudge, as we have said, was no gambler, and his idea of a "dead cert" was not quite the same as a sporting man's. He was flattered by the possession of this special information, but it did not occur to him to make any use of it; indeed, the whole affair had faded from his mind when a chance circumstance recalled it. It was on the evening of the first day of the races that he happened to be in the bar of the "Black Bull" with one or two of his acquaintances. The occasion was a somewhat special one, for, having lured some misguided rustic – much against the advice of his friends – into a bet, he had just brought off a "dead cert" of his own kind, and was in the very act of receiving payment, when a gig stopped at the inn door, and a stout, red-faced man got down and entered. The new-comer was well known to the denizens of the "Black Bull," being none other than Mr Sandys, the famous bookmaker; a gentleman of suave and genial manners, especially on the present occasion, he having, as he expressed it, done rather a good line during the day. He was even disposed to be facetious, for having assuaged his thirst with a preliminary gulp, he smiled round on the awe-stricken yokels, and invited them jointly and severally to try a bout with Fickle Fortune.

"Hey!" said he, sticking a fat thumb into Barnabas' ribs, "what do you say? Smart-looking chap like you ought to be ready to back his fancy. Come now, what can I do for you?" and here he produced a fat, leather-covered volume and licked the point of a lead pencil.

And then it was that Barnabas Mudge went stark mad. And yet, perhaps, not so mad as he seemed; for in that moment, it flashed upon him that even to lose money gloriously, magnificently, was to add to that reputation that he was so carefully cultivating.

"How do the odds go?" he asked carelessly; and the yokels drew nearer with dilated eyes, while the landlord rested his knuckles on the counter and leaned forward inquisitively. Mr Sandys produced a list of the fixtures, and began to read off numerical statements which sounded like the delirious mutterings of an insane stockbroker.

"What about King Tom?" inquired Barnabas. "He's in the first event I see."

The bookmaker shook his head. "No class," said he, and added, altruistically, "Don't you go chucking your coppers away on dark 'orses."

"And then," pursued Barnabas, ignoring Mr Sandys' really well-meant advice, "there's Columbine. She's in the second event, I see."

Mr Sandys emptied his glass with an impatient gulp. "Another outsider," said he. "Hasn't got a bloomin' look in. You take my tip, and put your money on a horse that's known."

Barnabas took a quick glance round at the circle of open-mouthed rustics, and then announced bumptiously, "I'm a goin' to back my fancy, and I fancies them two 'orses. What'll you give me on the double event?"

The bookmaker was so taken aback that he had to call for another whisky and soda.

"Double event," he roared. "I won't do it. It would be just picking your pocket, and I don't pick the pockets of working men."

"Very well," said Barnabas, "then I must take my money to someone else."

"Oh, if you're going to make somebody a present," said Mr Sandys, "it may as well be me as anyone else. I'll give yer a hundred to one. That won't hurt you. How much shall we say? A bob?"

Barnabas turned to the bulging-eyed landlord and asked in a casual tone: "Tom, can you let me 'ave such a thing as twenty pound? You shall have it back in half an hour."

There was a breathless silence for two or three seconds. But the gambling fever had seized the landlord as well as Barnabas. Without a word, he retired to some secret lair whence he presently returned with four new five-pound notes.

"Well," said the bookmaker, "if you're clean off your onion, there's nothing more to be said; only, I warn you, you'll lose your money. Won't you think better of it?"

"I'm a-goin' to back my fancy," said Barnabas doggedly; upon which Mr Sandys formally registered the transaction, explaining that he could not receive the money in a public place, but that it was to be sent to his office.

Having once committed himself to this rash enterprise, Barnabas acted his part consistently. The entreaties of the excited yokels that he would attend the race in person and see that he got fair play, he ignored with magnanimous calm and went about his ordinary business as though a twenty-pound wager were a mere unconsidered trifle, and the oaken chest, from which he had extracted the bulk of his savings, were the repository of untold wealth. But he was the only calm person in the village; and when, in the waning afternoon, he betook himself to the "Black Bull," to await the return of the bookmaker, he found the tap-room packed and overflowing into the bar, where the landlord was compressing a month's business into a couple of hours.

In the interval, his brief attack of speculative mania had died out, and he had come prepared to increase his growing reputation by a stoical indifference to the loss that he had already accepted as inevitable; and while a mob of agitated yokels stood out in the road, eagerly watching for the returning party, Barnabas sat in the Wycombe armchair and stolidly read the morning paper, an object of respectful and admiring astonishment to the other inmates of the tap-room.

About five o'clock, there suddenly arose a clamour from without. A score of heads, round-eyed with excitement, appeared at the open window, and a score of voices strove to break in upon his philosophic calm.

"He's a-comin', Barney! He's a-passin' the fingerpost now! He's opposight the pond!" and then, after a brief, but clamorous interval: "Here he is!" and the unmoved Barnabas, with his eye glued to an advertisement for a respectable housemaid, heard the gig stop, and was then aware of an irritable, but familiar voice calling out in the bar: "Where's that feller Mudge? Is he here?"

Barnabas laid down the paper and yawned. Then he rose and stretched himself, and, sauntering out into the bar, perceived Mr Sandys, surrounded by a closely-packed mob of yokels, and grasping a cheque-book and a fountain pen. But he was no longer genial, nor in the least inclined to be facetious. On the contrary he greeted Barnabas with a sour grin and slapped his cheque-book down on the only clean spot on the counter.

"So, here you are," said he. "Confound you! Do you know you've eaten up the whole of my earnings?"

Barnabas muttered an apology, being somewhat confused by the unwonted conduct of the usually genial Sandys, and stood by, watching in some bewilderment, as the bookmaker scribbled on a cheque, accompanying the process with disparaging comments.

"S'welp me! Cleaned out by a bloomin' chaw-bacon! Better get a bloomin' nurse to come round with me next time! There 'y'are!"

There was a soft sound of rending, and the astonished Barnabas found himself regarding an elongated slip of mauve paper that flickered at the end of his nose. With slowly dawning comprehension, he took the cheque and laboriously spelled out its mandate to pay to Barnabas Mudge the sum of two thousand pounds; and he was still staring at it, in absolute stupefaction, as the wheels of the bookmaker's gig rolled away down the road.

It is notorious that circumstances alter cases. As Barnabas betook himself homeward with the two thousand pound cheque in his pocket, the jar of gold which had hitherto monopolised his field of mental vision, sank into sudden insignificance. He even debated whether it were not better publicly to announce the discovery of the treasure and so put himself definitely on the right side of the law; but a renewed inspection of the jar, with its glittering contents, produced the inevitable result. Cupidity overcame discretion.

It was two days later that he set out for the neighbouring market town for the purpose of opening an account at the bank to which the landlord of the "Black Bull" had introduced him. Before starting, he had once more brought forth the jar from its hiding-place, with a half-formed intention of taking that with him, too. But the singular identity of date on the coins deterred him; for the strange coincidence would inevitably be noticed by the officials of the bank, and notice was precisely what Barnabas did not desire. So he returned the jar to its hiding-place, to serve as a store to be drawn upon for current expenditure, but first, he took from it ten sovereigns, which he dropped into his trousers pocket. With two thousand pounds at the bank, he could surely afford to jingle a little loose gold.

It was not unobserved by Barnabas that his appearance at the bank in his very indifferent best suit created a somewhat unfavourable impression, and he decided anon to furnish himself with raiment more suitable to his new station.

Meanwhile, the eight-mile walk had developed an appetite and an agreeable thirst which he decided to assuage, regardless of expense, at the "King's Head." But here, too, his costume exposed him to humiliations; notwithstanding which, he worked his way stolidly through the entire bill of fare, watched superciliously by an obviously suspicious waiter, by whom the rather startling bill of costs was laid beside his plate before he had fairly finished his fourth slab of cheese.

Barnabas, however, was not offended. On the contrary, the bill afforded him the means of vindicating his position; which he did by carelessly dropping on it one of the golden gifts of benevolent Providence. The effect, however, on the waiter was not quite what he had hoped; for that supercilious menial, as he retired, turned the coin over and over in his palm as if he were a numismatist inspecting a specimen of some rare and ancient coinage. If Barnabas could have followed him into the office, he would have seen that this numismatic enthusiasm was actually communicated to the manager; by whom the coin was closely examined, rung on the desk and finally weighed in a very queer little balance.

"Now then," said Barnabas to the waiter, who lurked furtively in the vicinity of his seat, with a futile pretence of having forgotten him, "how much longer are you going to be with that there change?"

"Yessir, coming, sir, in one minute," the waiter replied, casting an expectant look towards the door; which at that very moment opened to admit three persons of whom one wore the becoming costume of the local police. The three strangers and the waiter deliberately converged upon Barnabas, and the waiter remarked, more lucidly than grammatically: "This is 'im!"

Barnabas rose, with a chilly sensation at his spine and a premonition of evil. One of the strangers, who looked like a guardsman in mufti, held out his hand, on which lay a sovereign, and opened his mouth and spake:

"I am a police officer. I am going to arrest you on a charge of uttering counterfeit coin, and it's my duty to caution you that anything you say will be used in evidence against you."

Barnabas broke out into a cold sweat. "Do you mean to tell me," he faltered, "that that is a bad sovereign?"

"Rank bad 'un," replied the officer, suddenly dropping his legal phraseology, "and I want to know if you've got any more." Here Barnabas was led unresisting, to the office, where, his pockets being expertly turned out, the other nine sovereigns were brought to light, and laid in an incriminating row on the desk.

"Same old lot!" said the detective, as he ran his eye rapidly over them. "I thought we'd seen the last of Fred Gilbert's masterpieces. Where did yer get this stuff, young man?"

Now Barnabas, as we have said, was a man of intellect; and, at the first appearance of the police, had been completely enlightened by a flash of intuition; and he now saw clearly that his only chance lay in a frank statement of the actual facts. He accordingly recited in detail the circumstances attending the discovery of the treasure, and he was encouraged as he proceeded to observe a slow grin spreading over the officer's countenance.

"Where do you say this house was?" the detective asked.

"Harebell Lane, Baconsfield. Last house on the right 'and side."

The detective chuckled. "That's the place," said he. "We went through it most carefully after Freddie was nobbled at Newmarket, but couldn't find a single piece. Rare downy bird was Frederick. Kept all his moulds and stuff at his place in London. However, you'll have to come along, young man, for if you didn't make this snide money, you prigged it, on your own showing, though I don't suppose the magistrates will be hard on you."

As a matter of fact, they were not. On the contrary, they were disposed to be hilarious to the verge of impropriety; for when Barnabas was charged with "having unlawfully concealed from the knowledge of our Lord the King the finding of a certain treasure," the entire Court, including the prosecuting detective, broke into the broadest of grins; and when the Clerk rose to point out to their

Worships that the word "treasure" was defined in the statute as "any gold or silver in coin, plate, or bullion, hidden in ancient times," whereas, the present treasure consisted in a quantity of base metal, the grins gave way to audible chuckles, and the amused justices agreed to take advantage of the legal quibble and acquit the prisoner.

On the very same day, Barnabas surrendered the fateful jar to the detective as "Trustee of our Lord the King," and ventured smilingly to express the hope that His Majesty would make no improper use of his newly-acquired wealth.

It is now some years since these stirring events befell, years which have justified Fortune in the favours she was pleased to bestow on Barnabas Mudge; whose honoured name has since then not only adorned a multitude of contractors' notice boards, but has occasionally appeared at the foot of cheques compared with which the memorable draft of Mr Sandys would be a mere bagatelle.

R AUSTIN FREEMAN

THE D'ARBLAY MYSTERY

When a man is found floating beneath the skin of a green-skimmed pond one morning, Dr Thorndyke becomes embroiled in an astonishing case. This wickedly entertaining detective fiction reveals that the victim was murdered through a lethal injection and someone out there is trying a cover-up.

DR THORNDYKE INTERVENES

What would you do if you opened a package to find a man's head? What would you do if the headless corpse had been swapped for a case of bullion? What would you do if you knew a brutal murderer was out there, somewhere, and waiting for you? Some people would run. Dr Thorndyke intervenes.

R Austin Freeman

Felo De Se

John Gillam was a gambler. John Gillam faced financial ruin and was the victim of a sinister blackmail attempt. John Gillam is now dead. In this exceptional mystery, Dr Thorndyke is brought in to untangle the secrecy surrounding the death of John Gillam, a man not known for insanity and thoughts of suicide.

Flighty Phyllis

Chronicling the adventures and misadventures of Phyllis Dudley, Richard Austin Freeman brings to life a charming character always getting into scrapes. From impersonating a man to discovering mysterious trap doors, *Flighty Phyllis* is an entertaining glimpse at the times and trials of a wayward woman.

R Austin Freeman

Helen Vardon's Confession

Through the open door of a library, Helen Vardon hears an argument that changes her life forever. Helen's father and a man called Otway argue over missing funds in a trust one night. Otway proposes a marriage between him and Helen in exchange for his co-operation and silence. What transpires is a captivating tale of blackmail, fraud and death. Dr Thorndyke is left to piece together the clues in this enticing mystery.

Mr Pottermack's Oversight

Mr Pottermack is a law-abiding, settled homebody who has nothing to hide until the appearance of the shadowy Lewison, a gambler and blackmailer with an incredible story. It appears that Pottermack is in fact a runaway prisoner, convicted of fraud, and Lewison is about to spill the beans unless he receives a large bribe in return for his silence. But Pottermack protests his innocence, and resolves to shut Lewison up once and for all. Will he do it? And if he does, will he get away with it?

OTHER TITLES BY R AUSTIN FREEMAN AVAILABLE DIRECT FROM HOUSE OF STRATUS

Quantity		£	$(US)	$(CAN)	€
	A CERTAIN DR THORNDYKE	6.99	11.50	16.95	11.50
	THE D'ARBLAY MYSTERY	6.99	11.50	16.95	11.50
	DR THORNDYKE INTERVENES	6.99	11.50	16.95	11.50
	DR THORNDYKE'S CASEBOOK	6.99	11.50	16.95	11.50
	THE EYE OF OSIRIS	6.99	11.50	16.95	11.50
	FELO DE SE	6.99	11.50	16.95	11.50
	FLIGHTY PHYLLIS	6.99	11.50	16.95	11.50
	THE GOLDEN POOL: THE STORY OF A FORGOTTEN MINE	6.99	11.50	16.95	11.50
	HELEN VARDON'S CONFESSION	6.99	11.50	16.95	11.50

ALL HOUSE OF STRATUS BOOKS ARE AVAILABLE FROM GOOD BOOKSHOPS OR DIRECT FROM THE PUBLISHER:

Internet: **www.houseofstratus.com** including author interviews, reviews, features.

Email: **sales@houseofstratus.com** please quote author, title and credit card details.

OTHER TITLES BY R AUSTIN FREEMAN AVAILABLE DIRECT FROM HOUSE OF STRATUS

Quantity		£	$(US)	$(CAN)	€
	Mr Polton Explains	6.99	11.50	16.95	11.50
	Mr Pottermack's Oversight	6.99	11.50	16.95	11.50
	The Mystery of 31 New Inn	6.99	11.50	16.95	11.50
	The Mystery of Angelina Frood	6.99	11.50	16.95	11.50
	The Penrose Mystery	6.99	11.50	16.95	11.50
	The Puzzle Lock	6.99	11.50	16.95	11.50
	The Red Thumb Mark	6.99	11.50	16.95	11.50
	The Shadow of the Wolf	6.99	11.50	16.95	11.50
	A Silent Witness	6.99	11.50	16.95	11.50
	The Singing Bone	6.99	11.50	16.95	11.50
	The Unwilling Adventurer	6.99	11.50	16.95	11.50
	When Rogues Fall Out	6.99	11.50	16.95	11.50

ALL HOUSE OF STRATUS BOOKS ARE AVAILABLE FROM GOOD BOOKSHOPS
OR DIRECT FROM THE PUBLISHER:

Hotline: UK ONLY: 0800 169 1780, please quote author, title and credit card details.
INTERNATIONAL: +44 (0) 20 7494 6400, please quote author, title, and credit card details.

Send to: House of Stratus Sales Department
24c Old Burlington Street
London
W1X 1RL
UK

Please allow for postage costs charged per order plus an amount per book as set out in the tables below:

	£(Sterling)	$(US)	$(CAN)	€(Euros)
Cost per order				
UK	2.00	3.00	4.50	3.30
Europe	3.00	4.50	6.75	5.00
North America	3.00	4.50	6.75	5.00
Rest of World	3.00	4.50	6.75	5.00
Additional cost per book				
UK	0.50	0.75	1.15	0.85
Europe	1.00	1.50	2.30	1.70
North America	2.00	3.00	4.60	3.40
Rest of World	2.50	3.75	5.75	4.25

PLEASE SEND CHEQUE, POSTAL ORDER (STERLING ONLY), EUROCHEQUE, OR INTERNATIONAL MONEY ORDER (PLEASE CIRCLE METHOD OF PAYMENT YOU WISH TO USE)
MAKE PAYABLE TO: STRATUS HOLDINGS plc

Cost of book(s): —————————— Example: 3 x books at £6.99 each: £20.97

Cost of order: —————————— Example: £2.00 (Delivery to UK address)

Additional cost per book: ————— Example: 3 x £0.50: £1.50

Order total including postage: ——— Example: £24.47

Please tick currency you wish to use and add total amount of order:

☐ £ (Sterling)   ☐ $ (US)   ☐ $ (CAN)   ☐ € (EUROS)

VISA, MASTERCARD, SWITCH, AMEX, SOLO, JCB:

☐ ☐ ☐ ☐ ☐ ☐ ☐ ☐ ☐ ☐ ☐ ☐ ☐ ☐ ☐ ☐ ☐ ☐ ☐ ☐

Issue number (Switch only):

☐ ☐ ☐

Start Date:

☐ ☐ / ☐ ☐

Expiry Date:

☐ ☐ / ☐ ☐

Signature: ————————————

NAME: ——————————————————

ADDRESS: —————————————————

——————————————————

POSTCODE: ————————

Please allow 28 days for delivery.

Prices subject to change without notice.
Please tick box if you do not wish to receive any additional information. ☐

House of Stratus publishes many other titles in this genre; please check our website (**www.houseofstratus.com**) for more details.